# Warning

**Warning**
This book touches on some dark elements.
Inside are scenes that talk about Cancer,
self-harm, cutting, attempted suicide, and rape.
None of the above elements are on the page but they are
talked about.
This is a stand-alone HEA

# Prologue

The empty bottle slipped from my fingers as my body slumped over, forcing me to empty the content of my stomach before my body fell back against the tall cold rock.

Fuck that hurt!

I slide to the ground, landing hard to my ass. A thick fog has overtaken my head, and I can no longer feel my limbs since I went numb an hour ago. Probably from the cold. Although I barely notice the bite of the air anymore. I don't know if I have the alcohol to thank or if I no longer care, maybe both? My head begins to slump forward and off to the side. I know if I give in to the black void that is calling to me, I'll sink so far into the ground that I'll never find my way back. I slam my back against the rock again, smacking the back of my head in the process.

My head lolled to the side, and I squint to see the shimmer of the fresh etched letters stretched across the rock next to me.

No. Not a rock. A stone. A headstone.

And it's not letters but a name.

Fuck, I'm going to vomit again.

I lift the bottle to my lips, needing the burn of the amber liquid to wash away the ache in my chest. But the bottle is empty. I toss it with disgust from my hand, not giving a shit where it lands. And it does land somewhere off to my side because I hear it crack and shatter.

My sore bloodshot eyes try to stay glued to the writing next to me.

I can't leave her here. Not alone. Not in the cold darkness of night.

She always hated being alone.

"Guess I'll have to live here now," I mutter my words to the stone.

"I'm not leaving here. I won't leave you."

Where in the hell did that bottle go? I look around at the ground beside me and find chunks of shattered glass. I pick a piece up in my fist, not caring it's slicing the shit out of my skin.

"Fuck you," I scream, tossing the glass away as if it were the item of betrayal. Anger once again runs through my insides.

My eyes are heavy, and I lean my head against the stone to close them.

I'm cold. But I can't leave her.

My eyes burn with tears, and the wetness pisses me off more. "I'm so sorry, baby. I'm so fucking sorry." I don't know if I'm speaking the words aloud because, in my head, they are screaming. I don't care. All I know is I'm broken. I'm broken, and I will never be whole again.

My life, love, and world are in the cold hard ground. I can't leave her.

"Declan?"

I lift my head noticing once again the cold wetness on my cheeks.

"Declan?"

"Dani?" Her voice. Is that her voice? Oh God, am I forgetting her beautiful voice already?

"No, sweetie, it's me. Rachel."

The pain in my chest bursts at the sound of my sister's sweet voice. My breathing stops, and my chest swells as a sob erupts from my broken heart. A wounded wail hits my ears, and I have no idea it's coming from me.

"Declan, I'm here. Brother, I'm here."

I hear her talking to someone. Telling them, she can't leave me here.

Yes, she can, and she will. I'll never leave her. I'll never leave my beautiful Dani.

My sister sinks lower until I see her face in front of mine. My gaze is blurry, and I can't make out her features.

"I need to take you home, Declan. Come with me, please."

I'm shaking my head so hard I feel the need to throw up again.

"No. I can't leave Dani here."

"Oh, honey. Please don't."

Another sob rips open my chest, and this time I struggle to breathe. "Please, Rach. Please don't make me leave her." I beg.

Her voice is faint and shaky. "Honey, I can't leave you here. Dani wouldn't want you to stay this way."

My eyes are heavy, and I can't fight them to stay open any longer. I let my head fall back against the cold stone. I won't leave her. I won't. I'll stay in this cemetery forever.

Tired darkness starts to wrap around me as I begin my inevitable descend. My mind and heart race to hold onto the vision of my beautiful wife in my head.

I need to keep her close to me forever. I can't believe she's gone.

My beautiful wife is gone.

# Chapter One

♥

*Two Years later*

"Thank you for coming out on such short notice, Quinn."

I shift my weight into the soft fibers of a plush white sofa and smile at the beautiful blond sitting across from me. I arrived fifteen minutes ago to the luxurious sky-rise apartment for this interview and have been try-ing to keep my gaze on the woman asking the questions ever since. No matter how uncomfortable I get from eye contact.

The woman shifted through some papers on a clip-board before bringing smiling eyes up to meet mine. "When I called the hiring agency, I was afraid I'd already gone through all the available personal assistants. I'm so glad you were able to meet with me today."

I hold my smile in place and return the practiced lines of thanking her for giving me a chance at this interview.

The woman interviewing me, Rachel Palmer, smiles a genuine smile lighting up her beautiful, well-sculp-tured face. Using the word beautiful to describe her is a gross understatement. Ms. Palmer is a classic beauty. A woman to whom people no doubt flock.

Her luscious locks of golden hair flow in soft waves past her shoulders, giving me the vibe that she would be a perfect model for a shampoo commercial.

"Quinn, tell me a little about yourself."

I pull in a nervous breath and start with the sugar coating. "Um, I'm not sure how far back you want, but I did return to work after taking some time off. Before that, I worked in California as a personal assistant. I just signed with the temp agency here in Washington yesterday."

"Yes. Monica at the agency told me you're new, and you also come with a high recommendation by their partner agency in California. She says you worked as a PA for a well-known Hollywood couple. Is that right? Wow! That must have been exciting.

I give her my practiced smile even though my stomach flips with the threat of vomiting. "It can be. The lifestyle seems magical to everyone on the outside looking in, but once you live it for a while...." Is a nightmare. "... the job not so impressive. My clients struggled with privacy all the time. It's a whole different world when you're inside the magic bubble."

"I suppose you're right." Rachael's gaze holds mine for a moment before dropping down to the paperwork in her hands.

Lounging comfortably in a chair that matches the couch, Rachel is noticeably pregnant and still appears like a woman who could work in the fashion world. A woman who wears beautiful trendy designer clothes and who would never be seen for a second out without makeup.

My hands shift to my lap, and my fingers find a loose thread on my shirt, and I mentally slap myself for fidgeting with my clothes. I can't help it. I nervously run my fingertips over the fabric again. I'm not comfortable with what I'm wearing. The black pencil skirt is out of the ordinary clothes I prefer to wear. My comfort level is jeans and t-shirts. I hate feeling like I'm exposed. Exposure does nothing but gain unwanted attention.

All my life, I never liked the way I looked. Clothes hide what you don't want others to see. A trick I learned a long time ago. Battling image issues through my childhood and teen years have made it impossible to feel good in anything outside my comfort zone.

I'm modest enough to know I'm not ugly but learning a few tricks with makeup from my sister has done wonders in the looks department.

Thinking of all my insecurities, I suddenly have a familiar burn along the tip of my finger as I skid my index fingernail down the soft tissue at the side of my thumb's cuticle. One of my unconscious nervous habits always leaves my poor thumb embarrassingly torn up along the nail bed. Try as I might, I can never break the nasty habit.

"Monica should have emailed you a copy of my detailed evaluations as well as reference letters from my former employers," I say, tucking my hands together on my lap.

"Yes, she did. I looked them over, and you have high recommendations. Do you mind if I ask why, you left your last job?" Rachel asks.

My gaze shifts down to my lap, and I quickly remember the rehearsed lines. "I was going through a rough time in my life, and I decided that it would be better for me to be close to family. So, I decided it was time to come back home to Washington."

Well, it was mostly true. I just left out a few key points, like my former employer didn't want to 'deal with my personal problems' after the attack.

I push any thoughts of that life as well as my self-conscious voice in my head telling me I'm not suitable for this job away.

"I have to tell you; I'm glad you did come back. We haven't had luck in finding the right person for this job. My brother Declan is how can I put this? He can be challenging to work for."

Challenging. No single word has more red flags attached to it in my line of work. No personal assistant wants to hear challenges while describing their employer. Challenging always means the person is a jerk, difficult to please, or a horrible human. Regardless, it makes my job as a PA a lot harder than sending emails and doing Starbucks runs.

"Has he gone through many PAs in the past?" I ask, trying to understand what I may be getting myself into.

Rachel smirks and shakes her head at the question before uncrossing and re-crossing her long legs looking to settle deeper into her seat.

"My brother has gone through them all. He has an unnatural ability to find fault with any and everyone. Too tall, too short, too plain, too muscular, too feminine. Ugh. The list goes on and on. I love my brother. I do. But I don't know how much more understanding I can be for him." She pauses for a moment as if choosing her words carefully.

"Declan is going through a challenging time in his life right now. He is learning to stand on his own two feet again, and I understand it is hard for him, but I don't know what else to do if this doesn't work out?"

"Does he want a PA? I mean, it sounds like he might be finding faults on purpose." I ask.

"He doesn't have a choice. This job opening is to find a temporary replacement for me. I've been my brother's assistant for years, but as you can see, I'm going to need some much-needed time off soon."

Her hands drift over her round pregnant stomach. "Whether he likes it or not." She smiles, bringing her hands to rest over her swollen middle "As much as it displeases my brother, I'm not going to be able to continue controlling every little detail for him for too much longer."

"Do you mind if I ask what kind of tough time he's going through? If I take the job, I would like to be prepared for what I am to help with. I like to meet challenges head-on."

There is nothing worse in my line of work than to accept a seemingly perfect job only to find out two weeks later your new employer loves to party with young girls while getting handsy with you after doing a line of coke. It wasn't only the employer who needed to be doing the interviewing. It's necessary I feel safe and comfortable at any job from here on out.

"I understand. I want to keep the personal details quiet and focus on the job tasks. Of course, if you want the job, and we hire you, I'll make sure you are up to speed with all the necessary information," Rachel says with a slight frown of concern.

"Of course. I'm used to being on a need-to-know basis. Drawbacks of working with the famous," I say to help make conversation lite once again.

The truth is, I've felt my whole life has been on a need-to-know basis. My parents sure didn't have a problem keeping things a secret from me. And getting into the line of work I did, employers aren't much more forthcoming. I've always felt like the last to be picked, the last to know. The one that is always the last to the party.

"One of the job details is being an assistant to me. I need someone who can take my place for a few months and who can help take most of the workload on a more permanent basis when this little one comes." She said, rubbing her rounded stomach.

"You will need to be heavily involved in social media and be comfortable doing blogs and phone interviews. Declan can keep strange hours, but nothing is too difficult. Besides, you seem like a smart woman. I'm sure you would have no problems with any of the workload."

I thank her for the compliment, pleased the overall job does sound promising. I need this interview to go as smoothly as possible. Not only do I need to get my life back on track, but Doctor Lynn, my therapist, says landing a job will help me obtain my goal of becoming independent from my parents and a crucial step in my recovery.

No matter how grateful I am to my parents, they're not easy to deal with them. My father's disregard for me and my mother's uncontrollable coddling of my every move makes me think the two of them are silently waiting for the hypothetical bottom to drop out.

Again.

Rachel's lips curl with a sincere smile. "Also, one of the things we would need you to do is some light house-keeping. Nothing too heavy. Declan lives alone, but his house is a substantial size. In my opinion, his house is too much for one person. However, he insists he needs the space. Half the house never gets used. I tried to convince him to move closer to the city into a condo or a smaller house, but he wouldn't hear of it.

"He works from home and doesn't go out often. He rarely leaves his house anymore. He used to love to travel all around the world. He would be so excited to see different countries and meet new people, but now, he prefers to stay home and write."

"Write? Is he a writer? Anything I might have read?"

Rachel's cheeks instantly tint with a flush of pink. "Are you a reader of romance fiction by chance? Romance on the spicier side?"

Spicier? My entire romance collection could be considered downright triple rated. I found my first erotica romance by chance after one of my employers turned me on to an author who wrote nothing but adult erotic romance. I've been hooked ever since.

"Yes. I've read some." Or a lot.

"Declan writes romance fiction, but he uses a pen name. Back when he first started writing, he thought it would be too taboo to be a male romance writer in a world full of women, so he publishes in his initials." Rachel said.

"Is there anything else I should know about him?" I ask. She hasn't given me much information about Declan, which has more red flags of warning written all over it. Then again, I don't want to make something out of nothing either.

Rachel takes a drink from her coffee cup as her cell phone buzzes, alerting her of a text message.

"Speak of the devil," She smirks, picking her phone up. Her fingers flew over the keyboard sending back a text.

"To be completely honest with you, Quinn, I like you. I think you and Declan would get along just fine. I think you should meet. I'm heading over there to drop off a few things when I'm done talking with you. Why don't you come along with me and meet him yourself? We can talk some more on the way over there, and you can meet Declan and see first-hand if you think you want to give this job a go."

"That sounds great."

Gathering my purse from the floor, I stand and wait for Rachel to grab her items before following her from the apartment. Entering the elevator, we ride in silence down the ten floors to the parking garage levels. I parked on the first level, where the signs indicated for visitors to park. As a resident, Rachel's BMW is parked on the third level of the garage in a personalized slot.

Sliding into the cool smooth black leather seats of her sleek Audi makes me wish for a moment I could splurge on myself and buy a car like this one day. I'd been in plenty of expensive cars over the years, but none of them had ever belonged to me. All were the property of my wealthy employers or household cars for all the house staff to use while running errands.

Quiet remained between us as Rachel pulled out of her parking spot, out of the garage, and headed for the freeway on-ramp.

"Where does he live?" I ask as downtown Seattle begins to disappear in the car's side mirror.

"Declan's house is about ten minutes out of the city. The actual address is in a smaller town near the water. He's not much for company these days and prefers to be out here where no one can bother him. I tease him that it's his way of staying away from our parents who live in the city. Plus, he's had a few fans find out who he is, and by not stepping out into the spotlight, he hopes people won't recognize him."

"Can't say I blame him. A few of my past employers couldn't walk to the cars in their driveways without paparazzi snapping pictures of them. It's hell when you need to put on a full face of makeup and hair to drop your kids off at school. Otherwise, you're afraid someone might take a picture of you with your bed head and have it show up on the cover of all the gossip magazines saying you're an addict."

"They assume drug-addicted by a no-makeup day and bed head?" Rachel asked.

"The paparazzi can be horrible. And the kids have it just as bad. God forbid, they are on the thinner side without having a full-fledge eating disorder or enjoy eating real food and be fat-shamed because they can't fit into the standard size zero of a designer dress." I try not to full-fledge sound too bitter.

"I think that's another reason Declan is so adamant about not having his name out there. He can go shopping or go to the movies, and no one stops him since not many people know who he is. Of course, he's a writer, not a movie star. He's no Mr. King but, he still has millions of fans and followers."

"He sounds pretty successful."

"He is. His books are popular in the romance world." Rachel said as she turned the car off the freeway to head down a minor two-lane highway. Her car is the only one on the road as the city falls further behind them. She slows down and prepares to turn to a private road.

"My brother has done well for himself. Sometimes, I think he wishes he could take the credit. But other times, he's happy being alone out here with no one being the wiser."

"If your brother's books have that much fan following, maybe I've heard of him. What name does he use?"

"D.C. Palmer. Ever heard of him?" She asked with a grin.

I shook my head. "No. I can't say I have. Maybe I'll look into picking one up."

"If you do, remember, they aren't for the weak reader. Consider your self-warned," she says, smiling.

Five minutes later, Rachel drives us through a tall black iron gate that she had to type in a code to open. The narrow driveway is wide enough for a single car and is lined along the sides with white wooden fencing that suggests an upscale ranch-style home. Following the curved driveway, the house came into view. Rachel wasn't joking when she said the house was too large for one person. The grand structure standing in front of us is sleek and modern yet holds a hint of classic country with its gray brick exterior, white and black trim, and bright red front double doors. The entire place should be featured on the pages of the Country Living magazine.

"Wow. This is incredible." I sit up straight in the seat, getting a better look out the window.

"This place is crazy, right? Declan would never have bought this place if his wife hadn't fallen in love with it at first sight."

"His wife? I didn't realize he was married. I thought he lived alone?" How had a wife not made it into their conversations before now?

"Declan is widowed. Dani died two years ago. A topic we will discuss further in more detail if you decide to take the job." She said, bringing the car to a stop across the red front doors. "Are you ready?"

No. I say in my mind. I take a deep breath in and offer Rachel a shaky smile. There's no real reason for me to be this nervous. Unless realizing that this could go so wrong, learning Rachel's brother is not only a problematic client but a difficult client who is mourning the loss of his wife that is causing me to be nervous. Two things I don't handle well myself. Death and anger.

"Sure," I say the quick one-word answer. Not knowing just how much this job is about to change my life.

"Great. Let's go meet my brother."

# Chapter Two

♥

"Declan? That's an Irish name, isn't it?"

I fight the urge to roll my fucking eyes. "It is where my grandfather was born, and since I'm his namesake, I would think so." My words come out snarky, and I sound like an asshole, but I don't apologize. The new interviewee, my sister has dragged in here twenty minutes ago, stares at me like a deer in headlights. She looks at me like she's never seen a broken man before, and in my opinion, isn't very professional of her. Weren't experienced assistants supposed to know how to handle their surroundings and how rude it is to stare at their potential employer? Did Rachel lie to me when she texted to tell me she found someone qualified to handle all my bullshit? Her words, not mine.

This meek curvy blonde doesn't strike me as someone who could handle me on a good day. Shit, she doesn't look like she could deal with Luc, my German shepherd, on a good day.

As I sit across the room from her and Rachel, I notice a slight tremble in the girl's hand. Nerves?

Great. All I need is a weak assistant who acts like doormat material. Where's the fun in that?

"Where did you go to school?" My question sounds more like an interrogation command than a harmless job interview. Maybe I should slam my hand on the table and shine a bright light into her eyes as I quiz her. I don't care who likes it or not. This is me. I have one voice, and I can't help if I come off like a hard ass. The girl probably thinks I'm a dick.

Good. I am.

I'm aware of how I behave, and I won't apologize. Life is a dick, and so am I. If I don't like you or what you bring to the table, I have no use for you. Why should I apologize for that? And although I'm a grown-ass man and should act differently, I don't.

I don't care what people think of me anymore. I used to but not anymore. I learned the hard way life's too short to give a damn what anyone thinks about you.

I drag my bored gaze over the curvy interviewee once again to take in her outfit. I'm not an expert on women's fashion, but I was married once and knew a few things. I take in the smart blouse, and the perfect knee-length skirt finished off with dull black flats. If I had to describe her appearance, I'd say she's like a new age Mary Poppins. All she's missing is the jumbo bag of tricks and the ridiculous hat.

As my gaze lifts back to hers, I see a sparkle in her eyes, holding a strength behind them that is silently daring me to comment on her boring attire. For a split second, I believe I see a glimpse of the woman Rachel promised me.

A fighter.

Maybe she wasn't as afraid of me after all. Could it be she has perfected the art of pretending? This could work for me. The last thing I need or want is some damn fearful damsel in distress mousing around my house, shedding tears every time I open my mouth.

I never wanted to hire anyone, to begin with. Rachel insisted I need help around here to make sure all the day-to-day happenings are taken care of. So I can focus on work. Hate to rain on my sister's parade, but a stack of dirty dishes and unanswered emails are not the reason the muses living in my head have grown silent. They've been silent close to two years now.

What's so wrong with wanting to be alone?

After Dani, I've grown accustomed to being alone.

"WSU. I graduated in the top five of my class. My degree is in public relations, and I minored in Business. I've since gone on to be a personal assistant as well as an estate manager." The meek girl says, answering the question I forgot I asked.

I scuff. "I don't need an estate manager," I comment as I ignore my sister's frown and questionable brow raise. Her way of implying I need to rein in the attitude.

"True. You need a personal assistant. I can assure you I have years of experience working for clients in demanding and challenging lifestyles."

I draw out a full minute to observe her fully. She balances on the edge of the couch cushion with a straight spine posture looking like she's ready at a second's notice to defend her work experience. Her legs are crossed at the ankle, and her fingers are linked together and folded neatly in her lap—a perfect practiced pose to gain herself an A-plus at any high-bred finishing school.

Too bad she doesn't look the part. Again I'm no fashion expert, but I can tell discount shoes and off-the-rack clothing when I see them—confirming my thoughts that she has had years of pretending. Years of pretending to be someone she isn't.

She has the proper posture, the correct manner, and the right yes sir, no sir, down to an art form, and fuck me, that is not what I need. I don't want a submissive female hanging around my house all damn day waiting for me to throw a command here and there to get shit done.

I agreed to make Rachel happy, but she's not the one who will be here all day and night dealing with the outcome. I will.

I need someone who could think for themselves and stay out of my damn way.

I let my gaze trail over her boring outfit once again, not hiding my lack of impressiveness. It wouldn't be too hard to keep this one far from my thoughts. She's an attractive woman but, her body holds more curves than I typically prefer. Not to mention the lack of larger breasts. I realize it makes me sound like a pig, but who cares.

I also don't do blondes. If I did decide to start dating again, which would be a cold day in hell first, blondes are the first ones scratched off the list.

Sizing her up, I'm relieved to realize she has nothing that interests me. Maybe it wouldn't be a bad idea to hire her after all. At least she wouldn't tempt me by flaunting herself around the house like the last assistant had tried. I couldn't even remember that one's name. But what I could remember included red hair and huge tits and the fact that she was too eager to work here after she learned who I was.

No matter how attractive she was, her appearance didn't matter when she opened her mouth, and I realized she was playing with a few cards shy of a full deck. Not to mention she had offered to give me a blow job by the second night of working for me. I gave her the boot after that. There's no room in my life for distractions, sex, or my old lifestyle. Not that I would have let her blow me anyways. Sex, no matter how hot the woman, is off the table. All things in the BDSM lifestyle are off the table.

As a writer of erotic-based romance, I spent all day thinking and writing relationships between a Dom and sub. At least I did before I lost Dani. Now, anything to do with love, intimacy, and all that other bullshit remains strictly in black and white.

"What has Rachel told you about the job? Knowing my loving sister, she has a notorious way of sugar-coating shit."

Rachel took that cue to put her two cents in the mix. "I told her you live alone, and you're a writer. Oh, and you like your privacy. We didn't go into many other details. We could discuss other things if she agrees to accept the job.

"So, the meek little mouse has no idea how fucked up I am? Or how much of a prick I can be? Or that I work long hours to drown my thoughts, and I sometimes can't sleep because I worry, I'll wake up in the middle of the night screaming for a ghost who no longer lingers near me.

She wouldn't be so eager to work for me if she knew about all the skeletons in my closet. And I'll be damned if I'm about to open the door and let them fall out.

"Rachel told me you write romance books. I'm excited to pick one up and read it." The girl says, giving me a shy smile. Another hopeless romantic. Yet another reason to stay as far away from her as possible. I'll be damned if I get caught up in it.

"Even if you don't take the job, I hope you will remember to be discreet about the information you hear here. I've jumped through many hoops for many years to make sure my name stays hidden."

"Of course," she agrees.

"If you take the job, your salary will be bi-weekly with no charge for the room and board. I like..." She interrupts me with a surprised arch of her brow. "Room and board? I'm confused. Is this a live-in position?"

I can't deny her surprise doesn't give me pause. "Rachel? Did you forget that key part of the interview?"

"I assumed she knew since I asked the agency for live-ins only to apply."

"I'm sorry if I sound surprised. Normally live-ins are for nannies." She interjected like a true professional. She hid any glimmers of shock, replacing it with calm and skill.

"I don't keep normal hours. I'm a writer, and I write when I'm inspired. I need someone who can be available to me and here when needed. You can't do that if you leave at night and come back in the morning. If the schedule doesn't work, this isn't the job for you."

"No, I'm sure it will be fine. Living here will work out for me. I'll have to let my...roommates know."

"Fine." Standing from my chair, I motion toward my sister. "But before you sign on for this, I want you to know, Rachel is the one pushing for me to have someone here. I think this is her way of needing to know I'm being taken care of so she can have her own life back. Besides the assisting needs, I don't want anyone here, but since it will make my sister happy for me to have a babysitter, I'm willing to try it one more time."

"Declan, that isn't true at all. I've explained how I feel about this." Rachel's hand drops to her stomach again. "You knew this day would come for the last six months."

I don't let her finish. "I know you need time when the baby comes. I'm not a complete monster. We can try having someone here once more. But this is it. If she doesn't work out, I'm done, Rachel. Let me be alone in what peace I have."

"Declan...?"I raise a hand in the air between my baby sister and myself. I shouldn't have called her out like that in front of—what was her name again?

"We can talk about this later. Why don't you show, um...?"

"Quinn," Rachel hisses between clenched teeth, annoyed I hadn't bothered to remember her name.

"Yes, show Quinn the pool house where she will be staying. I have some business to deal with for the rest of the day. Make sure you lock the door when you leave. Come on, Luc."

Leaving the room, the German shepherd who had been patiently waiting trailed behind me as we headed down the hall to the furthest room in the back of the house.

My office used to be the best room in the house, with the best views from the large picture windows overlooking the backyard, pool, and the other outbuildings.

When Dani and I first bought this house, I made my office here in the back bedroom because my wife had made her studio in the pool house. Not to mention she enjoyed spending her summer mornings swimming and lounging poolside, and this room just happened to have the perfect view to appreciate her beauty.

It allowed me to watch her as I got words on paper. She loved to swim in the nude also played a factor in my perverse need to watch. Dani knew what it did to me and would go as far as to do a little show of stripping her clothes off. Knowing all too well, I watched from behind my desk.

She called it being my muse. I know she loved the attention I gave her, and to be fair, I loved giving it.

Closing the door to the office, I slumped down into the fading plush fabric of my office chair behind the desk as Luc circled twice before curling up on his pillow on the floor next to me. Reaching over, I flick the computer monitor on, hearing the low humming of the machine wake and wait for the monitor to fire up.

My gaze slid back toward the windows that had long ago been closed off from the outside world with a thick layer of dust covering the wooden blinds. Not one drop of light has entered through these windows in two long years. I don't want to peer out of them and see that damn pool and have a constant reminder of what I'll never have again. All it is, is a reminder that I'll never see my wife dive into its cool depths or laugh and smile as she splashes chlorine water at me again.

I thought about having it filled in with dirt. To have it covered up as if it had never been there in the first place. Doing that won't fix the shambles that is now in my heart. If anything, it would make me hate myself more at the thought of destroying the one thing Dani loved the most about this house. It's also the damn reason I couldn't move away and sell it. The reason I fight myself every day to stay.

I can still hear my therapist's toneless words now. "Don't sell the house just yet. Instead, lease an apartment for a few months, see how things go. Moving into a different space may help the healing."

I couldn't do it. I couldn't bring myself to let the house go any more than I could bring myself to fill in that damn pool. To let everything about Dani go. Not yet. I'm not ready yet.

I've been taking it one day at a time. At least my therapist calls it that. I am learning to cope and live with a loss of a loved one.

In the beginning, there were days I couldn't make it out of bed. There were nights I would wander through the house, a lost soul-searching for my missing mate. Tears fell freely, and my heart ripped and bled. There's no getting over a woman like Dani. My world, my life, my love, my partner. I'm never going to get over her. All I can do is learn to live without her.

Cancer is a raging bitch, and if it were a living, breathing organism, I would be more than happy to shove a stick up its ass. It became my beautiful wife's silent killer. On our wedding day, I vowed to serve, protect, and cherish Dani, not realizing then, there were things in this world I couldn't protect her from. Though not from lack of trying.

I spent hours in those first few months after her diagnosis begging, praying, and bartering with every God from Christian to Greek to take me instead. But fate can be a fickle bitch just like her twin sister Karma, and I was punished by having to watch my beautiful wife die in front of me and not being able to do a damn thing to stop it.

Walking down memory lane forces a ball of rage to ignite in my stomach. I look around the office, my gaze skims over the empty surface of my bookshelves and desktop. Knowing I'm not going to find the items my eyes and heart search for.

I had taken them all away. Every picture of Dani from the desk and walls are stored away in the meager attempt they would no longer haunt me.

When I first felt that I might return to writing, Dr. Matt, my therapist, suggested taking the pictures and removing them from the room. From the office, where I need to keep her memories away long enough to get words on paper. I hadn't stopped there. I had taken every picture I could find down, breaking glass and shredding photographs. At the time, destroying every shred of our happy lives together felt like the right thing to do. I was also knee-deep in the second stage of grief, also known as anger.

A shaky sigh escapes my lips as I rake fingers through my hair. Looking down, the light on my phone screen lights up, catching my attention and signaling I have a message. I pick up the phone, and my finger moves over the screen, seeing Rachel's message. I tap on her name and wait as the text comes up on the screen.

*Hey brother, just letting you know we left, and I locked the door behind us. Quinn seems interested in taking the job, so I will fill her in a little more and get the paperwork started. Will you please try to make this one work? You don't have to like her, but please stop acting like a dick. You were a little rude to her, and you promised you would try harder this time. I Love you. I'll be back tomorrow.*

I hit the button to erase the message, swing back around in the chair, face the computer monitor, and pull up my current work in progress. As I touch fingers to the keyboard and the words begin to flow, I feel the peace my writing gives me as it takes me out of my head and leads me out of the darkness, I now call my life.

# Chapter Three

♥

"I'm sorry about my brother," Rachel says after we're back in the car and heading toward the freeway.

"It's okay." Telling my potential new employer that her brother is an ass isn't going to work in my favor.

Declan Palmer was the complete opposite of the image I had in my mind. If someone asked me to picture a male romance writer suffering the loss of his wife, I would have described a small, frail empty man. Boy, did I have it wrong?

The man who stared back at me, as I unconsciously ogled him, had been anything but frail. Handsome didn't come close to describing Declan's stunning handsome features. The word didn't do the man justice. The genes in their family are excellent.

Standing shy of six-foot, his short black hair and demanding brown eyes complete his dark, moody features. I tried my best to look beyond the lines of his hard-set face in the few short minutes I could spare to gaze at him without his noticing. When he turned those rich brown eyes toward me, I had the urge to crumble under their stare.

"Dr. Matt, his therapist, says Declan is still going through the five stages of grief." Rachel's gaze moves to the side, catching mine.

"He hasn't always been like that. When Dani, his wife, first got sick, Declan started changing. The illness took her fast. She started complaining one day that she didn't feel well. She had all the usual flu symptoms, cold sweats, chills, and headaches, all the typical signs. When a few days turned into a week. Declan took her to the doctor, thinking what anyone would that his wife had the everyday run-of-the-mill flu.

"However, after a blood test came back with abnormal readings, they admitted her into the hospital to run more tests. We learned she was already entering the last few stages of Chronic Myeloid Leukemia. Cancer starts in the blood cells of the bone marrow and invades the blood. With a late diagnosis, the doctors were skeptical about chemo working." She pauses to wipe a tear from her cheek.

"If they had found it earlier, she would have gone through treatments and would have had a good fighting chance. But Dani had never been a huge fan of doctors, to begin with. Her parents raised her to believe if she wasn't seriously sick, she had no reason to be seen by a doctor. They were the type of people to do home remedies first before buying over-the-counter medicines. No one knows if she had other symptoms. She never complained about anything."

My eyes drift close as I think of how awful it must have been for Dani and Declan. Too many people ignore the early warning signs, unfortunately. That horrible illness takes too many lives every year.

"They started her on immediate treatments, and she fought for months, but the treatments took a lot out of her. To understand, you need to know Dani oozed beauty. All her life, she had been a feminine girl who didn't have a mean bone in her body. She loved pink, loved makeup, and adored beautiful clothes.

"After a few months in treatment, she began to lose her hair, and her body became so thin and frail that her cheeks sunk in as she lost close to fifty pounds she didn't have to lose." Rachel paused, wiping another tear from her cheek with a swipe of her fingers.

"After months of hospitals and trial drugs, she begged my brother to let her die. She told him she no longer wanted to fight for her and only fought for him. She wanted the pain to stop."

Hearing Rachel's story made it hard to breathe around the heavy lump lodged in my throat. I force a cough in the attempt to remove the damn thing.

"Oh my God. That's so sad."

She nods, clearly needing a minute to control her emotions before continuing.

"Declan lived in denial about how bad cancer had got. When it became clear the sickness was taking everything from her, in his eyes, she remained just as beautiful as she had been the day they were married. He punched a doctor in the face after the guy called Declan selfish for keeping her hanging on. Wrong of the doctor to say, but he had a point. Dani wouldn't go anywhere without knowing Declan would be okay without her."

"Do you think she stayed for him?"

"I do. Those two had a marriage a little different from most relationships these days. Dani had a... submissive personality. She needed Declan to accept her illness and be ready to let her go. She wouldn't let cancer come between the two of them."

"But he couldn't let her go," I say, confirming what I already know. My heart broke right along with the couple in her story.

Rachel shakes her head. "No. He couldn't. But in the end, he did what he had to do to make her comfortable. The five stages of grief overpowered my brother. Of course, denial started before Dani left us. After her funeral, anger, and rage consumed him. He tore through the house, destroying any and everything in his path. He still carries rage tucked inside his heart. Everyone says time will heal the wounds, but I'm not so sure I believe that anymore after two years. I think no matter how Declan tries to move on, he will always carry anger in his heart for the pain Dani went through. The other two stages of bargaining and depression were hit-and-miss. He recently went back to work. I pray his depression is finally getting better. I long for the day he will enter the fifth stage, acceptance."

"Were the two of them together for a long time?" I ask.

"Yes. I mean, for Declan, his relationship with Dani ranked up there to the longest relationship of his life. They were together for five years, and for my brother, who used to be a man whore before Dani came along, it was a lifetime."

"I think I could see your brother as a player. She tamed the wild beast in him, huh?"

*Don't you wish you had someone to love you that much?*

I ignored the voice inside my head, wishing that I had kept on the medication the last doctor had given me months ago.

Smiling, Rachel wipes the moisture from her eyes once again. "You could say that."

I turn my attention to the window giving myself a minute to clear the voice from my mind. Somewhere in the middle of their story, my heart began to soften and to slowly understand, if only just a little, why Declan acts the way he does. It's the caretaker inside of me who wants to show compassion toward the husband who had to watch the love of his life die. I don't pity him, only understanding.

Rachel's heavy sigh breaks my attention. "I know, I just dumped a heavy load of information on your shoulders, but here is the bottom line. My brother is trying to weave his way through this world with a broken heart. He can be mean, and there will be times you want to run screaming from the house. But knowing that, I'm still going to ask you, will you please, at least, give this a try? I'm running out of options. No one seems to understand the grief he's in."

I turn my attention to the freeway in front of us. I give Rachel's question some thought as skyscrapers begin to fill my line of vision, telling me we're about to enter the city once again. We would be back in the parking garage in less than ten minutes. I don't have a lot of time to make a decision I will have to live with.

My fingers softly drum against the leather interior of the inside door. I wouldn't say I liked having to make this decision on the spot. On the one hand, I could make more than enough money to get out of my parent's house. I've not been home long but living with my mother would drive any sane person to madness.

Not having my sister Kate there to help keep me sane while my mom can be a little overbearing. Mom tried her hardest to pry herself into my life. She always makes sure I'm okay and not ready to plunge off the edge.

Not that I can blame her after the few rough years I put my family through. The years I want to forget. The hell I put myself through. Not to mention hearing about how much pain Declan struggles with every day over his wife's loss was the same pain I could have given to my own family. No one knows what self-inflicted pain feels like unless they struggle with it.

My father is another reason not to want to be back home. The man barely notices when I'm there. Although mom assures me it's because football season is in full swing. Beings he's a season ticket holder, he takes the game seriously. Mom says, "If you're not a Seahawk or a ref, he has no use for you until February." Mom doesn't say that my father still hasn't forgiven me for the night I tried to change their lives forever. I put my parents and sister through hell. Dad loves me. He just can't forgive me.

As Rachel pulls her shiny sports car into the parking garage once again, I think about what my life would have been like had my family walked away from me while I was at my lowest.

My parents struggled to understand my sickness, but they never once gave up hope that I would get better. I had feared that one day my family would give up on me, and I would be tossed aside and left alone.

Even though Declan wasn't my family, he's someone's family. He's Rachel's brother. I can't give up on someone so easily. My parents and sister didn't give up on me, and I need to pay that forward.

"I'm going to give it a try. I've worked with challenging people before, and your brother doesn't seem all too different."

The car suddenly fills with beautiful laughter. "Honey, you have no idea how difficult he can be. But I'm glad you're willing to try. I'll call him in the morning. You and I can go over your contract and paperwork once we get back to my condo." She tells me with a wide smile.

"Are you sure you don't want to interview anyone else?"

She shakes her head before catching my gaze. "There's no one left. You're our last hope."

# Chapter Four

♥

"Damn it, Declan. We talked about this. You said you would give this arrangement another try. You know I need time off after the baby comes. I've worked non-stop for you in the past, but I'm not giving in this time. There's nothing I do for you that Quinn can't do while I'm gone."

I hold the phone to my ear, but I do not comment. I know my sister, and she's not done telling me off yet.

"Declan, you need someone who can dedicate time to the hundreds of tasks that need done every day. Do you think book blogs and media presses set themselves up? It all takes time. So does all the crap you want to be done at the house. I can't do it all. And I won't keep trying to keep up anymore either. I'll soon have a little one who does need me for everything, and that's where I'm needed more. It's time I put my family in front of my career for once."

I keep the phone away from my mouth, so she can't hear my heavy sigh. Rachel's voice teeters on a thin edge between anger and frustration. I know my sister too well to know if I don't stop pushing her now and back off a little, she's going to break. All hell will break loose if that happens. I won't see her again until after the baby's here.

I hear a female sigh come over the phone line as Rachel lets out a breath calming her emotions. When she speaks again, her voice is soft.

"Why don't we think of Quinn as my assistant, okay? I need to know she's there getting things done so I can put all my focus on what I need to get done here. My doctors are telling me I'm bordering bed-rest if I don't start taking it easy." She pauses for a moment, and even though I couldn't see her, I knew my sister was doing that thing where she closes her eyes and silently counts to ten to calm herself down. When she's ready to speak without yelling at me, she continues.

"Did the pallet of books arrive yet?" The change in subject is on purpose, but I don't call her out. I don't want to upset her again. I hate hearing anger and sadness in my sister's voice, primarily when directed at me. Knowing I cause her irritation of any kind makes me feel like an asshole.

Sitting back in my office chair, my gaze darts to the book invoice my new assistant left on my desk this morning.

"Yeah, it's here. As we speak, I have our assistant opening the boxes in the dining room. You know a thousand books are needing signing, right?"

"Isn't it great? We stopped at a thousand, but we've been getting emails from fans asking if they can still pre-order. I think this autographed release is a wonderful idea. We might have to reopen it for another thousand."

"Are you out of your mind? Do you have any idea how long it's going to take me to sign all these books?"

Doing a pre-order for the newest release is a wonderful idea for sales and the fans. But for me, it's a pain in my ass. I just want to write. I've never liked the business side of this job. That was always Dani's area and then Rachel's.

"That's one of the things Quinn is there for. I already sent over the order forms for her to print out with the reader's mailing addresses on them. You sign them and have her package and label. You're smart. Figure it out."

"Fine. Are you coming out tomorrow?" I sigh into the phone.

"I'll be there tonight. Remember, I told you I would stop by tonight because I'm taking tomorrow off?"

"Tomorrow is Tuesday. What do you need the day off for?" Not that she needs my permission to have a day to herself, but I don't tell her that.

"I have stuff going on, Declan, God. What is wrong with you today?"

I close my eyes and rub my forehead with my fingers out of frustration. Rachel's right. She has a life of her own to live and a baby to get ready for. How can I expect her to spend every minute here with me?

"I'm sorry. You're right. You don't have to tell me what you're doing. You're a big girl, and you don't need my permission." And soon, she will be a mom. It still blows my mind. My baby sister is going to be a mother soon.

"Thank you for saying that. I'll grab food before I head out to help you two with the book signing in a few hours. Is there anything special you want me to pick up?"

I tell her to pick whatever sounds good to her and end the call. I release a heavy breath as my gaze moves to the closed office door. I hesitate, knowing my new PA is out there. I hate this. I don't have the slightest idea what I'm supposed to talk to her about. All the other PA's Rachel brought over here were closer to my age.

Quinn strikes me differently from the others, and it's not just her young age. I can't put a finger on it just yet, but something about her tells me she's not the type to run screaming for the hills.

Is there a possibility we could have something in common? A woman ten years younger than me? I don't even find the girl attractive. Not that she isn't beautiful. She's just not my type.

Running my sweaty palms over the leg of my pants, I push to my feet and take the steps toward the door. Holding the door open, I wait as my trusty sidekick takes his sweet time getting up from his bed. "Come on, old man. We have work to do." I say as Luc walks past me and out the door. He doesn't seem happy about leaving the comfort of his bed. "I know the feeling, pal."

I reach the dining room coming to a halt as my gaze scans the room. Boxes upon boxes are stacked in rows of four tall lined up against the far wall. No doubt they were piled only so high because the person doing the stacking lacked the upper body strength to go any higher.

Some boxes are empty, and piles of D.C. Palmer's newest smutty romance sit waiting for me on two six-foot-long folding tables. Had she done all this in an hour?

I feared I would have to give outlined details for her to follow as I've done for past assistants, and yet, here she's taking the initiative and getting things done.

The floorboard under me groans with my weight. A startled squeak is ripped from Quinn as she quickly turns to face me and forces a tight smile over her lips. The sound makes me think of a mouse coming upon a fat house cat.

"Will this setup work for you? Do I need to change anything?"

My new blonde assistant is on the other side of the table, holding a small stack of books in her arms. Judging by the stray strands of hair that have worked their way out from the once neat tight ponytail, it's clear she's been working her butt off on her first day.

I appreciate the drive she shows.

Looking around the room one more time, I nod. "This will work. You're going to need to find the pile of order forms and labels. Rachel said she emailed them earlier today."

"I printed the forms and put them right here on your table. I thought you could sit here and do the signing. Once they are signed, I'll move them to this table to get them packaged and ready to ship. Rachel said the first pick-up will be tomorrow?"

"Sounds like a plan." I say, taking a seat in the rolling office chair she placed at the table for me. A small pillow sits on the chair at my lower back for my comfort. Who told her to do that? Had Rachel asked her to do it? Or could it be she put thought into setting the room up to my liking and comfort?

My back stiffens. I don't want Quinn to think I need her to treat me with kid gloves. The last thing I need is someone smothering me. Rachel more than fills that role, and when she doesn't, my mother never has a problem filling me in on all the aspects of my life she wants me to do differently. I don't need anyone fussing over me. I prefer to be alone in my misery. The thought of this mouse of a girl treating me as such pisses me off.

Glancing over the table, I eye the favorite gel pens I prefer to use when signing books. Holding one in the air, I catch her gaze and arch a brow in question.

"Your sister left those. I figured they were meant for you. Are they the ones you use?"

"Yeah," I snap. It seems petty to be annoyed with someone who just wants to see after my comforts. I manage to drop my gaze away from hers and start on the first stack of books.

It doesn't take long before book three hundred is signed and moved to the other side of the table, where Quinn is consumed with the task of stuffing the books into envelopes. I drop the pen down and lean back in the chair, raising my arms to stretch over my head. I watch as she glances over at me and smiles. "Do you need a break? I could bring you something. Do you want Water, Soda, or Coffee?" Her cheery voice cuts through the awkward silence, and I'm reminded of my mood.

"If I do, I can get it myself." I watch hurt flash quickly over her face, and I wince as my tone echoes back to me. Why does this girl bring out my worse traits? I feel like I need to see just how far I can push her before she pushes back, and for the life of me, I can't figure out why.

Guilt creeps in, and a heaviness unfolds in my chest. I can't breathe. I don't like acting like a dick. In the last two years, I've had few people around me. I don't want to be around people living their perfect lives with seemingly no cares in the world while my Dani doesn't get the chance to. People say it's okay to still be bitter. Others, like Rachel, say I have no excuse to be a jackass.

I push away from the table, needing to get out of the room and get some air. I catch a glimpse of concern in Quinn's eyes before she turns back to packaging the signed books. Another ping of guilt stops me at the entryway to the kitchen. Cursing my damn remorse, I look over my shoulder at her.

"Do you want anything? Since I'm going into the kitchen." My voice is stern, but I can't help it.

Without looking my way, she shakes her head. I'm sure she's annoyed with my bitchiness." Suit yourself." I say and disappear down the hall. I grab a can of soda from the fridge and hear the front door open and close.

"Hey, you two. Wow, great start on the books. Look how many are done." Rachel steps into the room with her hands full of brown paper take-out bags.

"Are you ready for a dinner break? I brought Chinese. I'll get some plates," Rachel says, walking past me, letting the aroma of the delicious-smelling take-out fill the air as she passes.

"This is going to take forever, Rachel. You think we can do another thousand?"

"Have Quinn sign half of them. Take some of the load off your plate. I'll help too."

My head is shaking before she can finish.

"No. My fans deserve to get a genuine signature from me." I say, taking my seat back at the table.

Rachel turns in the doorway of the kitchen. The look on her face tells me she's not buying my bullshit. "It's not as if the readers know you on a personal level. Or know who you really are. They wouldn't know the difference."

"No." The word is stern "Either I sign them, or they don't get signed." Why, all of a sudden, does it feel like I'm having to explain and defend myself all the time?

"We still have a few days before they all have to ship, so just keep working away at it. It will get done."

"Yes, Mom." My mood is starting to slip into the bottomless pit of annoyance again.

"The fans have reacted to the virtual signing better than we had hoped. We have to do it with the next release," Rachel says, sinking into a chair near the table with her plate tucked between her chest and her arms as if the food she's about to consume is her own precious young.

"Easy for you to say, you're not the one here doing any of the work."

Lowering her fork with food still on it, Rachel looks toward Quinn. The two women share a look I'm sure men all over this earth could recognize as 'did he just say that?

"Has he been this way all day?" Rachel's gaze zeros in on Quinn.

Quinn's gaze flickers my way. "This is the most he's spoken all day."

Shit. Here we go. Rachel will have a field day with this little piece of information. I should stop her before my loving sister, and business manager turns into the incredible hulk.

I jump to my defense when Rachel swings her raised brows and angry mama bear glare toward me.

I raise my hands in the air as part of my self-defense. "I've been preoccupied. It has nothing to do with her." Pausing, I steal a glance toward Quinn, who is watching us from her seat across the room.

"Look, I'm an ass. You know that. I'm not good at this, but I promise I'll try my hardest not to be a dick anymore. Okay?"

Rachel snorts but goes back to eating. "My dear brother, you truly have a way with words. I'll give you that."

Before I have a chance to regret my words, my sister thankfully changes the subject.

"Quinn, I showed you around the house a little the other day, has my brother bothered to at least show you around the rest of the house?"

"I've seen the garage. It's where the pallet of books was placed after delivery. And of course, the pool house."

"How thoughtful of him not to give you a tour. After we finish up here, I'll show you around. It's not a mansion, but I wouldn't hold my breath at the notion if you did get lost, my brother would spend one-minute thinking to go look for you. It's basic survival."

I glance up, meaning to glare at my sister but instead, I catch a soft, beautiful smile curl over Quinn's lips.

I peer back at my sister and shrug. "I've been busy. I'm on a deadline right now. By the way, do you have any news on the script edits? If they don't get them back to me for final approval soon, production is going to be pushed back."

"Production?" Quinn asks, popping her head up.

"One of the series is getting a three-part miniseries for Netflix. Cool, right? To think the world of romantic erotica is finally making its way into mainstream media. Even if we do still have those stiff asses sticking their noses up at us. The genre is gaining more and more fans every day, and that's all that matters."

Rachel says with a heart as if she's the writer in the family. I have to give credit where it's due. Besides Dani, Rachel has always been my number one fan.

"That's exciting. Congratulations. Which series?"

"The Dark Desires series."

"Wow! Really? I just picked up the first book. One girl is torn between two brothers. Sad, but hot."

"Sad? How do you figure it's sad? It has a happy ever after." I said, not caring that I just spoiled the ending for her.

Quinn takes another small bite from her fork and wipes her mouth with her napkin before setting her plate down. The look on her face says she's tried to find the words to argue her point.

"I mean, the struggle Sarah goes through with loving both brothers and having to choose between them is the heart wrenching part. Oh, and then there's the baby, and they don't know which one is the father because she has been with both men. It's not sad in a depressing way. It's sad that even though she loves them both, she would rather give them both up to save their brotherhood before they tear it apart. It's what's so moving."

"I thought you said you just got the book?"

She shrugs. "I'm a fast reader."

Hearing someone talk about my books with so much passion makes pride swell inside my chest. For a moment, her strong argument took me back in time, and for a brief moment, my mind landed on one of the many disagreements Dani and I had over characters and story plots. She had once told me the same thing, and it felt good to hear someone talk about my stories with emotion again. Something I didn't think I would experience again

The distant memory brings on the familiar ping of emotion. Therapy has taught me that memories of my wife won't cause so much pain and hurt inside me one day. I wish that day would come sooner rather than later. She's gone, and nothing is changing that.

Deep down, I know I'm ready to move on. My heart can't take any more of the pain that has lingered for far too long. Dani wouldn't have wanted me to mourn this long.

"Excuse me, ladies."

I push out of my chair, leave my dinner plate sitting untouched, and walk from the room. At this moment, I don't care if I'm being rude by walking away because being rude feels better than flying into a rage, I'm not sure I could contain.

The need to get out of the house and breathe fresh air overpowers me. For the first time since Dani's death, I start feeling like I want to move on from the dark corners I've crawled into. Even if it's just to myself, I can admit that it may be time to move on.

# Chapter Five

By the time I pulled the door to the pool house closed, the morning sun had worked its way up the sky to peek over the tree line in the backyard. Wrapping my sweater-covered arms around my middle, I try to hold off the chill lingering in the morning air.

My first three full days working and living here have been nothing like I thought they would be. After Declan stormed out during dinner the first night, I spent the entire next day worrying myself to the point of anger about what I could have said to set him off. Rachel tried to reassure me his mood swings were normal and pleaded with me not to make them personal. I struggle with confrontation.

Do you blame him for not wanting to be out here looking at you all day?

I shake the inner voice from my head. He has locked himself inside his office for the last two days, not opening the door for anything. Not even the food I cooked for him. The previous two mornings, it grew cold on the tray outside the door to his office, sitting there until I removed it out of fear of attracting ants.

Feeling frustrated, I make my way to the kitchen and begin pulling ingredients out of the fridge to make breakfast. I think about throwing bread in the toaster for myself since cooking is a waste of time and food for a person who won't bother to eat it.

I won't waste more time being ignored with my irritable mood this morning. Turning on the stove, I crack eggs into a bowl, add the milk and whip up a plate of scrambled eggs and toast. This time, I don't bother making a plate for my employer. If he wants to ignore the efforts I put in, I might as well stop wasting the food.

As I eat, I turn on my iPad and pull my plate closer to my seat. I open the emails Rachel sends daily on everything that needs tending to for the day and any preparations I might have for the up-and-coming days.

Today's first email is already waiting for me. The message is short, with just one line.

Has he emerged from the room yet?

Rachel's question forces my eyes to roll back as I quickly type a reply.

Day three. Nothing yet.

A few minutes after hitting send, the distant ringing of a phone echoes through the air. I don't bother to look for it because the sound is coming from behind the home office's locked door down the hall.

By the time I get through with my breakfast and place my dishes in the dishwasher, Declan's voice breaks the silence as he emerges from the room.

"I did leave the room. Yes, I did. I'm heading to the kitchen now. Wait..." Declan holds a cell phone out toward me, bouncing it up and down, indicating he wants me to take the phone, which I do bring to my ear.

"Hello?"

"Oh, good. He did leave the room. He needs to get moving today, please. He has two days to have all those books signed. Sign them yourself if you have to. Oh, and he needs to be in the city by one this afternoon to meet with production. Do you think you can have him cleaned up and ready to look professional in time?"

I glance at the digital clock on the microwave, just after nine twenty. That leaves just over three hours to work a miracle. "He'll be there."

I hand the phone back to Declan, who doesn't bother getting back on but switches it off before tucking it in his back-jean pocket.

"I should jump in the shower."

"That sounds like a good place to start," I mumble, turning my gaze back to the iPad.

Declan turns his back to me but doesn't make a move to leave the room. His head turns so he can see me over his shoulder. He looks as if he wants to say something but instead walks out of the room.

God, that man frustrates me.

I force myself to take a calming breath as irritation gnaws on my insides. I'm not sure I can do this. I thought I could, but I can't. Declan needs professional help. He needs someone educated on how to deal with grief. Like a light bulb flickering on, an idea comes to me.

Grabbing my cell phone, I head back to the pool house as I pull up my contacts and scroll down until I come to the one person who would know how to handle this situation as a professional. I'm sure I'm going to regret this.

*Quinn*

You need to be firm yet helpful.

Those are my mother's words playing over in my head. Like a chant, I keep repeating them.

It wasn't easy growing up with a therapist for a mom. Especially when she has a fucked-up daughter like me. I kept her busy, that's for sure, raising an unstable daughter with multiple self-harm and self-image issues. My mom's been a therapist for twenty years. She's seen just about every type of situation walk into her office.

I took a minute to explain the loss of Declan's wife to my mom. I also made sure to mention the mood swings and anger. I talk with her as I wait for Declan to shower and dress for his meeting. Even though she tells me to stand firm, she also reminds me just how unstable people in Declan's situation can be.

Not that I think he would hurt me. Declan seems to be dominant by nature, and if I took a guess, I'd bet that he pulls his character traits for most of the heroes he writes about.

A warm heat wrapped around my neck at the thought of Declan being like the heroes in his books. Considering his novels are Dominant/submissive relationships and bondage romance, it isn't too hard to imagine him in one of his scenes.

I have to mentally push those thoughts away as I prepare for the rest of the day and the new start to this working relationship. He is my boss, and I will not think of him as anything but that. One of two things is definitely about to happen. Either my mom will be right, and standing my ground to Declan will open him up to our professional relationship, or... I'll be back to filling out job applications.

After a twenty-minute car ride into the city and another three hours of discussion around a table with the production team, we are back inside Declan's Jeep submerged in silence. I desperately tried not to inhale the aroma of musk and sandalwood as it filled my nostrils. The delicious smell made it near impossible not to see the man sitting no more than a foot away from me. God, it's been forever since I've had sex.

Shit.

Where in the hell did that thought come from? I shift my weight in the seat, quickly changing positions as if my body can shield my thoughts from Declan.

"You, okay?" he asks, glancing over at me. He must have noticed the sudden change in my demeanor.

"Fine. Fine. Just fine." God, I sound like an idiot.

Declan's lips curl up at the ends with a sneer.

"Do you think those writers are going to be able to do your work justice?" I ask, hoping to start any conversation with him.

Declan remains quiet as if he's giving my question some thought. His head, resting back on the headrest of the driver's seat, slowly rolls to the side to gaze at me.

"What are you talking about?"

I meet his gaze.

"I overheard what the production staff said about the storyline and how they want it to go through a rewrite. How do you think your fans will react to the new storyline?"

He's silent for a moment as his gaze moves back to the road in front of us.

"It's a small plot change. Do you think the hardcore readers will mind or be upset about it?"

A silent breath leaves my lungs as relief fills me. Declan could have told me to butt out and mind my own business. Or better yet, he could have continued to ignore me, but he didn't. He's asking for my opinion. One step forward.

"Of course, the fans are going to notice. You can't touch the hot factors. I'm a new fan of the Dark Desire series. So if I'm worried, what will the lifelong fans think? I think making some of those changes the writers mentioned in the meeting will be a mistake."

I watch from the corner of my eye as he shifts in his seat, resting one hand on the top of the steering wheel.

"What changes do you think would be mistakes? Speaking as a fan, of course." He grins as he says the last part with a subtle eye roll.

Looking toward me, he meets my gaze for a second before turning back to traffic.

"Well, for starters, I don't think you should take out the part about her getting pregnant. Half of the appeal of the love triangle is that she doesn't know which brother is the father, and in the end, they both decide it doesn't matter to them because they both want to be the father. Those kinds of things you just can't take out of the plot. It will ruin the fantasy for some of the book lovers."

"Removing the...what did you call it...the hot factor?" He throws my words back at me.

I smile. "Exactly."

"Alright. We keep the baby. What else?"

My smile widens. At least I'm getting him talking to me. Even though it shouldn't, having this conversation feels like I've just won a small victory in the invisible war between us.

"Speaking only as a fan, of course," I tease.

"Oh, of course," he mocks. There are faint traces of a smile touching his lips, so I decide not to linger on it.

"You can't let them take away any of the threesome scenes either. Those are the hot wow factors your readers will be expecting. The fans will be expecting them, but you know that already. It's the reason you wrote them in the first place. If you take those out, half the shock factor is gone. A forbidden romance is super-hot."

Declan doesn't respond right away. He keeps his attention on the front window. The stern expression on his face gave me the sense that he was pondering our conversation. Minutes pass before he speaks again.

"I want to apologize to you for the way I acted the past few days. Especially that first night we met. Please believe me when I tell you my intention wasn't to upset you." He pauses to take a long breath letting the air fill his lungs for a moment before exhaling. Running his palms over the thighs of his jeans, he seems to be ridding his palms of nervous sweat.

"When you were talking about the series, it reminded me of...." He paused a moment before beginning again with a shaky breath.

"It reminded me of Dani. After she would read a new manuscript of mine, she would go to work breaking it apart to discuss the flaws. I guess in my mind, you were doing the same thing, and in some weird way, it made me realize I've needed to make some changes. My reactions have nothing to do with you. I just took it out on you, and I'm sorry."

My gut twists with sorrow as I listen to him. I never intended to bring up bad memories for him.

"I'm sorry too. I'm not sure of all the triggers yet. Like in any relationship, even a professional one, we need to teach each other what we can deal with and what we can't."

"My whole life feels like a trigger." He turns away to the scenery passing us.

I think back to my mom's advice this morning. 'If you want him to open up and let his guard down, you have to make him believe that you are trustworthy. Most people struggling with loss have a hard time letting people in.'

"Does talking about Dani bring on anger?" I keep my gaze straight in front of me as I ask. My fingers tighten around each other, and I can't bring myself to look at him. I can't let him see how nervous I am talking about this.

After a lingering pause, Declan finally breaks the silence.

"It took me a year after it happened to accept the fact my wife is gone. Believe it or not, this last year hasn't been too bad. I know I have my moments, my behavior the other night, but on most days, I'm...learning to weave through my life without her."

I offer a reassuring smile, not sure if it looks genuine. "Did your therapist phrase it like that?" I ask, darting my gaze toward him.

"Is it that obvious?" The sides of his lips twitch like he wants to grin.

I hold my hand in the air turning my gaze toward him again. "Twenty years of therapy, right here."

"Wow. You're a lifer, huh? You might be more fucked up than I am. What did you do to receive that life sentence?"

"I was born." My gaze holds his for a moment, and I think I see a flicker of concern in his eyes. "My mother is a psychologist. I lay on the couch for free."

"Shit. What was that like growing up?"

"How do you think? Every time I did anything that most people would shrug off as stupid childhood or teenage adolescence, my mom sat me down and made me 'talk' it out," I say, using my fingers to make air quotations.

The next sound echoing through the car is the sound of male laughter. The deep, hearty chuckle makes my heart, honest to goodness, melt just a little. He has a great laugh and smile.

"That had to be fun growing up?"

"Fun? Trying to explain to your mom you already know all about and have tried masturbation isn't what I call fun. Not when she wants you to talk about how it makes you feel."

He turns away once again, still holding a smile on his face. It's great to see him smile. Something tells me it's been a while since he had last done it. Besides, his features just went from handsome to downright fuck-able when he smiles.

God help me.

"Did she ever walk in on you while you were in the middle of doing it?" He asks, keeping our conversation going.

"God, no. I would have died. Don't tell me...you?" I laugh as the smile fades from his mouth, and I try hard not to picture him stroking himself into orgasm. The heat rose to my cheeks again.

"When I was twelve. I got ahold of one of my dad's dirty magazines that my mom didn't know he had. I thought I had locked the bathroom door. I had double-checked it every single time except for that day."

I laugh harder. "Oh no. what did she do?"

"What could she do? She quickly closed the door leaving me to clean up and cover myself. When I went down for dinner that night, she acted like she hadn't just seen me whacking off in the family bathroom."

"You're lucky. My mom would have made me keep a masturbation journal or something, so we could talk about how it makes me feel."

His deep throaty laugh fills the car once again.

"I guess if you look at some kids, we were both just lucky to have our parents when we were growing up."

I nod in agreement. I don't bother to tell him that those memories are all before the shit-show of my teenage years began. By the time my sixteenth birthday rolled around, I was already deeply depressed, medicated, and suffering from self-harm. I wish I could block all those memories permanently.

Pulling the car through the gate, he came to a stop in front of the house. As he shut off the engine, I unhooked my seatbelt, pausing a moment before climbing out.

"I hope I didn't overstep my bounds about the whole production thing. I just...want you to have the best for your fans. I've been on the fan pages and media sites. There's a lot of people out there, like me, who love the stories. We invest ourselves in the characters. I would hate to see your fans turn on the series all because of a bad rewrite." I reach for the door handle to step out when his words stop me.

"Thank you. I'm glad you said something. Not many people in my life will give honest feedback straight to my face. They just listen to what I want and try to give it to me. What happens when I'm lining their pockets with money? Only a few people in my life ever had the balls to voice their opinion with me on anything. It's refreshing."

Later that night, while I busied myself preparing dinner, Declan sat in the dining room with his favorite ink pen in one hand, open book in front of him while signing the pre-orders. It felt domestic. I'm working, but I'm also enjoying spending time with Declan.

"Ready for a little dinner break?" I ask, carrying two dinner plates out into the dining room and setting his plate on the table next to him.

"Perfect timing. I just finished another box. I think I'm down to a few boxes left. I guess they can wait until I get some food in me."

I leave his plate and walk over to the chair on the opposite side to sit down and indulge in my cooking.

"This is good. I'm pleased to know you can cook." He says, taking another bite of the flaky fish I baked in the oven.

"You would have known that three days ago if you weren't sulking in your office." My words sound harsh though I don't mean them to be. I'm relieved when he offers a smile instead of a frown.

"True."

"Your last assistant didn't cook very well?"

His head shakes as he pops another bit of salad in his mouth. He swallows before answering. "My last assistant wasn't here long enough for me to find out."

"Did she not like your charming personality?" I ask, grinning to let him know I'm teasing and bit into the flaky white fish.

He kept his eyes on his food. "No. The opposite, actually. She offered me sexual favors on her second day here."

My fork dropped from my fingers, making a loud clink as it landed against the plate. "Seriously? Wow. What did you do?"

"There wasn't anything I could do. I made her leave the next day. Who knows what kind of shit she's capable of? The last thing I need is to be accused of sexual assault."

He had a good point. In this day in age, women have been standing up for their rights, and that's great. However, some women will take advantage of the 'Me too' movement, and innocent men like Declan can end up getting hurt because of it. Those situations are not unheard of for a pissed-off woman to cry assault when things don't go her way.

It makes me wonder why he feels safe with me. Maybe he can see that I'm not that kind of person and that I would never do that to him.

Or maybe because he knows how ridiculous you are, and no matter how hard you try, you will never be pretty enough to turn the head of a man like Declan. Who would believe you anyway?

I silently tell the nagging voice in my head to shut up and quickly change the subject.

"Do you mind if I ask what you're working on now? Are there any new projects in the works?"

His gaze drops back to his plate. "I guess you can say I have a work in progress. I haven't written anything new in two years. My newest releases are all manuscripts I finished before Dani got sick."

"When does production begin on your series?"

"I should receive my final copy of the manuscript in a few weeks." He said between taking another bite of his dinner.

"Your fans are going to love the series. I can't wait to see it myself. And, if you ever decide you want to give writing a go again and need someone to beta read for you and give you their non-professional opinion on it, I would love for you to think of me."

His head nods in consideration. "Thanks'. When, or rather, if I'm ever ready to let someone look at it, I'll think of you."

We fall into a comfortable silence. Declan finishes eating and pushes his plate to the side.

"Dani was the reason I got published in the first place."

His sudden confession has my fork freezing from moving lettuce around my plate.

He continues, so I don't have to say anything.

"As soon as I would finish drafting a novel, she would read through the pages marking up the margins with red ink pointing out all the things she thought I should change. Things she wanted me to change." His voice holds the promise of a smile at the memories.

"She said she liked knowing she was always the first person to read what I wrote."

I drop my gaze away from him. At the moment, I realize I appreciate that he needs to keep the memories of his wife private. Not that I mind if he shares her with me, I can imagine how hard it must be to share any of his memories as precious as they are.

"Her voice is strong in my books, especially in the lead female point of view. She would tell me when I needed to take it slower, make the female nicer, or be more aggressive. She showed me how to get into the female mind and write scenes of how "real women" would do things. I'm not sure I can write without her."

"Is that why you haven't written anything new?" I ask though I shouldn't. I'm supposed to listen and let him vent and get things off his chest.

"I haven't felt the spark in a long time. My muse has grown silent."

He takes a moment as if to collect his thoughts. "Luckily, I have a backlog of manuscripts I can dust off and send to my editor as I'm waiting to see where I want my career to go. If I decide to take it anywhere."

My heart hurts for him. Rachel was right. Declan didn't just lose his wife, but he lost his muse, writing partner, his world.

After the dinner dishes are taken care of, Declan busies himself in the task of signing the last of the books, and I go to work getting the books packaged and ready to ship to the awaiting fans.

With nothing left to say between us, we work in silence for the rest of the evening. We've made such great strides and progress between us that I don't want to push my luck by pushing Declan too hard. He has opened up with me today, and Dani has even been in the conversation. Those were giant steps toward a promising relationship between us.

We both settle in, knowing that we have a long night ahead of us. We're both prepared to pull an all-nighter if we have to.

Mostly, we're both ready and eager to get Rachel off our backs.

# Chapter Six

♥

"Declan, we need you in here." Rachel hollers out the front door of the pool house.

The roomy one-bedroom that sits three hundred feet from the backdoor of the property has officially been my home for the last two weeks. The exterior of this smaller house matched the main house in color and style, but the similarity stops there. The main house is dark and cold. The pool house is full of light and is airy, with windows on every wall.

Today, Rachel and I have set out to clean the remaining items from what had once been Dani's art studio. The front room of the pool house appears the same as it did two years ago. All the furniture and remaining items in the space were covered with fading white drop cloths. Left behind, paint supplies of Dani's sat unused and full of dust.

Rachel said Declan had refused to pack the supplies away, demanding they all be left right where she had left them when she became too sick to continue her painting. She said it felt as if he expected Dani to come back and pick up where she had left off.

Rachel had finally convinced Declan that it was time to do something with all the art supplies. She found a local program that holds art classes for low-income children. Rachel reminded Declan that Dani would have loved the idea of giving back to underprivileged kids. After an hour, he had agreed and told Rachel that she would have to do it. He didn't think he could physically be the one to haul her stuff away.

"You hollered?" Declan asks, stepping into the doorway. He's dressed in the same loose-fitting blue jeans and a white cotton shirt that I've come to realize is his go-to outfit. Not that I'm complaining. The man has a stunningly beautiful body that any woman in her right mind could stop and appreciate.

His white t-shirt is stretched tight across his chest and arms, forming a second skin. His jeans hang from his hips, loose in the butt and thighs, hiding the yummy mouthwatering body I imagine is under those clothes.

Declan's soft demeanor slips from his face as his gaze meets his sister's before dropping to the empty cardboard boxes she piled next to her.

Running a shaky hand through his hair, he steps back, turning his body until he's hovering halfway between the open doorway. He looks as if he's on the verge of running. His gaze drops down to Luc, who has come to sit next to his master's feet.

"I didn't think you meant to do this today. When you ask me if I was ready...?" He pauses, leaving the words from falling from his mouth. "You never said it would be today."

I cross my arms in front of my chest, dropping my gaze to Luc, who waits patiently for Declan. Looking between the two siblings, I feel like an intruder for witnessing their uncomfortable conversation. Rachel asked for my help today, and my job is to do the things that need doing around the house.

"If not now, when, Declan? You said so yourself. You asked me to help you move on. That's what we're here to do today." She explains, looking at me and back to her brother. He doesn't glance my way. Not once.

My mind is reeling over the fact that he had asked for this. The fact that he can admit that he is ready to go on with his life is a good sign.

A shaky sigh escapes Declan, and both his hands move to the wooden trim around the doorframe gripping it between his fingers until his skin turns pale white. His head hangs heavy between his shoulders. There is no movement in him for the longest moment besides the rise and fall of air filling his lungs. He seems to be struggling with the internal battle that no doubt rages inside him. It wasn't easy to let go of the past. It's scarier to move on with your life.

Rachel steals a glance my way but doesn't move toward her brother. Instead, she gives him time to gather his thoughts and emotions. He deserves that much. I admire him and the strength he regains with every passing day. It makes me wish I could reach out and hug him. No one should ever have to make a decision as big as this one on their own.

Raising his head, he meets his sister's gaze, lingering for the briefest moments before he shifts to mine and back to Rachel.

"You're right. She would prefer if someone could enjoy using all of this. She wouldn't want it just to sit here collecting dust. Do me a favor? Any paintings you find, could you bring them into the house. I promised her parents I would send some to them when I was ready to let them go."

"Got it, boss." Rachel's light heart tone eased the situation. She seems to have the ability to make a crappy day better somehow.

We wait until Declan goes back into the house before Rachel opens a few empty boxes, spreads them out around the small room, and begins collecting art supplies from the nearby tables and shelves. I go to work on the other side of the room, grabbing up bottles and jars of paint.

It takes us a little over two hours of packing to collect it all. We don't stop until every paintbrush and blank canvas is wrapped, packed, and placed against the wall next to the door awaiting pick up. I stand back next to Rachel and stare at all our hard work and the space we created. It no longer resembles the same room I moved into a few weeks ago.

Our clothes and hands are covered in dust and little splatters of spilled paint, but we have the satisfaction of knowing the daunting task is finished. Looking down at all the boxes, Rachel places her hands on her hips.

"I can't believe we finally got this done." She turns her head to peer at me.

"I mean it. Declan and I have been talking about doing this for the last few months, but when we set things in motion, he backs out and throws a tantrum. Now, if we can get the guys from the center with the truck and get this loaded up before he changes his mind, we will be in the clear."

To hear her put it that way forces an uneasy feeling to creep over me for boxing his wife's things away, especially if he isn't ready yet.

"Are you sure he can handle this? I mean, no one knows how long it takes another person to come to terms with a loss like his. Maybe he isn't ready. You said yourself they had a marriage different than most."

"Trust me. He's ready. He just needs a little nudging, is all." Her phone buzzes in her pocket, forcing her to pull it out.

"Cool. The guys from the center are here to pick the stuff up. I'm going to head to the front and show them in. Will you take those paintings we found into the house?"

Before I can answer, she turns and leaves the pool house. Gathering the loose drawings and paintings, I roll them together, placing the bundle in the crook of my arm, and head to the house. A comfortable silence welcomes me as I step inside and make my way through the kitchen. I do not doubt that Declan has himself held up in his office with the door closed and locked. I realize just how much I dreaded the job of giving him the paintings in the first place. Afraid they may trigger unwanted memories.

Moving down the hallway, I listen closely, trying to analyze any sounds coming from behind the door. But today, the door isn't closed and locked. Instead, it sits ajar, allowing me to peek around the door, I spot Declan standing next to a big wooden desk with a laptop open, but he's thumbing through a notebook in his hands. His brown gaze darts in my direction from behind a pair of glasses. His gaze locks on mine, his fingers come to a halt. I've seen him nearly every day for weeks, and still, my breath catches in my chest at the sight of him. This time is no different. This time it's worse because those glasses have only made him sexier. "I didn't know you wore glasses." I want to kick myself as soon as the words are out of my mouth.

"I do when I'm working on the computer, mouse."

"Mouse?"

A corner of his mouth curls. "You like to sneak around the house like one."

"Oh." Not the worst nickname to have. He doesn't summon me to come in, but I push my way further into the room anyway. "Sorry to interrupt, but we found some paintings you might want." I held the roll of papers in the air so that he could see them. Luc picks his head up off his pillow, showing more interest than his master.

"Thanks. You can put them over there on the window bench for now. I'll deal with them later." He nods toward the window to the left of his desk. Of course, it would have to be in the furthest corner away, forcing me to walk through the room and in front of his desk to reach it.

*Your shirt is too tight, showing off your muffin top, and your hair is a mess. Yes, walk right in front of this gorgeous man who wants nothing to do with you.*

What can I say? My inner voice is a bitch.

I take a deep breath in an attempt to calm my jitters as self-doubt overwhelms me. With Declan's gaze watching me, my nerves kick into overtime. "Sure."

He drops back to the chair behind the desk as I make my way to the window. Passing next to him, I notice the typing on the screen.

He notices me staring and leans back, lacing his fingers together and bringing them to rest behind his head. The new position shows off the tight white t-shirt as it strains over the muscles on his stomach.

Could he be any sexier?

"Is there something else?" he asks.

"You're writing again. You must have felt inspired."

"I'm editing a finished piece." His hand moves toward the keyboard once again, getting ready to dive back at the moment I leave the room. I should take that as my cue to leave and let him do just that, but my mind doesn't work that way.

"Not that your work is any of my business, but what are you going to do when sellers and fans want to meet you in person? Hire an actor to play the part? As a fan of romance books, I have to say I would love to meet the author in person, and I'm sure others feel the same way. You don't want to disappoint your fans, do you?"

His face grows serious as his gaze lifts to search mine.

"People are disappointed every day."

Shit. That's not what I meant at all. I had no intentions of bringing up reminders of sadness.

"I guess all I'm saying is, I'm sure your fans won't care that you're a man if you are honest with them. If you make some appearances, you could gain a bigger fan base. There are a lot of authors that write under multiple names."

His gaze darkens, and I know I have overstepped.

"Are you finished?" His voice had lowered, and the look of annoyance was visible.

My chin fell toward my chest as if I were tucking tail. But the truth, I couldn't lose this job because of my mouth. "Yes. I'm sorry. I'll keep my opinions to myself."

I make it to the door just as Rachel's voice echoes on the other side.

"Here you are. Did you give him the paintings?"

Declan answers for me. "She did. I'll look through them later. Did everything get loaded?"

His sister smiles at him, leaning into the open doorway as she rubs her hands over her rounded stomach. "Yes. The delivery men were just beaming about the amount of stuff. They said they had never had that large of a donation at one time before. They said the kids are going to be so excited."

A soft smile touches Declan's lips, and for a split second, contentment flashes in his eyes. "I'm glad to hear it. Now, if you two will excuse me, I have something that needs seeing to."

Holding the door open, I wait for Rachel to hug her brother before joining me back in the hall. Just before I can turn away, Declan's soft voice stops me. "Mouse?"

My heart softens at the sound of my nickname on his lips. My face beams at his soft smile. "Yes, Declan?"

"Close the door behind you?"

My heart sinks.

His words just hurt my heart a little bit more.

*Quinn*

Two months into my new job, the green leaves on the trees have faded into yellow, orange, and brown and now littered the ground. The warm blue skies over the Pacific Northwest have long since disappeared under grey clouds that insist on pouring inch after inch of rain.

Thanksgiving's a week away, and though Declan has assured me that I will have the holiday weekend off, the thought of going home to my parent's house doesn't sound appealing in the least. Not this year. I'm not in the mood to play patient and have mom analyze everything in my life right now. Or hound me with questions about my job or, better yet, quiz me about Declan. I've already opened that can of worms when I called to get her professional advice. I've been dodging her calls ever since. My mom isn't going to stop until she gets every detail out of me. Besides, I can't bring myself to leave Declan alone on the holidays. Rachel offered to spend the last two Thanksgivings since Dani's been gone with him, but he turned her down each time, telling her he would rather be alone.

If he wants to be left alone, I'll respect his wishes, but after spending time with him these last few weeks, leaving him alone would be harder on me than I care to admit.

Over the last month, Declan and I have spent a lot of time together alone in the house. He has merged from spending his days locked in his office to join me for at least one meal a day and sometimes, two.

On the first two days that he came it out of his room for a meal, we didn't speak a word to each other, but by the third day, we got to talking about my days as a personal assistant and living in L.A. After that, our conversations led to all sorts of topics. We agreed that anything and everything was open for discussion, except our love lives. He didn't ask about any past boyfriends, nor did I bring up Dani. I don't mention her unless he brings her into the conversation first, which I noticed happened fewer and fewer times.

The days can be a little touch and go. Declan has bad days where I leave him alone to wallow in his misery, and there are great days where he is smiling more and eager to tease.

I've begun to realize I like the fun laughing Declan. The guy lets his guard down long enough to let his dark features fade into softer tones as he relaxes into a smile. Or whose brown eyes crease and crinkle at the corners with every genuine laugh line.

He has a beautiful laugh.

One that I'm afraid will melt my heart if I'm not too careful and guarded. That's the last thing I need. P.A.'s find themselves unemployed once personal feelings develop between them and their employers. I've seen it happen, and I'm not going out like that. I need this job far too bad to screw it up with a stupid fantasy. Besides, men like Declan with their firm muscled bodies and G.Q. magazine features don't go for the plain slightly chubby girls like me. If all my years working in Hollywood has taught me anything, it's that we don't fit in their world. He's a ten, if not a strong eleven on the scales of hot and sexy. I average somewhere near a six or seven on a good day when I'm not bloated.

With Thanksgiving coming up, I want to talk with Declan about his plans for the holiday. But like yesterday and all evening the night before, the door to the office remains closed to me and, no doubt, locked.

It wasn't until I stood in the kitchen fixing a protein shake for dinner that the door opened at the end of the hall. I took a moment to glance down the front of me to make sure I wasn't too frumpy and wince in embarrassed shame as I took in the sight of my oversized sweater and black leggings.

I quickly bring my hands to my hair, pushing away the loose strands that have fallen out of the bun I wrapped my hair in this morning. I'm not sure why I care about my appearance every time Declan walks into the room? It isn't like he sexually notices me anyway.

"There you are, Mouse." He says as if he's been looking all over the house for me.

"Hey. Are you ready for dinner? I can whip something up for you. I didn't know what time you would be done tonight, so I just...."

His frown cuts me off. "Didn't you make anything for yourself?"

I hold my glass up, giving it a little wiggle, showing him that I have already had dinner.

"Right. You and those damn protein shakes. Don't you ever eat real food anymore?"

I laugh. "I try not to."

When he doesn't respond, I glance back at him to see that he's staring back at me with a grim look across his face. His features are somewhere crossed between pissed off and concerned. I can't help getting the feeling that he's angry with me about something.

"Damn it, Quinn. These things aren't meant to keep you alive. They help supplement a meal or two, not replace every meal. Your body is going to need more than those can give you."

As he lectures me, the familiar cringe of talking about my weight creeped up. Next thing I know, he'll be telling me the run-of-the-mill speech about 'if only I would work out and eat less saturated fats' or tell me 'If I go on a vegan diet, I will drop the pounds.' The problem is, I've tried all those things. Diets like that don't work for me. I go on walks and runs and sweat for hours doing cardio. The truth is, not all diets are meant for everyone.

My defenses go up, and I lower my glass with a plop on the countertop. "I'm well aware all about the shakes. Can we talk about something else? Please."

He raises his hands in the air between us. Turning my back to him, I curse myself under my breath for being bitchy with him. I'm sure he doesn't mean anything by it, and I'm sure he thinks he's helping me.

I face him and change the subject. "I was thinking. Thanksgiving is coming next week, and I thought...."

"Next week is Thanksgiving? Where the hell have, I been?"

I smile. "Are you kidding me? He is locked away in that room, knocking out another panty-dropping love story. Or, at least, I hope that's what you've been doing. And yes, Thanksgiving is next week, and since I don't have the need to go this weekend, I thought perhaps we could do a little something here instead." It can't be that weird of a request. We ate dinner together almost every night.

He moved to the fridge sticking his head inside as he rummaged through it. "What did you have in mind?"

Pressing my back into the counter, I brace my hands on either side of me. I note how his firm ass looks in the low-waisted sweats as he bends over, peering inside the fridge. Good lord, the man has an award-winning body. I drop my gaze shaking the image of my boss's ass from my brain.

"I was thinking I could cook a traditional dinner and invite Rachel and Max to join us."

"That sounds fine."

Now comes the part I fear he may struggle with.

"I thought maybe we could invite your parents? Rachel said the four of you haven't spent a holiday together since— a while."

Declan's head stayed submerged inside the fridge as he dug around for something to eat. I'm not sure he could hear me. I wait until he finds what he's looking for and stands straight before shutting the door and dropping leftovers on the countertop next to me.

"What do you think? Do you think your parents will like that?"

One of his brown brows raises. "If you have met my parents before, you wouldn't be too eager to have them here for a holiday."

"Rachel says they would like to come. Besides, if I continue working for you, it's probably a good idea for me to meet them. That way, I can at least put a face to the voice every time your mother calls, and I'm forced to produce another excuse for you not wanting to talk to her."

"Is it my fault she calls when I'm working?"

"You're always working, so that's a little unfair." I smile, showing him I'm not serious. He seems to be in a better mood this evening, so I decide to take advantage of his happiness to push a little further. "I'll make all the food, and I can keep it small."

"You don't want to go to your parent's house for the holidays? Or have other plans?"

"My dad and their neighbors and closest friends who she invites to dinner every year. My mom and some of the other ladies will spend all day cooking while my father sits in the living room watching football with the guys."

"Why don't you invite them over here? It doesn't make sense not to. If you're going to be here, then they should be too. Maybe our parents will like each other Plus, I wouldn't mind meeting them."

My stomach buzzes with the fluttering of nerves. Have our parents in the same house? A holiday together? It feels weird enough to think about my parents spending a holiday with my new employer but thinking of them here with his parents as well...

"Trust me when I say you don't want them here. My mother is pushy. She'll spend all night analyzing everyone at the table."

He smiles. "Great. She can start with my mom. That will keep her busy for hours."

He's not going to give up on this. "I know my parents would like to meet you as well. Thanks for thinking of them."

After popping the tops on the leftover containers, he puts one in the microwave and presses the digital buttons.

I watch him as he builds a plate with every leftover in the fridge. The sight of all the miss-matched items gives me the giggles as I think of him eating it.

"I could make you something fresh, so you don't have to eat that," I say, watching in horror as he licks the spoon.

He peers down at the plate he's working so hard to assemble and shrugs one shoulder. "There's no sense in wasting all this food you already cooked."

"If someone ate the food the day I cooked it, there wouldn't be leftovers."

Grabbing the bowl from the microwave, he turns back, gliding his gaze between mine and the protein shake on the counter. "I could say the same thing about you."

I smile. That's fair. I can let Declan have that one.

Once his food is hot, he grabs a fork and jumps on the countertop with his plate planted in the other hand.

"So, tell me about these parents I'm going to meet in a week. What do they do for a living?"

"I already told you about my mom. She owns and runs a small psychology office. She works mostly with kids in the system. Foster kids, damaged teens, like that. My father is an electrician. He has a small company that keeps him busy most of the week. And on weekends, when he's not watching football or cutting the grass, you can find him outside in the shed or the yard. He and the neighbors have an ongoing debate over who has the best mower with the most power."

Declan laughs. The sound of the beautiful melody makes me happy. Declan could pass as good-looking when he's pissed off and frowning, but when that man smiles... I get a small glimpse of the sexy dominant author behind all those books. I'm blessed since so few people get to experience this side of him.

"I didn't know people actually fought over things like that. I thought it was only something you see in the movies."

"If it is, no one told my dad."

"He's a football fan. A season ticket holder?"

"You know it. Every year. He and some friends from work rock out the entire season. My dad makes it no secret that he's disappointed he never had a boy. He always wanted a son to share his love of football with but after my sister and I came, our mother couldn't have any more kids. He used to joke that he would turn me into the first woman on an NFL team. As you can see, that didn't work so well for him. What about your parents? What do they do?"

I can't stop my gaze from dropping to his throat, watching the solid corded muscles work as he swallowed his food. An ache roars to life deep in my stomach, and my tongue darts out to moisten my lips.

"My dad works in private banking, and mom used to be a teacher but now that dad has made a little money, mom spends her days at the country club or taking care of the house."

"What do they think about your career?"

He takes another bite chewing slowly, and swallows before answering.

"My dad is supportive no matter what Rachel and I do. Mom...struggles with it. She doesn't understand how anyone finds my books interesting."

Tearing my gaze away from him, I turn to the sink to wash my glass.

"I hope you are inviting your sister?" he says.

"She's on location right now. She is a makeup artist for a Hollywood production company. Last I heard, she won't be able to come home for the holidays. By the way, I'm going to get the shopping for dinner done tomorrow. Is there anything you want me to pick up? Anything that's a traditional item that you or your family has to have?"

Leave it to my luck that I could ruin Thanksgiving Dinner without the traditional raspberry pie? He slides from the counter and moves in behind me. His arm reaches around my side to place his dishes in the sink. I'm pressed between him and the counter. His chest presses against my back, and I can feel his breath in my hair.

"Please, buy anything you think we might need for dinner. Make sure you use the credit card Rachel gave you. I don't want you spending your own money on dinner." We are standing so close that butterflies start to flutter in my stomach. I feel the brush of his nose at the tip of my ear as if he's smelling me. Before I can turn around, he quickly moves away.

I watch him leave the kitchen and disappear down the hall. My heart pounds in my chest. What the hell just happened?

*Quinn*

Thanksgiving proved to be more hectic than I planned for. Even in a house the size of this one, there doesn't seem to be enough room for the few people invited to Declan's first Thanksgiving hosting. He insisted that if we were going to have dinner in his home, neither of us was leaving either set of our parents out. Even though I've warned him about my mom's uncontrollable need to interrogate, he still insisted they come.

Once my parents arrived and introductions were made, my dad was itching to find a room with a TV. The man can't go without watching the Thanksgiving Day football game. His Seahawks weren't playing, but next to the hawks, Dad would root for the Cowboys any day. My mom teased him about liking them purely to enjoy watching the famous cheerleaders. He'd smiled and asked her why he would want to watch them when he had the most gorgeous woman in the world sleeping in his bed at night.

Cheesy, yes. But still, a moment with my parents makes me realize that true love does exist outside of Hollywood movies. As corny as they are, my parents live most people's fantasies. They aren't rich or famous, and they both work forty-plus hours a week, but they love each other harder than anyone I've ever seen.

I called Kate to see if she would be able to fly home for the holiday, but she said they were only wrapping up filming for the weekend. The director wanted to stay on time for the film since the release date was announced. I'm going to miss her as I do every holiday we are apart, and lord knows I could use her help against our mom.

If we make it through the night without any significant problems, I would consider the night a success.

To my relief, Declan, his father, and Rachel's boyfriend Max joined my Dad in the living room to watch the game together, leaving us women to mingle in the kitchen and finish the last touches of dinner.

More like my mother helped me with the food while Ms. Palmer opened, poured, and drank the bottle of two thousand and nine Chablis Grand Cru Les Clos she had brought to dinner. Rachel joined us in the kitchen, but mainly for the attempt at sneaking food.

The Palmers looked different from the image Declan described to me. When he said his mom was a teacher, I pictured in my mind a middle-aged woman with a sweet smile and a pencil tucked inside a messy bun looking like she had spent the last twenty years playing with kindergarteners. But what I saw today was the furthest from that image. The woman across the kitchen island from me gave off a cold and distant atmosphere. Not to mention, I haven't seen the woman smile not once in the hour and a half she has been here.

I glance up from the cutting board as Rachel all but attacks the veggies, eating them as fast as I can cut them. Hiding my grin, I duck my chin to my chest.

"Quinn, Rachel tells me you worked in Las Angeles for a famous couple. Anyone we might know?"

"Are you a fan of action movies?"

"Not really." She said matter-of-factly

That didn't surprise me. "Then probably not. Besides, I've signed a non-discloser for my former employer, which means I can't discuss who I worked for."

"I see. Well, I'm glad that you take your job seriously. It makes me less anxious about your working here for Declan. We all know how he likes his privacy." She tells me in a rude and closed lip manner.

"Is there anything you need me to do, Quinn? I feel bad standing here doing nothing while you and your mom work to cook us dinner." Rachel rubs at her belly as she rounds the kitchen island, moving closer and scouting out more food.

"There's nothing left to do. The turkey is nearly cooked, and I'm finishing the veggie tray now." I wipe my hands on a towel as I gaze up at them.

"You heard her, Rachel. We will be more in the way than helpful. Let's visit with your brother and father." Ms. Palmer led her daughter out of the room. Rachel offers me a smile as she wiggles her fingers in a sad attempt to wave goodbye. I can't help the smile that curls over my lips. Connie Palmer is a pushy take no-nonsense kind of woman.

"Is it just me, or does being around that lady make you want to apologize for breathing her air?" My mother asks as I open the oven to check the turkey. Turning back to face her, I find her grinning.

"I thought it was just me. I'm glad I'm not the only one that thought she's a little stuffy."

"Nope, I'm feeling you."

I raise a finely plucked brow at my mom. "You feel me?" I ask, mocking her choice of words.

Her smile lights up her face. "I thought I would start brushing up on all the slang words the kids are using today. I want to keep it fresh and cool. It helps me to relate to the kids that I council."

My head shakes, and I laugh. "Lord, help us all."

"Finally, we can talk just us girls. So, tell me how things are going, Sugarbean?"

My mother's nickname for me hasn't changed in all these years. The name used to piss me off, but I didn't let it bother me anymore as I grew older. Besides, I'm not the only one with a nickname. Since she was a baby, we have called my sister Kate, Kit Kat.

"I'm fine. Declan doesn't talk much to me. He's normally locked in his office working. When he comes out, he's pleasant enough. If we could get a chance, I know we would become friends, not to mention, I could get a better understanding of how he likes things around the house."

"Just keep working on him. You have one of those personalities people can't help but be drawn to. He might be fighting it now but trust me; I'm sure it's because he's wearied of getting too close to others. A fear that is completely understandable given what he went through. Give it time, and he'll come around."

"Thanks, mom."

"I mean it, Sugarbean. You are so easy to love. Always have been. You have an invisible pull that tethers people to you. He'll be no different, you'll see."

"I don't need him to love me. He's, my boss. I just want to help any way I can." I pause and look around the kitchen to find what else needs tending. "I need to set the table for dinner. Why don't you go mingle for a little while check on how dads doing in there?"

A relieved sigh left me when she disappeared, and I finally felt a weight being lifted. My mom will never be a burden to me, but her need to make sure her family is happy and content all the time can consume the day. I'm relieved to be on my own for a minute to re-gather my thoughts and clear my mind before joining the others.

"Please give me something to do so I can stay in here," Rachel demands, entering the formal dining room as I'm placing placemats around the table.

"Here, if you want to finish putting these out, I'll go grab plates." I point to the placemats and silverware. I turn to head to the kitchen and run straight into a wide chest. His musky scent engulfs me, and I sigh.

"Please tell me you have something for me to do? Why did I let you talk me into this?" Declan groaned walking around the corner.

"Which one? Mom or Dad?" Rachel asks.

"Mom. Man, she's at it again. Why can't she just leave things alone? She's been drilling me about Quinn every chance she gets. What's her deal?"

Has his mom been drilling him about me? Why? Why is she questioning him about me?

"You know how she gets Declan. She worries about you. She doesn't like you being alone out here."

"I'm not alone. Quinn's here. You'll protect me, won't you, Quinn?" He turns his gaze toward me and gives me an innocent, playful wink. My heart seizes in my chest. It aches for him. Aches for the pain of his loss. Aches because I so desperately want to hug him and take all his pain away. I hate that my stomach flutters every time he looks at me. That look brings back some feelings

I haven't felt in a long time. Shame washed over me, and I quickly look away. He's my boss, and I need to remember that.

I hate that I'm betraying his trust by having these feelings. That is the last thing he needs right now.

I quickly shift my gaze away. A simple nod is what I manage as a response to his teasing.

"Of course, I would. After all, I'm on the payroll." Joking back at him, I lift my gaze, and for the slightest moment, I sworn I saw a tiny sliver of disappointment cross his brown eyes.

He turns back to Rachel. "Give me something to do before mom comes back in here."

It's funny how all three of us adults are hiding away from our parents. "You can help Rachel finish setting the table. I'm going to check on the food."

Leaving them in the dining room, I enter the kitchen and stop short as I encounter Connie Palmer.

"Oh, there you are. I was beginning to think you had run off somewhere." She says with a scoff.

I offer her a smile despite the cold chill I suddenly feel running over the back of my neck. "Is there anything I can get you?"

"I'm fine, dear. I was hoping to catch you alone for a moment. I thought it would be good for the two of us to talk. Woman to woman." She glances over her shoulder to secure the fact we are indeed alone. Turning back to me, she sets her wine on the counter and reaches for the bottle to give herself a refill.

"I wanted to speak with you about my son." She tops off her glass before lifting it to her lips to take a sip.

"We are both women here and being blunt is the best way to put matters to rest. I'm aware that you have noticed my son was blessed with excellent looks and a successful career?"

I clear my suddenly dry throat as I nod. "Yes, of course. He is a nice-looking man." Where is she going with this? I think I have a pretty good idea what she is about to say, and an all too familiar acid starts churning in my gut.

"He also has a big heart that has already been crushed when Dani passed. There for a while, I didn't think he was ever going to come back to us."

These were all facts I knew already, but she's not finished making sure I am aware.

"I'm sure you've heard everything about Dani by now. She and Declan were together for years. We all loved Dani. She was good for him."

I want to ask her what this has to do with me, but I don't. Instead, I stand there waiting for her to continue.

For a brief moment, sadness touches Connie's eyes, and she quickly blinks it away. She had genuinely loved her daughter-in-law.

"I just want to make it clear how disappointed I will be if I find out that someone has waltzed in here and tried to take advantage of my son while he's still grieving over his late wife."

The older woman might as well have slapped me across my face. I went speechless. Stunned that out of everything she could have said, those words were the last things I expected.

"Are you implying that I'm interested in your son romantically? Because that would be...."

"Crazy. Right? I knew it was a long shot, to begin with. I mean, let's face it, you're not exactly my son's type of woman."

Her words sting and the air is painfully knocked from my lungs by the force of the slam.

"I have to admit I was a little put off when Rachel said she hired you as a live-in assistant, but after coming here and seeing you for myself...." She pauses a moment as her cold eyes run down and back up the length of my body. "Well, I feel better about you being here with him. You're the type of girl he needs. Not some sexy little thing that may distract him from the work he is finally getting back to. You seem like a wholesome girl who could be a sister to him when his family can't be here."

Unwanted tears burn the back of my eyes as I stare at the woman standing in front of me, filling my ears with insults. She couldn't have made it any more transparent. In her eyes, I'm not good enough for her son.

The thought of shedding a single tear in front of this woman infuriates me. I will hate myself if I give into the salty urge. The woman is heartless. Cruel isn't the word to describe her sharp tongue. Fleeing the room is my only option.

At the moment, all I can think of is getting away. I need to escape the pain her words inflict on me. Unwanted memories come rushing back like a broken dam. My legs won't move. My body is frozen in place. The heat of embarrassment flares across my cheeks.

"What the hell did you do?" Declan's stern icy voice comes from the doorway. My head turns in time to catch the cold stare and icy voice he directed on his mother. His brown eyes drill holes into Connie.

"Honey, I didn't do anything. Quinn and I were just having a little get-to-know-you conversation."

Hot tears of shame sting the edges of my eyes, threatening to spill over my lashes. I can't be standing here when they fall. Turning away quickly, I all but ran to the back door needing the safety and privacy of my own space.

"Quinn! Wait." Declan yells behind me. Raising a hand in the air, I hope he can understand that I need a minute alone to gather myself and plaster back on the smile that is expected of me.

I escaped without a second to spare. The kitchen door closes behind me as the first tear falls against my cheek.

# Chapter Seven

♥

A half-hour and a quick reapply of makeup later, I duck back into the house, where I hear raised voices drifting out from behind the closed office door. I recognize one of the voices belonging to Declan. The softer female voice no doubt belongs to his mother.

I don't want them to fight on Thanksgiving because of me. Being the center of an argument between my employer and his family is not where I want to be.

"I thought you left." Rachel said, stopping in the doorway of the kitchen.

"What the heck happened in here? Declan is pissed at our mom and... oh no. What did she do to you?" Rachel braced her hands along the kitchen counter. "She does this, you know. She speaks before she thinks. What did she say?"

I can't tell Rachel that her mother called me unworthy of her son. I don't want to be more involved with their family than I already am. All I want to do is finish this dinner, say goodbye to my parents, return to my room, and drink my weight in Rum before passing out to sleep this damn holiday away.

"It's nothing. I'm fine. Really." I say, hoping Rachel will drop the matter. I'm sure she didn't mean for it to sound the way it came out."

"Oh, she probably did," Rachel said, but she doesn't push the subject any further.

The digital timer on the front of the oven blinks and beeps, indicating the turkey is ready to come out. I move across the kitchen and busy myself with the meal.

Within minutes, we are sitting around the formal dining table. Declan's place is at the head of the table, with both of his parents flanking either side of him. Rachel and Max are opposite my parents, with my seat at the other end. My eyes drift over everyone as I take in their low chatters and clinking of spoons against glass bowls. I meet my mom's gaze, and I know she wonders what happened. The questions are there in her eyes. I give her a soft smile and a slight shake of my head, begging her not to ask.

Declan's weary frown matched his mother's. Both sat quietly as everyone else carried on the conversation around them. Their silence made me feel more like an outsider than I did when she told me I was out of her son's league.

Rachel and Max kindly turned the awkward silence away from the pouting duo and conversed with my parents. She asked them questions about their careers, trying to keep them both engaged throughout dinner. I could have kissed them for that kindness.

My mom soon got wrapped up in asking Rachel a million questions about the baby. Not bothering to hide the fact that she's disappointed she's not a grandmother herself yet.

As empty plates multiplied across the table, it gave me an excuse to leave the awkward meal and begin clearing them away. Connie stops me as I pass behind her chair.

"This was a wonderful dinner, Quinn. Very well done."

I force an uncomfortable tight smile over my lips. I can't be rude to Declan's mom, even if she's only offering her pity gratitude to make Declan happy.

"Thank you. I'm glad you enjoyed it." I say, picking up the empty plate in front of her.

After collecting the dirty dishes from around the table, I head to the kitchen, putting them in the sink before bracing my hands along the edge. I need a moment to catch my breath.

Making it through dinner has been so awkward it bordered painful. Sitting at the table, knowing everyone could see the red puffiness of my eyes due to crying made me want to start crying all over again. My mom kept stealing glances at me all night, but she never once asked me what was wrong. For once, she finally left something alone, and I was so grateful for that. If I could find a dark hole to hide from their sympathetic gazes, I would.

It wasn't too often I let others get under my skin, but Connie Palmer has the ability. The torment of old wounds opening again was a pain I hadn't felt in a long time.

The urge to yell and scream at her that I was here to do a job, not to steal her son, consumed me. Declan is good-looking, and yes, my heart flutters with every rare smile he gifts me. But our relationship isn't like that. He's not ready for anything more, and I'm not sure I am either. I haven't had any relationships since I was in California.

"Do you think now is a good time for pie?" Declan's voice catches me off guard, making me jump as I push away from the counter, and I turn to face him.

"Sure. I'll bring it out in a minute."

"I can get it. I didn't mean to say we are ready for you to serve us, Quinn. You are not the help. I'm more than capable of carrying dessert out to our guests myself. You're not a servant."

"That's not what I meant," I assure him.

His lips curl softly, and his eyes crinkle with tiny lines at the sides, softening his stern features and, for once, showing off his older age. My heart melts into a puddle of goo inside my chest as I notice for the first time there's a small shallow dimple at the corners of his turned-up lips. The man is too handsome for his own good. His mother's spiteful words come rushing back.

Dropping my eyes down to the front of myself, I take in the sight of my loose-fitting sweater and black leggings. Connie is right. Dani had been a gorgeous woman. Just like Rachel.

Everything I'm not.

I turn back to the sink switching the water on to distract myself. I promised myself I wouldn't cry again. Not now. Not in front of him.

"The pies are on the counter if you want to take them. I'll be right out with plates." I say, focusing on the dirty cookware.

I suddenly feel the air shift around me. The faint smell of Declan's cologne swirls in the air. It's undoubtedly him, and for as long as I live, I'll never forget what it smells like.

His hand softly touches my shoulder, and I let him urge me to turn and face him. I'm pressed between the sink and his chest, but I keep my gaze down, not wanting to see his eyes.

Strong fingers slide under my chin, forcing my head and gaze to rise to his. "I don't know what she said to you. But judging from the sadness in your eyes, it was pretty bad."

I make a meek attempt to brush the soft words off by smiling at him. "I'm fine."

My gaze drops away from him in the hopes he doesn't see the moister building in my eyes.

His voice is soft but firm. "Bullshit. She said something that hurt you. I'm sorry. She can get pushy and overbearing sometimes."

When I don't meet his gaze, he nudges my chin again, and I have no choice but to look up at him. His fingers on my skin feel like silk, and my stomach knots up with butterflies. His body is close to mine. His chest rises and falls with soft even breaths as my lungs stop filling with an air altogether.

I don't dare step away, afraid of breaking the spell he has me under. It feels so good to be this close to him. Even if he is trying to give me comfort, his nearness makes me remember just how long it's been since I've had a good man this close to me.

A shiver runs through my body.

Not wanting to embarrass myself any more tonight, I quickly step to the side and out of his reach, making the hand on my face fall away. I move to the counter where the dessert plates and serving knife sit and grab them in my arms.

Turning, I nearly drop the load to the floor as I bump into his rock-hard chest. He's now holding two pies, one in each hand as he stops suddenly, his dark eyes landing on mine.

"We aren't done talking about this. You will tell me what my mother said before this night is out."

Speechless, I nod and lead the way from the room because I have no doubt, he means it. Hopefully, by the time our parents leave, and he remembers I agreed to talk to him, I'll be locked away in the safety of my room halfway to the bottom of a bottle.

*Quinn*

I pour my second glass of wine and turn the speaker to my iPod up. There was nothing like a sweet taste of red wine and the vocal talents of my favorite female badass pop singer to make me forget about today's shit show.

An hour after dessert was served, I walked my parents out to their car. Dad went ahead to start and warm up the engine, and mom used that time to ask me once again what had happened tonight. I tried to convince her it was nothing and ended up pleading with her to leave it alone. She did, but I saw the afraid look in her eye as she hugged me goodbye. She's worried I would do something to hurt myself. I won't, of course, but I can't say I blame her for the fear.

After my parents drive away, I immediately head to the back door calling out to Declan from over my shoulder that I would see him in the morning.

His parents decided to linger with their visit, and I wasn't sure how much more I could take for one night. Declan tried to stop me by calling out, but like any mature adult acting like a child, I pretended I didn't hear him and sulked out the back door and over to the pool house. That had been an hour ago.

Closing my eyes, I try to block out the emotions from earlier. For a person who has struggled with body image most of her life, having people judge me for these flaws opened old wounds that had scarred over. My kind of scars run deeper than my outer skin. It is a pain that no one understands unless they, too, have suffered from self-hate.

Body image issues have made it impossible to allow myself the easiest pleasures. Heading into the single bedroom of the pool house, I strip the heavy, oversized sweater over my head and fling it to the nearby chair in the corner pausing in front of the full-length mirror that stands next to the dresser. I stare at myself in my boots, leggings, and black bra. The skin that circles around my midsection is pale from lack of exposure to the sun since I never entertain the idea of wearing anything that shows off my midsection.

I peer at the skin that no longer hangs over the top of my pants. I'm still far from toned, but I have worked hard to get it this small.

My hands lower to my hips, angling out my elbows as I turn right then left, looking over the many different profiles of my body and my butt. Over the years, my parents and Kate tried to convince me of how great I looked, but I couldn't see it. Not when all I see in the mirror staring back at me is the imperfections of myself?

My gaze rose to my bra-covered breasts. The best part of my body has always been my breasts. Most women complain that theirs were too big, small, or saggy. Not mine. There is one part of me I don't wish to change.

Releasing the hold of my hips, I let my arms fall to my sides, and my gaze catches sight of the small white scars stretched across my arms in the mirror's reflection. Gazing at them now brings back haunted memories of when my depression had hit rock bottom.

It took me years in therapy to talk out my feelings to figure out what had made me crave the burn the razor's sharp edge brought me. Depression is an actual disease, and I suffered terribly from it. For so many years, I thought myself not worthy of my parent's love or anyone else for that matter. Life got worse for a while after my mom caught me cutting my forearm in the bathroom. As a therapist herself, she had immediately gone to try to fix me and my problems.

She found me the best doctors and made me go to therapy three times a week. I saw the disappointment in my parent's eyes, and it made me more shameful than the white scars covering my forearm and wrist.

"Quinn?"

Turning from the mirror, I jump at the sound of a masculine voice.

Shit. Declan's in the next room. I was so wrapped up in the past that I didn't hear him enter the house.

"Hold on a second. I'm changing." I holler out, but it was too late. He rounds the corner to the bedroom, and his gaze lands on me and the exposed skin my bra isn't covering. His tense brown eyes soften as they run over the length of my body. I swear I see a speck of heat flare inside his eyes as his gaze roams over me. He quickly turns away as if he just remembered he had entered a bedroom that didn't belong to him. He spits out an apology to me from the other room.

I grab the first shirt within my reach and go after him. He's standing in the living room, his back to me with one arm resting high on the door frame. His forehead is pressed against his forearm as if he's fighting pain.

"Declan." His name is soft on my lips, and I'm not sure he heard me.

Moments pass before he drops his arm from the door and glances toward me. "I'm sorry for walking in like that. I called out to you. I guess you didn't hear me." His handsome face flushes with embarrassment. I notice a slight tremble in his hand before he shoves them into the front pockets of his jeans.

His unease stares back at me. I shrug it off as if it matters little that this gorgeous man has just seen me in my bra.

"It's all right. Don't worry about it. Did you need something?" I hope he didn't. I'm already a slight buzzed from the multiple glasses of wine I had throughout dinner.

"I wanted to make sure you were okay after tonight. You were quiet through dessert and skipped out so fast. Will you please tell me what my mother said to you? It has to have been pretty bad for it to affect you like this."

Maybe it was the two glasses of wine I just drank, but it suddenly seemed stupid not to tell him.

"It's no big deal. I'll be fine." some of her words just made some old wounds reopen.

He leans his massive body back against the door frame as his gaze holds mine. His expression was wavering on the debate of believing me or not.

"My mother can have no filter. She doesn't stop and think before she attacks with her words. I talked with her. I need to make sure she's aware of the effect her harsh words have on people."

Oh, she's aware. A woman like Connie Palmer knows exactly what she is doing.

"That's not necessary. Really. I'm fine."

Crossing his thick arms over his broad chest, I watch the muscles in his forearms tighten and stretch with his stance. My fingertips tingle with the thought of tracing the bulging veins.

"It is a big deal. To me. Tell me." He demanded.

I immediately fell into defensive mode, crossing my arms over my chest.

I take a deep breath and release it slowly. "She commented on you and me. Nothing I haven't heard before. Not like what she said is false."

His brows dip low in the middle as a frown form.

"I'm afraid I'm lost. Just spit it out already."

"Fine. Your mom thought that I needed to know that you're still in the grieving process after your wife and that she doesn't want me to take advantage of you."

"That's ridiculous."

"That's what I told her. She isn't accusing me of using you, especially not after meeting me anyways. She said, judging by my looks, she was relieved knowing I was here with you for that very reason. The last thing you need is to have an attractive assistant. So, she was pleased I didn't fit into that category."

His mouth dropped with shock for a lingering moment before he pushed away from the door. The familiar sting of tears burns again behind my eyes, but I'm not about to let them fall again.

Turning away, I quickly brush any moisture from my cheeks and eyes before I sense a movement behind me. I don't bother looking over my shoulder. I can't let Declan know how badly his mom's words hurt me.

"The old wound you talked about...?"

"It doesn't matter. Everyone has a past."

His strong presence grows closer behind me. His gaze lingering on my body. We don't touch, but his heat engulfed me, wrapping around me as if a blanket to protect me. A delicious shiver tickles down my spine.

I slowly turn back to face him. His hands raise to gently brush the strands of hair away from the tops of my shoulders. I try to step out only to find myself pressed against his chest and wrapped in his arms. I tense having his hard body pressed into mine. My mind races to a dark place, and for a moment, I'm transported back to a time I wish I could forget. I open my mouth to demand that he let me go, and I inhale the musky scent that I have admired in the past few weeks. The smell relaxes me and makes me feel safe. I don't step back; instead, I let him decide to drop his arms away. He doesn't. They stay around my shoulders.

"There is nothing wrong with you or your body. You are a beautiful woman." He says, slowly brushing my cheek with the back of his fingers. The tender touch sends my heart fluttering and my breath to catch in my lungs. He's standing too close and touching me in ways that are too intimate for a boss and employee relationship.

I need to take a step away from him. I know I should put some distance between us, but I don't want to lose the heat his body has me wrapped inside of. The aroma of his cologne mixed with the lingering scent of the wine he had with dinner has my stomach in knots. His words have worked their magic on me, and for a moment, I let myself believe I'm as beautiful as he makes me feel.

I drop my gaze to the floor as embarrassment begins to fill me, and I imagine what I must look like to him. A tipsy blubbering mess with blotchy, red-stained eyes.

"Thank you. I'm just being ridiculous." I try to shrug off the entire encounter by pulling away.

He lets me step back but grips my chin with his fingers once again, raising my face to his. "I don't think you're ridiculous at all." His voice is smooth and low.

Existence as I know it slows to an immediate crawl. The air surrounding us freezes as if frozen in time forever. I'm afraid to breathe for fear of ruining this moment and breaking the spell he's cast over me. All I can do is stare into his heavy-lidded, soulful brown eyes that hold me captive.

It has been too long since someone has looked at me with concern in their eyes. Not concerned that I might hurt myself again or self-destruct, but with worry that I'm in pain.

"Thank you, but I'm..." my words are silenced as his lips cover mine. For the briefest second, my heart stops beating. Rational thoughts and feelings flee as my eyes drift closed, and I breathe him inside me. His mouth presses softly against mine for a moment before his lips part, and he takes my lower lip between his, sucking it into his warmth. No rushing or hurried force. Just gentle, soft, and slow.

His chest presses harder against my breasts, making my nipples stiffen under my shirt as they become aware of our connection. My fingers itch with the need to reach out and touch him, but all thoughts leave me again as the tip of his silky tongue sweeps across the padded softness of my bottom lip, coaxing me to open for him.

Without thinking, I part my lips, letting my tongue slowly glide into him, seeking the warm wetness of his mouth.

My hands lift to lay against his chest, and his heart races under my touch. The kiss is affecting him as much as it is me. But before I have the chance to slide them around his neck and pull him closer to me, he quickly drops his hold as if touching me burns his skin. He steps away, bringing a hand to cover his mouth. Shame fills me as visible regret takes over his face.

"I'm sorry. That shouldn't have happened." He says, dropping his gaze away from me.

In another breath, he's out the door, not bothering to take the time to close it behind him. Tears burn once again down my cheeks. Pivoting around, I slam my hand against the wall before sliding down into a puddle on the floor.

Mixed feelings of anger and embarrassment fight for the upper hand in my head. The familiar sense of shame and regret pull at me. How could I let my emotions get in the way of my job?

Figures you would fuck this up.

I want to tell the voice in my head to shut the hell up, but it's right.

How in the hell have I let this happen? He was being nice, trying to comfort me. I'm the one who read more into the kiss than there was. I'll apologize in the morning. That is if I still have a job to save.

# Chapter Eight

♥

Early morning frost cast the illusion of crystalized snow across the ground and the marble headstones surrounding me. Snowfall in this part of the state is few and far between, but if the temperature drops low enough, white icy frost will form, making the ground slick enough to make driving dangerous.

Clutching my coat around my waist tightly, I hunker deeper into the soft wool of my knit scarf, covering my mouth and rapidly freezing nose. Time is going on around me, but I've lost all sense of it. I decided to avoid the clock after I laid awake in bed half the night, tossing, and turning with no chance of sleep-in sight.

My head hasn't stopped spinning since the kiss. I tried to shake the emotions from my mind by telling myself to find forgiveness for the slip-up and that the kiss didn't mean anything. Or at least, the guilt has me convincing myself it meant nothing.

I tuck my frozen hands deeper inside the warm pockets of my jacket. My gaze drops to the beautiful cold gray marble headstone. The name that once lingered on my lips with a smile stretched across the surface.

Danial Elizabeth Palmer. Loving daughter and wife.

Not mother. She hadn't gotten a chance to get to that part of her life. There were times when we had thought about having children, but before we had an opportunity to begin trying, she would convince me she wasn't ready. I knew she denied her want of children because of me. She thought I couldn't be bothered with the idea of kids, and as the selfish ass I was back then, I didn't correct her either. The truth was, I wasn't ready to share her with anyone. I regret that decision more than ever.

I had my wife, my life partner, and my writing. I always thought there would be time for kids later. Days like today, I wish I hadn't been such a selfish bastard. If I had only thought of Dani and her needs and wants as a woman, I would still have a piece of her here with me today. Now, all I have is this cold stone staring back and me and the haunting memories of how much I took for granted.

"Your husband is a cheating bastard." I blurt out to the cold headstone.

I haven't kissed another woman besides my wife in seven years. Dani's lips had been the last ones to touch mine, and now that too is lost forever. If I were being honest with myself, I would at least admit it wasn't the kiss that's made me an asshole. It's the fact that deep down inside me, I liked it.

"I wish I could stand here and tell you that it didn't mean anything to me. I wish I could sound like the typical cliché, but you know me better than that." I gaze skimming over the etched words once again.

On most days, I would sit on the ground leaning against the stone as I talked to Dani for hours. The cold, wet ground made that gesture less appealing today.

Hunching down, I drop to eye level with my wife's name. "I don't understand what's going on in my head right now. She's nothing like you, and you were everything I thought I ever wanted. But she's sweet, and she loves to help others."

I stop myself before I say the words. I've never talked about another woman to my wife in our years together.

"Well, you know what I'm saying. Quinn is nice. You would like her. Rachel likes her too. The two of them do the same thing you and her always did, they gang up on me when I'm being a stubborn ass. I'm still not sure why girls do that? Stick together like you do. It's fucking annoying."

I kept going. "Anyways. They cleaned out your studio a few weeks ago. All the supplies went to a low-income children's center. I thought you would be okay with that. I know you love kids, so it felt right to give them your things. Rachel found the place, so I know you would approve. I also had them keep out some of your paintings while packing things up. I sent them to your parents. Your mom has asked about them, but I..." a lump lodged in my throat, and I coughed to clear it. "I... uh, I wasn't ready."

I stood back up and waited as the tingles settled and the feeling returned to my feet.

"I'll never be ready to say goodbye completely to you, but living is finally getting easier now without you. You were right. But I still miss you every day."

Lifting my gaze away from her headstone, I peer out beyond the graveyard. The morning sun slowly rises in the sky, bouncing off the winter frost on the monuments surrounding me. The sparkle catches my eye, forcing me to squint against the shine. Dani would have found the sight beautiful. Even though most people say graveyards are creepy, she was the type of person who would have busted out her paints or coal chalks, inspired. She was an inspiration herself. She was always mine.

"Okay, love. I'm freezing my balls off out here, so I'm heading home. I wanted you to hear about Quinn from me. I love you."

After a moment of picturing my wife's beautiful face in my mind one more time, I turn and find the path that led me back to where my car is parked. In the beginning, right after Dani passed, I would come to the cemetery a few times a week. It eventually slowed to a few times a month. Every time I came here, it turned out the same. I would be on a drunken bender where I would go out cussing and screaming up a storm where the groundskeeper would have to threaten to call the cops if I did it again. My anger would turn to sadness, and I would sit out here and cry until I fell asleep from the overwhelming emotions.

Today, walking back to my car, the urge to cry or scream with fury weren't consuming me. There's a peaceful calm inside my heart and mind today.

It's a strange sense of tranquility settling over me that makes me want to smile. Like invisible arms are surrounding me, wrapping me in an embrace. If I believed in all that spooky ghost shit for one minute, I wouldn't for a second argue that Dani somehow is telling me she understands.

Before she passed, she told me she wanted me to move on after her. She made me promise that when the time is right, I would find love and be happy again. Of course, I agreed as a grieving husband to his dying wife would. I wanted Dani to have peace when she passed, and I knew she wouldn't find it if she had to worry over my well-being, so I agreed to her ridiculous terms—never giving them another minute of thought...until now.

Once I'm back in my car with the engine on and the heat blasting warm air over my frozen body, I reach for my phone and send a text to Rachel, telling her where I was. She responded by asking if I needed her to come to pick me up. Figures she would think I'm not fit to drive. I can't say I blame her for all the times before this. That would have been the case.

I sent a text back telling her that I was okay and that I hadn't had a sip of alcohol and asked if she wanted to go to dinner tonight. We owed Quinn an apology for our mother yesterday and my actions last night, but I leave that last part out of the text.

Her return text is simple with the word sure and a question mark. She must be confused about the sudden dinner plans.

Good.

I smile and send a text back, telling her I'll send her the information once I have it before tossing my phone on the seat next to me and heading away from the cemetery. For the first time in two years, I'm leaving this place with a sense of peace around my heart and shoulders. It's both welcoming and unnerving.

*Quinn*

I stare at my reflection in the full-length mirror and cringe at the sight.

Dresses were never my thing. I've never liked how I looked in them, but I like the classic little black dress if the occasion calls for one. A girl can never go wrong with that decision. Turning to my side, I observe the back of the dress, making sure everything's in place.

Declan spent all morning held up in his office. After the kiss that happened in the pool house, there was no telling what kind of mood he would be in. I knew the kiss bothered him. The look of complete horror on his face when he had left last night said all I needed to know. When I woke up this morning and found the house empty, it worried me he had taken last night harder than I realized.

When he did return to the house, he explained that he wanted to take Rachel and me out to dinner tonight and said to wear something semi-formal.

Taking a step away from the mirror, I skim my hands down the baby-soft cotton fabric skirt before double-checking the bobby pins securing my hair in the twisted up-do. Small gold hoops hung from my ears and a thin gold chain with a heart pendant settled in the middle of the tiny dip between my collar bone. The dress was short sleeve capped at the shoulders, and a modest neckline cut just above my breasts. I paired it with a black satin faux fur-lined wrap for added warmth. My heels were the only pair I had thought to bring with me when I moved in, and since I didn't know I would need a formal outfit, the black boring two-inch pumps were all I had. I skim my gaze over my subtle makeup of concealer, mascara, and lip gloss.

A soft knock echoed through the room, pulling my gaze away from the mirror.

"Quinn? The car is here. Are you dressed?" Rachel calls from the small front room of the pool house.

"Yes. I grab my purse, double-check, and walk out of the bedroom. One minute I'm coming out."

"Wow. You're stunning." Her eyes light up as she looks me over from head to toe.

"You're making me rethink this old thing." She says, looking down at the cute red dress she's wearing. Of course, Rachel's simply gorgeous, even with her enormous pregnant belly pushed out.

Her red dress is longer than mine and tight everywhere, showing off her round middle and the rest of her toned body underneath it. She slipped on red flats, and her blonde hair lay in fat ringlets cascading along her shoulders.

After seeing her, I'm confident I could wear a ballgown fit for the Queen's inauguration, and no one would notice me next to her. I'm still not sure why I was invited tonight or agreed to come.

"I feel underdressed next to you," I tell her.

Her smile fades. "You're beautiful. Guys love the daring little black dress. It makes us women appear more mysterious. Now, let's go before Declan leaves without us." She teases and loops her arm through mine, walking us out the door.

Declan and Max are at the front door waiting for us.

"It's about time. I was starting to think we were going to miss our reservations." Declan says, hurrying the three of us out the door and to the awaiting car.

We climb into the backseat of the stretched limo, taking up two of the three bench seats. Declan and I are on the seat facing the driver while Rachel all but sits on Max's lap on the right-side chair. The cute couple giggles and kisses as they whisper little things into each other's ears. I try to pretend I can't hear them and avoid watching the display of affection or making eye contact. Declan seems to be doing the same and picks up a bottle of Champagne that has been chilling on the sidebar.

Popping the top, he pours a glass of the bubbly drink handing one over to Max, who tears apart from Rachel long enough to take his glass. Declan then runs two more glasses handing one to me before he deposits the bottle back into the bucket. Opening the small compact fridge, he pulls out a can of apple juice and pulls the tab before handing it over to his giggling sister.

"Here's to a wonderful night out. I hope everyone has fun and enjoys themselves."

"Here, here," Rachel says before taking a drink from her can. I raise my glass to my lips, letting a small amount of Champagne slide down my throat.

I hold the glass in my hands as I sit back into the leather seat, taking in my surroundings. Rachel and Max are back to kissing and laughing in their private world, making it painfully obvious they are so in love. My gaze moves to the scene of the highway passing beside us. We are heading towards the city, but only Declan and the driver know where.

"You look great, by the way." Declan's voice is soft and close to mine. Glancing his way, I notice that he has turned his body on the seat to face me, sharing the same window.

He doesn't take his gaze from the moving land beside us, so I quickly turn back to it.

"Thank you. You're not half bad yourself." I say with a smile on my lips.

He snorts a half laugh as his gaze continues to eat up the outside. He has a window of his own to view, yet he is leaning closer to peer out of mine. The nearness of his chest to my back is causing my body to shiver. I quickly run my hands over my exposed arms to chase them away. I don't want him to see the affect he has on me.

I'm not sure I can handle the truth of how he makes me feel yet. How do I expect him to?

Turning my full attention away from the man beside me, I watch as our car merges onto I-5. Glowing lights from high-rise buildings dust the city skyline, and the lights from Century Link's field glow brightly, marking a home game. My father is no doubt at home watching on his flat screen in the living room.

"Where are you taking us tonight? Seeing that we are all dressed up, I'm going to assume it doesn't have a drive-through window." Rachel says, climbing off Max's lap and onto the seat next to him.

Declan's lips curl up at the ends. "Wait another twenty minutes, and we will be there, and you can see for yourself."

Just as he said the words, the driver exited the freeway heading straight into the busy downtown district of Seattle. Fifteen minutes later, the car slows and turns into a parking lot. As the state's monument comes into my window's view, I glance over to Declan, Rachel, and Max.

"I've never been here before."

"Never? Haven't you lived here for years?" Rachel asks.

I nod as the car rolls to a stop. The driver leaves his place and walks around to open my door.

I step from the car, and my head lolls back as I take in the sight of one of Washington State's most iconic buildings. The Space Needle. "Have I ever mentioned that I'm deathly afraid of heights?"

Declan chuckles as he climbs out of the car behind me. "You have five hundred and twenty feet worth of a climb to get over it. Dinners in twenty minutes.

As a group, we walk into the bottom of the building, waiting our turn for the elevator.

My stomach crawls into my throat, and my nerves stretch so tight I'm afraid they're about to snap. He wants me to go into that small glass cage and head hundreds of feet into the air? There's no way I can do this.

I squeeze my hands together, trying to rid my palms of sweat as my breathing becomes heavier in my chest. I can feel a panic attack coming on, which is the last thing I want to do in front of them. I can't do it.

My stomach clenches into a knot as the doors to the elevator open. My chest is tight, and I can feel the tears starting to prickle the backs of my eyes. I'm going to have a full-on anxiety melt-down in about thirty seconds.

Great.

As the doors slide open, the three of them step forward, and it's then that Declan looks back at me. He must have noticed the panic look on my face because he quickly steps out next to me, grabbing my hand in his.

"Are you okay? Seriously, Quinn, you're scaring me a little. Fuck, this was a bad idea. I never thought you would be this scared."

He reaches for my clenched fists, and the warmth of his hands on mine calm me a little. "I'll tell you what, I'm going to hold your hands all the way up. It's a forty-three second ride. It's less than a minute. Do you think you can do it?" He asks.

I don't know why I nod my head. Maybe it's the warmth of his hold on me, but I don't pull away. Before I know it, he's leading me into the elevator, never releasing my hand as others file in. Max and Rachel are on the other side of the elevator, with strangers dividing us.

Declan wraps a comforting arm around my shoulders, pulling me tightly into his side. I tuck my chin toward my chest and lean my face into the shoulder of his coat. I remind myself to breathe, and as I do, his closeness helps calm my nerves.

The soft fabric of his jacket brushed against my face, and the warm scent of his cologne entered through my nose, and I wanted to melt.

He smells fresh, clean, and intoxicating. I don't recognize the cologne he's wearing, but the smell is playing tricks on my pheromones. My heart slows from the rush of the elevator climb but begins to rev as I realize I'm wrapped in his arms, and my face is pressed into his body. My eyes drift shut, and I let the noise of the other guests fade away as I cling to Declan's arm, shielding my view of the climb. The low rumble of his chuckle vibrates through him, but I don't care if he's laughing at me. Fear makes people do things they wouldn't normally do. Showing a weakness, even to heights, is one thing I hate doing.

"We're here, Quinn."

Pulling my head away from his arm, my eyes fly open, and we're entering the restaurant SkyCity.

Our coats are taken, and we are shown to our table without waiting. Our table, of course, is next to the glass showing off the proud view of the city below. Thankful-ly, Declan offers me the seat furthest from the window.

We order wine and oysters for the three of us, and Rachel orders cider and a salad. Declan insists we try the lobster tail for our entrees.

"You have never been here before?" Rachel asks, taking a sip of her water.

"I haven't always lived here. I lived and worked in California for a few years. I never had a desire to come here before. I'm afraid of heights."

"Really? I couldn't tell by the way you were digging a hole into Declan's arm." Max teased.

A blast of heat blisters my cheeks with a blush. I hadn't meant to cling to him the way I had, but fear and his manly scent toyed with my senses more than I could fight.

I offer an apologetic look to Declan, but he only grins, taking another bite of his oyster.

"You know what they say about oysters, don't you?" Rachel asks Max as she holds a shell to his lips. His eyebrows wiggle at her intimate teasing.

I shift my gaze away from the couple in love. Even though Declan's here as well, it's not like we're here on a double date. I'm beginning to feel like I'm the third wheel to their loving play.

Are we?

The conversation turns in circles to all different subjects as dinner goes on smoothly. Before I notice, an hour has passed and two full bottles of wine. When the waiter asks if we want to see the dessert menu, I'm too full to think about any more food.

"Who's up for a trip to the observation deck? Are you feeling up to it?" Declan asks, turning to catch my gaze. I want to say no, but I also don't want this night to end yet. I'm enjoying myself, and it's been a long time since I've gone out and had fun with people I like being around.

"I made it this far," I say, no doubt finding courage from all the wine I drank.

His smile stops my heart. "That's what I want to hear. I promise I'll stick right by you in case you start to feel anxious."

The observation deck sits above the restaurant and houses a three-hundred-and-sixty-degree view of Seattle and its waterways.

The lights of the city take my breath away. In one direction is the city's heart with the giant skyscrapers and high-rise apartments. Turn another direction, and the town levels out and spreads far and wide where homes sit beyond with the Puget Sound waters bordering on the other side. From this height, all I can see are the city lights sparkling like tiny diamonds over the tops of the water, making the crazy busy city seem calmer and peaceful. I feel like I'm standing on top of the world.

Rachel and Max sneak away, no doubt to get a few moments to duck into a dark corner somewhere, leaving Declan and me alone.

"Are you pleased you pushed yourself into coming up here?"

I turn to find Declan standing beside me, looking out beyond the safety glass at the edge. He steps in front of me, leaning against the railing as I stay back toward the center. Keeping the building at my back makes me feel more secure in being high off the ground.

"I am. Thank you for including me tonight. I'm having a lot of fun." My gaze roams over him, and my heart clenches again. God, this man is beautiful.

He's dressed up for the night in a dark suit, black button-up shirt, and a burgundy tie. Even his heavy winter coat is appropriate attire for the evening. His inky black hair, which had once been brushed back with perfection at the beginning of the night, has slowly begun dancing loosely around the tops of his head. The wind in the night air did not help in taming his locks.

"I... I want to apologize to you for the way I acted last night. My actions were uncalled for, and I'm sorry. All I can say is that with my mother and the things she said to you and the holiday, I..." he pauses for a moment. "The moment got away from me. I hope you don't want to quit and leave because of it. Because the truth is, I like you being at the house. You make me feel... comfortable."

Sudden wetness stings my eyes, and it isn't from the cool air.

"Thank you. That means a lot to me. I'm not going to quit. I like you too. I mean...I like working for you too. You are indeed a pain in the ass sometimes to work for, but you're starting to grow on me." I say quickly to lighten the mood.

If I hadn't already been braced against the center of the building, the wide bright smile he gives me would have knocked me right off the top of the building. My heart melts at the sight.

Moving into my side, his arm slides around my shoulders, tucking me closer and firmer against his side. As much as I want the gesture to mean more, I know it's the same he would have offered any friend.

I'll take being friends with Declan. He's proving to be a great guy under the mess of his broken heart.

"Come over here, you two. There's a selfie station to take our picture. Hurry up. It's freezing out here." Rachel calls out.

Declan and I join her and Max for our complimentary selfie photo. Rachel has her arms around Max, kissing her on the cheek. I lean into her back, smile up toward the camera, and feel Declan press into my back, resting his hand on my shoulder. At this moment, I see what it means to be happy. It's a feeling I haven't felt in a long time.

# Chapter Nine

♥

Christmas is less than three weeks away, and since the night at the Space needle, our dynamics have changed. Declan no longer locks himself in his office for all hours of the day and night. He works on his writing, but the door typically remains open. I leave him alone to do his work, and he no longer shuts me out. We also eat together as he makes it a priority to stop for meal breaks. In the evening, we challenge each other to games. Board games don't hold his attention long enough, and I hate puzzles, so we usually end up with cards. We're both surprisingly good at poker, and I taught him to play rummy. The only card game I draw a line on playing is Slap Jack, and that's because his competitiveness damn near broke his kitchen table.

I have the day off, so I decided to start my Christmas shopping this morning. Mom and dad were easy enough. I bought dad new slippers and a beautiful pocket watch. I picked up a new camera for mom. It was a little over my budget, but I can imagine how much she would love having it. Rachel and Max were getting a set of crystal liquor decanters she had pointed out on a trip to the mall the two of us had last week. I couldn't come up with anything for Declan.

Anytime I thought I found a gift perfect for him, I second guessed myself. I picked up a box with over a dozen different sets of cards. The box claims the ability to play over thirty other card games. But it was such a silly gift. I wanted to give him something more meaningful.

Walking through the kitchen, I'm just about to take my bags out to the pool house when Declan enters from the hallway.

"Hey, I'm going to bring in some extra wood. The weather station just put out a winter storm warning. They're predicting a pretty bad storm tonight. We might lose electricity. I thought you could sleep in one of the guest rooms tonight. If the power goes out in the middle of the night, you're going to freeze out there. We both may end up camping in the living room next to the fireplace." Declan says, pulling a jacket on.

I agree and head to the pool house to drop my bags and gather the cutest warmest pajamas I can find. By the time I gather up clothes and personal items I'll need for the night and morning, the wind outside has already begun whipping branches of the trees in the yard back and forth.

The howling sound of the forced winds scrape against the outside of the tiny house, and rain comes next. As if a cloud suddenly opened, the rain poured down by the bucket full. Loud hail the size of peas begins to pelt the ground tinging off the plastic pool tarp. Ducking my head for cover, I race around the pool to the main house and enter just as another gust of wind blows past, moving some patio furniture around.

Peeking back outside, I see Declan out in the shed, loading a wheelbarrow full of split wood. Behind him, the clouds are quickly turning darker shades of black. The wind roars, and the hail falls faster. Declan brings the wood close to the house, stacking it under the covered back porch patio.

"Guess the warning came just in time. Looks like it's going to get ugly out there." His arms are loaded with wood as he heads into the house and over to the living room.

As Declan continued to bring the wood into the house, I started making our dinner. I had just put the seasoned chicken in the oven to bake when the hail turned too heavy rain. The howl of wind screams in the distance confirming its presence. Standing at the kitchen island, I watch as the backdoor swings open and Declan strides in, soaked to the bone. His hands and arms are weighted down with another load of wood. I quickly move around him, closing the door as he shakes rain from his hair. His lips curl into a lazy smile as the wet drops drip down the sides of his face.

"The rains really coming down out there. This is crazy."

I glance out the window of the backdoor. It's no surprise with the noise the rains make as it hits the house.

"I cut as much wood as I could before the rain got too heavy. This will be enough to keep a fire going through the night if we need it to."

"I started dinner a little early. It will be another hour before dinner is done."

Loud rain poured at that moment, silencing my words. We both look out the rain-soaked kitchen windows with our eyes turned up to the sky.

"Typical Pacific North-West winter," Declan says, stepping away from the window and out of the room. He returned wearing dry clothes carrying a laptop in his hands. Sitting on a stool at the kitchen island, he boots up the notebook as I start cutting veggies for our salad.

An hour later, I set his food off to the side of his computer, I half expect him to ignore it. To my surprise, he shuts the computer down, pushes it to the side, and digs into the salad. Sliding my plate in front of the empty stool next to him, I move around the island so I can join him for dinner.

"Did Rachel have a chance to talk to you yet? She said she would have me take over most of the leg work the first year while she's on maternity leave. She's still going to help monitor the website for now, but she wants me taking over all social media sites."

He nods. "She did. Said she's officially going on leave as of next week. She said she needs time to get things ready for the baby. Max will be out of town on business, and they still need to set the nursery up. It would probably be nice of me if I offered to help."

I smile and decide to give him his sarcasm right back. "A great brother wouldn't have waited this long." I tease.

His eyes grow large with the pretend shock. "Ouch."

"I'm only teasing. You are the best brother from what I've seen between you two. A little demanding at times, but I think Rachel likes doing everything she does for you."

His smile slowly fades, and I'm sad to see it leave.

"I feel like a jerk sometimes asking her for everything that I do. But I also know that if we weren't related, there would be no question about the amount of responsibility I would give her."

After we cleared our plates and the kitchen's back to clean, I retreated to the living room, where my nightly belongings sit stacked on a chair. I want to give Declan peace and quiet to finish his work in the kitchen. I grab my newest book and curl into the far corner of the sofa. Wrapping a blanket around me, I dive in and get lost in the pages.

I'm three chapters into my book when the living room lights begin to flicker before going completely dark. The only light left in the room is the soft shimmering yellow flames in the fireplace.

"It's a good thing I started the fire up earlier," Declan announced, coming into the room.

"Were you able to finish what you were working on?" I asked, closing my book to watch him move toward the fire.

"I sent some emails out. My editor wants some chapters sent over."

"Are you getting closer to finishing anything new?" I ask, watching him stoke the fire.

I stare at his back as the muscles in his shoulders and biceps flex and bulk as he moves the burnt logs around to add fresh ones. His tight t-shirt stretches across his broad back, showing off the ridges of the muscles beneath. The glow of the flames engulfs him, casting him in a silhouette, and the sight is sexy as hell.

With the storm raging outside, the crackling of the fire, the beautiful handsome man was my only company what I wouldn't give to be someone else for the night. Someone who could turn his head. Not that Declan would be interested anyway. The man is still hung up on his late wife. Even after two years. Dani's everything to him.

Turning from the fire, Declan takes a seat on the other end of the couch, spreading his arm along the back. The tips of his fingers brush the back of my head as he looks to be settling in for comfort. "I'm rewriting an ending now. I'm not sure where I'm taking it just yet."

"I don't know how you do it. Have so many story ideas. Where would you say most of your ideas come from?" I ask, genuinely interested in learning his process.

His lips curl into a smile. The light of the fire flickers and dances across his features, softening them in a way that makes him appear so damn approachable.

Lord, what I would give for the chance to crawl up onto his strong, inviting lap.

"I guess you could say I hear voices in my head, but, mostly they're like a movie that's playing over and over in my mind. It won't stop until I give it all my attention and outline the story. Sometimes just getting the characters on paper helps to clear the visions, but other times I have to do a full first draft before the voices soften."

"You don't think you are responsible for coming up with the ideas for your stories?"

He shrugs off the question. "Mostly, they just come to me. I mean, different characters and storylines come out of different muses. Listening to music or seeing something unfold in front of me often helps. Dani used to help me brainstorm ideas. I would take an idea or sometimes just a scene that would play out in my head to her. She would help me by writing out story time-lines on little post-it notes, adding her thoughts and ideas."

"She played a big part in your writing, didn't she?" The tingling sensation of jealousy fluttered in my stomach. I hated that I felt them. I have no right and no claim on Declan.

"Yes. She sure did."

Silence sliced through our moment. I'm afraid to talk about his late wife Dani. Every time she is brought into the conversation, it ends badly. I need to change the subject entirely. We need a Dani-free topic.

Turning to stare out the large picture window that's opposite of the sofa, I watch as the rain splatters against the glass. "How long do you think the storm is going to last?"

Declan moves to my side, turning until he's facing me but staring out the window. His arm flung over the back of the couch, and his hand pressed along mine.

"I don't know. Hopefully not too long. It's getting pretty dark out there."

I couldn't find words to reply. All my thoughts zeroed in on his skin touching mine. My palms itch to reach out and take his hand.

As if he could read my thoughts, my heart stills as Declan closes the last inch that separates our hands, grabbing ahold of mine with his. His soft touch burns my skin. When he speaks, his voice is low and quiet.

"I want to thank you for everything you have done for me. My sister likes to point out that I'm not the easiest person to work for or with. I've been meaning to take a moment to tell you that even if I don't say it, or hell, show it, I do appreciate you and all you do for me." His voice is near a whisper.

I can't think. I try to wrap my mind around the right words. I turn to face Declan, his hand still in mine, and I'm aware of how close we are. My gaze meets his for a brief moment before dropping to his lips. My breathing ramps up inside my chest, and I lick my drying lips.

"You're welcome. I don't believe you're as difficult as your sister says you are to work with. You are indeed a bit of a diva." We both know that my words are dripping in sarcasm, and I want to laugh as his eyes widen, humor dancing back at me as he tries his hardest to look like my words have genuinely hurt him. It's a good thing he can write because his acting sucks.

"You think I'm a diva?"

"As Rachel said, being difficult to work with isn't your fault. " I laugh at the pretend hurt he displays.

"She said I was difficult?"

"Oh, she said a lot more than that, buddy. But I'll never rat her out. Girl code."

A high pitch shriek pierces the air as his hands lunge for the sides of my stomach. I try to jump to my feet to get away from him, but my legs tangle with him, and I topple back onto the couch sinking deeper into the overstuffed cushions.

Laughing so hard, tears are about to run down my cheeks. I latch onto his hands, trying desperately to unhinge his fingers from the sweet torture of tickling my ribs. Laughter erupts between the two of us. I haven't been tickled like this since I was a little girl.

My feet kick, and my back slips further down the cushion until I'm laying out flat beneath him.

"Okay, okay. Stop. I can't breathe." I gasp, trying to fill my lungs with precious air.

His fingers stop, but he doesn't remove his hands from my sides. Smiling, I look up into his face, and I'm pleased that his smile reflects my own.

Before either of us can say a word, his mouth is on mine. His soft lips are stiff against my closed mouth. The tip of his tongue pokes out, pushing against my lips until

I was awkwardly open to welcome him. His warm wet tongue glides over mine sends butterflies swarming over my body. My heart races as the taste of him intoxicates me. The smell of his cologne fills my nostrils and drives me crazy. One of his hands breaks away to find its way into my hair. He was holding me tighter against him as he deepened the kiss. My own hands circle his neck, pulling him down and holding him closer, holding onto him for as long as I can for as long as he will let me.

His mouth is growing more intense on mine. I feel the hunger in both of us as our hands start to roam over each other's bodies. I moan and arch my back, pressing myself closer to him.

He stiffens, and for a moment, I fear he will pull away from me. Instead, he deepens the kiss. The vision of him burns into my mind forever. It makes me ache for him and crave his flavor. He's both sweet and savory. Too good to be true.

His free hand works its way between our bodies, cupping my breasts from the outside of my shirt. Squeezing and rubbing, he holds the weight of my breast in his hand. His thumb brushed over my nipple, pulling a moan from both of our throats. His mouth dances over mine, stroking and licking at me inside and out. I nip at his lower lip, loving the dark sounds coming from his chest.

His cock hardens as he presses against me. His hips move back and forth as he rubs against my core. The weight of his chest on mine is pinning me deeper into the cushion of the couch. I buck against him, feeling my wetness starting to build.

My cell phone chimes from my pocket, and I recognize it as the tone I set for Rachel. We both ignore it as we are both reluctant to stop now. A chirp rings out, signifying a voicemail before it begins to ring again.

"Declan. I should answer it. Rachel's calling."

My words are like cold water splashed in his face. Within seconds, he's up and away from the couch, dragging his hands through his hair as he walks toward the fireplace. He needs a minute to process what the hell just happened.

"I'm going to call her back to see what she needs." I press the call back button.

Declan grabs his cell off the mantle where he placed it and holds it out for me to see. "She tried me multiple times, but my damn phone was on silent."

Just then, Rachel's phone picks up on the other end, but Rachel isn't who answers. As the strange woman on the other side of the telephone clues me in, my gaze darts to Declan, who's watching me as I listen to the voice on the other end of the phone.

"Thank you. Will you please tell her that her brother and I will be there as soon as we can?" Hanging up the phone, I caught Declan's awkward stare.

"Rachel's in the hospital. There's something wrong with the baby."

# Chapter Ten

Getting to the hospital in Seattle proved more difficult than expected. The rain continued to pour down, causing areas of isolated flooding along sections of the road. Thankfully, the freeway was near empty thanks to people staying inside and out of the storm.

We reached the emergency room an hour after the call. Declan went straight for the reception desk to check in as I entered the modest waiting room across the hall. I was still attempting to reach Max, with no luck.

"Hi. Are you Quinn?" I turn to the chairs along the wall and spot a middle-aged woman seated and clutching a wrinkled People's magazine in her hands.

"I am"

The woman looked relieved.

"I'm Ginger. I live in Rachel and Max's building. I'm their neighbor that called you. I'm so happy you made it so quickly. Is her brother here?" The woman's weary voice told me she was more than a little scared for her neighbor and friend.

"Yes, Declan's checking in and seeing if he can get an update from a doctor. What happened tonight?"

Ginger nervously continued to ring her hands over the suffering magazine.

"I'm not sure. I went next door to check on her every day since Max left for his business trip. Rachel has complained about back pains all day, and I feared she could be going into labor. Next, she's doubled over with rolling bouts of pain. The cramps were getting too intense she could barely stand. I convinced her to come here to be checked out to ease my mind. Honestly, she didn't look so great when we first got here. She's in the room with the doctor now. I hope nothing's wrong with the baby, it's still a bit too early for that little one to be coming out."

"She's thirty-three weeks. Whatever is going on, I hope they can stop her from going into labor." I said, trying my hardest to stay positive.

Declan appeared from around the corner of the waiting room.

"Did you find out anything?" I ask, watching him run a shaky hand through his hair.

"Yeah, the nurse said the doctor is in the room with Rachel now. They'll notify the doctor that I'm here, so he'll come to talk to me when he's done. I need to call my parents. Tell them we're here and what's going on." His gaze darts between Ginger and mine.

I introduce Declan to Ginger as we move over to chairs in the waiting room. Minutes seem to drag on like unfading hours waiting for the doctor to come out and give us news. Any news would be better than waiting out here not knowing anything. We try to busy ourselves making the needed phone calls, but it doesn't stop either of us from glancing up at the clock on the wall every few minutes.

"There's still no answer from Max. Were you able to get ahold of your parents?" I ask, sinking into a padded vinyl chair next to Declan.

"My father finally answered. They're on their way."

"It sounds like you have her family coming, and there's nothing I can do here except take up another chair. I'm going to head home. I promised Rachel I'd take care of her cat for her while she's away. It was the only way I could convince her to come to the hospital. She loves that furball." Ginger stood from the chair, turning toward me.

"If I give you my number, would you be willing to let me know how she's doing? My husband and I have known Rachel and Max for two years. Those two are like our family."

"Of course." Swiping the screen on my phone, I open the contacts and hand it over to her. After typing in her information, she hands it back to me.

"I will let you know as soon as we hear what's going on."

"Thank you for getting her here so quickly. I'm sure your swift actions guaranteed my sister and her baby to stay safe and healthy. Thank you for looking out for her." Declan said, extending his hand out to the older woman.

Ginger's face softened with the offering of a comforting smile. She ignores his hand and steps forward, leaning into Declan for a brief hug. "Don't even mention it, my dear. Please keep me informed."

We watch as the older woman leaves the room.

"Is it a bad sign that the doctors haven't been out here to tell us anything yet?" Declan asks low as he leans forward in his chair, resting his head in his hands.

"Maybe it's a good thing they're taking so long. Maybe it means the doctors are still in with her. That means they're doing what needs to be done for her and the baby."

"I fucking hate hospitals. I hated coming here when...." Declan clears his throat and avoids looking at me. We both know what he was going to say when Dani was here. "I fucking hate them." He says again.

Looking over at him, I stare at his back as he leans low close to his knees with his head hanging between his hands. I desperately want to place my hands on his shoulders and run my fingers over the swelling muscles under the cotton of his shirt.

As we sit here at a hospital waiting on news about his sister, I should feel ashamed that I'm having thoughts of groping him. I want to offer comfort and support, but after our evening together, I'm not sure if my intentions will come off in the way I intend.

I leave my hands in my lap.

"Mr. Palmer?" A woman's voice calls out his name from the opening of the waiting room. We both stand and turn to look at an older female dressed in a white lab coat with a name tag that read Dr. Malory Green with several initials behind it.

"Yes?" Declan met the doctor halfway across the room.

The doctor glances down at the clipboard in her hands. "You are Ms. Palmer's brother?"

"Yes. Is she okay? Is she in labor?"

"Rachel came in with some contractions. We were able to stop them. Your sister is also showing signs of early Pre-eclampsia."

"Pre-eclampsia? What does that mean?" he asks.

The doctor glances from Declan to me as I move up beside him, letting him know I'm there if he needs the support.

"It's a potentially dangerous condition that some women get during pregnancy that affects the blood pressure. She's been showing a few mild signs for the last few weeks, but she said she didn't think to come in to be checked. If left alone and precautions aren't followed, the condition causes high blood pressure and other health complications for both mother and baby."

"What do we do now? Does she stay here in the hospital? She won't be delivering the baby soon, will she?"

"No. The object is to keep the baby in for another three weeks. Two at best. We are finishing tests now and releasing her to go home tomorrow. But there will be rules that must be followed. And I mean followed to the tee if we have any chance keeping that baby from coming too early."

Declan folded his arms in front of his chest and widened his stance to tell the doctor he would take all directions as seriously as possible. "Shoot."

"First, she will be on bed rest. I mean complete bed rest. No moving around at all. The bathroom is as far as she can go. Not even to the kitchen for food so she will need someone's help. Twenty-four-hour help. No lifting anything over three pounds and, this is the main one, absolutely no stress or arguing. Nothing that may cause her blood pressure to rise."

"Okay. I'll have to get ahold of her boyfriend to inform him of all this, and my parents should be here any minute. We will figure this all out. Can I see her?"

The doctor tells Declan a nurse will be out shortly to retrieve him, and they'll be ordering a prescription for

Rachel when she's released tomorrow. I follow Declan back to the waiting room chairs. He takes a seat with a heavy sigh, and I slide down into the empty chair next to him. This time I let my hand move over the top of his shoulder.

"I need Max to answer his phone. I can't let her go to my parent's house. The doctor said no stress. Mom will have her stressed out before her first dinner."

"Isn't Max supposed to be away for a couple of weeks this time? Why doesn't she come to your place? You have more than enough rooms and besides the two of us are there all day. I will be more than happy to help out with your sister."

His face turns so he can look at me. The expression on his face is mixed between surprise and regret.

"I can't ask you to do that. It sounds like it will be full-time care for the next few weeks. Rachel sure as heck can't work, so you're going to have to take over all her work. You wouldn't have time to help her as well as the rest of the work."

"Sure, I can. Besides, you will be there if I can't be. And she'll be right there if I need her for a work question. Besides, you said yourself. You can't let your parents stress her out. Max is still traveling, so what are you supposed to do? Leave her with a neighbor?"

Letting out a deep sigh, he runs his hand through his hair, pushing it away from his face. "Your right. She's my sister, and it's up to me to take care of her while Max is away. We can set her up downstairs in the guestroom where we both can help her when needed."

He pauses, and his eyes squint closed as he looks at me. "Are you sure this isn't going to be too much trouble?

I mean, I'll help out as much as I can, but with deadlines coming up, it may be difficult for me to do a whole lot."

I offer him a reassuring smile. The truth is, I'm not sure about anything. "No problem. How much trouble can one pregnant woman be?"

That pulls a heavy laugh out of him. "You are under-estimating my sister."

*Declan*

I wonder if Quinn is asking herself what she got herself into.

Rachel's been here at the house for the last three days and I'm starting to go crazy watching Quinn stretch herself so thin. Between cooking, cleaning, running errands, taking care of Rachel's needs, and doing all the promotional tasks needed for my up-and-coming book release, she stays busy all day until she is drop-dead tired at night.

Not to mention the fact that on top of the day-to-day tasks, Rachel has asked her to pull out the damn Christmas decorations from the garage and put a few up. My sister convinced me that if she was going to be stuck in the house over Christmas, the least I could do was humor her and put up a few decorations.

I haven't decorated the house for any holiday in the two years since Dani's death. Decorating and hanging lights was always Dani's department. She was all about Christmas. My share of decorating had been carrying boxes into the living room and hanging lights off the outside trim of the house. Dani had done the rest since she was so particular about how she wanted things to look. I could care less if I had a tree, let alone have lights hanging off anything that stood still.

I helped carry in totes from the garage and searched for the damn artificial tree that was left over from years ago. We hadn't used it in years since Dani had a tree delivered to the house by a local fundraising organization. I had the service stopped that first Christmas without her. I didn't want anything to remind me she wasn't here to celebrate with me.

With Rachel's mind made up that we did in fact, need a tree, there was no use in arguing with her. I wouldn't win if I tried.

Quinn agreed to ride along with me to the local tree farm.

I grab my jacket, check to make sure my keys are in the pocket and head down the hall toward my sister's room. I knocked lightly on the door and wait for her to answer.

"Come in"

I push open the door and stop just inside the room. "Hey. Quinn and I are heading out to get the tree. Do you need anything else while we're out?"

Looking up from the book in her hands, Rachel gives me a pondering look as if she's ready to discuss war fair.

"Do we still have ice cream?"

The question makes me smile because the question isn't out of curiosity, it's asked out of sheer lust for the icy treat. Lord help my sister and her wonderful pregnancy cravings.

"Yeah. I think there's still seven different flavors in the freezer. You think that's enough for the baby?"

"Only seven? I guess we will see." She teases with a smile.

I love teasing her about how every time she has a craving for something new, she claims it's because the baby wants it. Just like the baby wanted waffles for breakfast yesterday and Oranges at lunch.

"We will be back in an hour or so." I push away from the open door.

"Hey, Declan?" Rachel calls out stopping me.

"Yeah?" I poke my head back into the room

"Let Quinn pick the tree. That way you know it will be a good one."

My brows furrowed and I give her a show of hurt on my face. "Do you think I don't have the skills to pick out a good Christmas tree on my own? I'm hurt sis." I pretend hurt as I close the door behind me.

Quinn is waiting in the kitchen for me. I allow my gaze to take in the sight of her body. Our relationship shifted after the night of the storm. I can't stop thinking about the taste of her mouth or the delicious feel of her body pressed against mine out of my head. And thoughts of that kiss gave me ready material for the last few nights jerk sessions.

"You look warm." I tell her looking over her ridiculous bulky attire. She's dressed in a baggy sweater that does too good of a job hiding all her womanly curves. Tight blue jeans hug her legs nicely, and a pair of knee-high black boots are pulled over the knee of her pants.

Her blonde hair is flowing loose around her shoulders and tucked neatly under a wool cap. She looks...stunning. I want to crawl under the knit sweater and wrap myself around her warmth.

She looks down the front of herself. "you said we would be outside. I'm not a fan of the cold."

I holler for Luc and the three of us head out to the garage. I unlock the passenger side of my old pickup holding the door open so she can climb in then lower the tailgate for Luc to jump in the back. Joining her in the cab, I open the garage doors with the visor remote and start the engine.

"How long have you had this thing?" Quinn asks shifting in the passenger side of the bench seat as she wraps the seatbelt around her.

"I got this truck the year I got my license. I had it restored, and the engine rebuilt after my second book hit the New York Times best sellers list."

She glances around the cab. "I like it. It's very...country."

I laugh. "That's because when I was sixteen, I was going through a cowboy faze."

I feel her gaze on me and I deliberately avoid looking her way. I ease the old tin can out of the garage and into the cold daylight before hitting the remote to close the door again.

Her gaze remains on me until we hit the main road. I can't take the heat of her stare any longer. "What?"

Her smile brightens her face and for a moment my heart flutters. Or maybe I just imagined it.

"You were a cowboy? You?" she acts shocked.

I grin. "Is that so hard to believe?"

She nods "Uh, yeah."

My lips curl into a full smile. As my eyes dart from hers to the road, I watch her eyes narrow to a squint. The sight of her wrinkling face makes me laugh harder. "What are you doing?"

"Trying to picture you as a cowboy with a large hat on. Oh my God, did you listen to country music?"

I don't answer her. I refuse to give her anymore fuel to make fun of me.

"Did you?" She asks again burning her gaze into the side of my face.

She turns away from me and pops open the glove box. Reaching inside she fumbles through the junk I've stored in there over the years.

"What are you looking for?"

"Where is it? I know you have one here. You have to." She mumbles as she weeds through the papers and loose items.

"What the hell are you talking about?" I ask as she pulls out a blank cd case smiling as she holds it in the air between us. "I'm going to bet this has country music on it."

I shrug. "I already told you, I got the truck when I was going through a country phase in my life."

"Yes, but you also said you had the truck redone just a few years ago. So, anything in this truck now, you put in here after the truck has been re-done."

She pops open the cd case and stuffs the blank cd into the reader. I shake my head and watch the road. She turns the volume up as a familiar melody comes over the speakers.

Her gaze burns into me and I avoid hers for as long as I can before I give up. She's grinning at me like the cat who ate the canary.

"Fine. I still like some of the music, okay? But come on, you mean to tell me you don't like Johnny Cash? Who doesn't like the man in black?"

Her smile is warming my insides and she shakes her head. "You never seize to amaze me, Declan."

That gets my attention. My smile falls, and I glance away from the road and back to her. "What do you mean?"

"A closet romance writer, deep down a nice guy and now...a Cash fan." She shakes her head before turning back to the stereo. She turns up the volume and we ride the rest of the way to the tree lot listening to the music.

The Christmas tree lot is spread out over acres of land. I park the truck in the one grassy area not over ran with potholes and mud. I grab my saw from the back of the truck and let Luc jump out. The two of us head out to explore the three acres of farmed trees with Luc weaving in and out of our legs.

"How big of a tree are we looking for? Your ceiling is what, twelve feet? Fifteen?" Quinn asks walking a few feet ahead of me.

*Declan*

"I have a sixteen-foot ceiling in the living room."

"That gives us a lot of options. Do you like full or thinner ones?"

My gaze drops to her body. I know she's referring to the trees but, in my mind, I immediately picture her curves. Not that she fits into the full-figure stereotype. But she's thicker than I have ever dated, and that fact doesn't seem to bother me in the least.

"Declan?"

I snap out of my thoughts and let her voice pull my attention to her. "We have enough room, so it doesn't matter."

We head further into the secluded line of trees. The further back we travel, the fewer people are around. All the families with little kids stay closer to the front of the lot. Quinn's convinced there are great secret trees further back than anyone is willing to go. If that's true, it's because other people are smart enough to know they don't want to lug a heavy ass tree out of the mud back to the main tree lot.

"Are you done with your Christmas shopping?" She asks me. I know she's making small talk, and I appreciate her for the effort of filling the silence.

"Almost. I got most of it done by shopping online. Rachel and Max are the last on my list. I have no idea what to do for them. How about you? All done?"

"Mostly. My mom keeps bugging me about going with her this weekend. She wants me to come home so we can go shopping and bake cookies and do all that family holiday junk."

"Why don't you?"

She stops walking and turns to face me. "Are you serious? My schedule is a little full right now. And I can't leave Rachel alone for you to take care of."

"Why can't you? She's, my sister. I think I can put up with her alone for a few days."

"Really? Are you going to help your sister in and out of the bathroom? Are you going to help her in and out of the shower or rub lotion on her swollen feet?"

I can feel the color drain from my face at the thought of seeing my sister in those situations.

"It's not ideal, but...Quinn? If you want to go home for the weekend, I don't want to stop you. You do so much for us that it wouldn't be fair to keep you any longer from your family."

"It's fine. My mom will manage without me."

"Quinn? Just go home for the...."

"I don't want to, okay?" She's suddenly severe.

What have I missed? I hold my hands in the air between us as if to defend myself. "Okay."

She drops her eyes to the ground as if she can't look at me any longer. "I'm sorry. I didn't mean to sound bitchy. It's just my mom has been trying to get me to come home for Christmas, and I don't want to be there."

"Why didn't you say so? I can understand that. Shit, I never want to be around my parents during the holidays either. Believe me. I know what you're saying. You've met our mom."

That got a little laugh from her. "She's not always like that, is she?"

I give her a severe glare. "Yes, always. I don't know how Rachel and I became so normal."

"Rachel, I can see as normal, but you...not so much."

My mouth drops open as I pretend to have wounded feelings.

"That hurt. You don't think I'm normal?"

She steps closer to me, closes the distance between us, and pokes my chest with her index finger. "You, my friend, are the furthest from normal I've ever met."

"Is that so?" I mock.

Standing this close, her head barely reaches my chin, causing me to gaze down to see her eyes. I slip my hand down to her side and poke at the soft spot on her ribs that I know will make her jump. A loud shriek rips from her, and she steps away in a hurry. I'm not going to let her get too far. I quickly close the distance between us, tickling the other side until she screeches and jitters out of my reach again.

Darting down a line of trees, I smile as I give chase with Luc barking with excitement and hot on my heels. A freeing bliss washes over me like a weight has been lifted from my shoulders. I dart in and out of uncut Christmas trees as Quinn laughs and runs ahead of me. She zigzags between rows of trees, making it hard for me to see which way she's going to head next. I cut straight through a line of trees, heading over a few rows trying to get ahead of her. My plan works as she cuts across another row of trees running smack into my chest. My arms reach out, encircling her as she lets out a yelp of laughter.

My fingers dive into her sides, tickling at her ribs. I know she can't fight the laughter, and the sound is contagious. The more she giggles and struggles, the more I tickle and laugh along with her.

"Okay, okay. I can't breathe anymore. My sides hurt." She wails between laughs. I pity her and stop tickling, but my hands don't fall away from her. We stand there with my arms wrapped around her as we stare at each other. Our laughter turns into heavy breaths that fog in the cold air between us.

"I didn't hurt you, did I?" I ask. My voice is low and rough from all the laughing. I haven't laughed like that in years. Doing things I haven't done in years seems to be a recurring thing when I'm around Quinn.

"No. What're a few bruised ribs anyways?" She smiles, staring up at me. My gaze locks with hers, and at this moment, we are all alone out here. I watch her smile fade slowly from her lips as her eyes drop to my mouth as if she's waiting for me to kiss her.

Do I want to kiss her?

I do. I need to.

Desire overpowers me, and I drop my mouth to hers. Quinn doesn't push me away or step back. Instead, she releases a soft moan and opens for my invading tongue to poke inside her warm mouth.

She's so warm and tastes so good. My mouth moves over hers. Slow at first, tasting and savoring. My hands crawl slowly down the sides of her ribs, moving toward her lower back to wrap her in my warmth. Her chest presses against mine, and at this moment, I curse the decision to wear a sweater of my own. I want to feel her against me. Her skin on mine. Warmth on warmth.

Heat spreads over my body, awaking senses that have been frozen for so long. My body jerks to life, and blood pulses through my veins. I deepen the kiss, eating away at her with a hunger I've been denied for so long.

Quinn opens to me. Her fingers move to the sides of my head as she pulls me close holding me tighter against her. I can't get enough.

I need more.

My cock swells behind my zipper, and I ache to be touched. The urge to rip off the clothes separating us is too overwhelming.

Her hurried breath matches mine as our mouths and tongues perfect a dance. Slipping a hand under the heaviness of her coat, I can no longer hold back my moans from escaping into her mouth when the pads of my fingers skim over her warm skin. Circling her waist, I bring my fingers up to trail lightly over her ribs, brushing over the soft silkiness of her arms.

I want to drop her to the frozen ground and cover her with the heat of my body. I want to rip our clothes off and drive my thick cock deep inside her. Before I can put any of my plans into action, soft giggles break into my senses, making me aware we aren't alone.

Ending the heated kiss, I gently pull away, keeping her in my arms as I look around to find the source of the interruption. Three teenage girls are standing together a few rows over, giggling as they whisper among themselves as their gazes dart our way.

"It looks like we have an audience." Quinn pushes away, stepping out of my hold, and I reluctantly let her go.

"They're a little too young to be an audience for what I want to do to you right now. Come on. Let's get a damn tree and get out of here. Rachel's been on her own long enough."

Neither one of us spoke a word about our heated moment. But if she thinks I'm just going to forget about that kiss or the undeniable heat between us once we get home, she has another think coming.

# Chapter Eleven

♥

"I think we need some more balls on the left side. Now move that ornament over just a little. Nope, too far, go back just a little." Rachel reclines on the end of the couch, watching Declan and I decorate the Christmas tree. Declan frowns over his shoulder at his sister as he picks up another ornament and moves it to meet her demands.

After the two of us got back to the house with the tree, Declan carried Rachel to the living room so that she could be a part of the festivities.

"There. That looks great. Full too." Rachel compliments us, tossing another kernel of popcorn into her mouth.

I watch the two siblings in silence. I don't want to step on toes and get in the middle of their family dispute but hearing them bicker back and forth brings a tinge of sadness to me as I think about how much I miss my sister Kate. No matter where we are in our lives, we have always made time to see each other at Christmas. This will be the first year we will spend the holiday apart.

"Do you have any more lights? I think it needs more lights."

Declan glares at his sister, placing his hands on his hips. "I'm not taking the decorations down to put up more lights. You gave your approval before putting all this other crap on here. It's too late now." He turns toward me.

"Will you tell her you to agree with me, so she will leave me alone?" The tone of his voice says he's serious, but he gives me a playful smile that suggests otherwise. This gentler playful side of him is entirely new. It's like a switch has been flipped, and he's become a different person. I find he teases more and often smiles now. Maybe this change is thanks to his sister being here around the clock—no matter who or what is to blame. The reasons aren't important. I'm not going to complain either way.

I hold a hand in the air. "I'm staying out of this. You both are my boss, and I won't choose sides."

"Good answer," Rachel laughs as her brother gives me a pretend look of hurt that I didn't jump to side with him.

"That tells me whose side you're on," Declan says. Turning back to the tree, he hangs the last few ornaments on the branches.

Needing a refill, I grab my coffee cup from the side table next to Rachel. "Anyone wants anything while I'm in the kitchen?"

"I would love cold water, please," Rachel asks without looking up from the package of candy canes she is struggling to open.

I head to the kitchen to pour another cup of coffee and duck down into the fridge to grab water. I gasp when I pop up to find Declan on the other side of the door.

I grab my chest and sigh dramatically. "You could have given me a heart attack," I tell him, closing the door. He doesn't answer as he stands staring at me with his hands tucked in his pockets.

"I had hoped we could get a minute alone."

Oh no, here it comes—the talk.

I need a minute to prepare myself before the blows of rejection come.

"I think I know what you're going to say."

"You do, huh? Are you going to say you think we should talk? Because that's what I was going to say. But let's wait until Rachel goes to bed. I don't want her to get the wrong idea."

Great! So, can we prolong my torture? I don't argue. "Sure, that will work."

"After I get her into bed tonight. I'll meet you out at the pool house?"

I nod in agreement, and he heads back into the living room to join his sister.

I need to keep my anxiety in check for a few more hours. How in the hell am I going to be able to pretend everything is fine for that long?

Rachel is curled on the couch, staring at the perfectly decorated sparkling Christmas tree. When Declan asked if she was ready for bed, she insisted on sleeping on the couch. He agreed after making her promise to keep her phone near if she needed him in the middle of the night. With him being down the hall in his room, he might not be able to hear her if she needs anything. And as it turns out, I needed to wait through three more hours of sibling bickering before it was time for me to say good night.

I head to the pool house needing time to change into my nightclothes and get the rooms warm and comfortable before he knocks on the door.

My stomach flutters with nerves. What will I do if he tells me that he doesn't want me to work for him anymore? It would make sense. When I first started this job, he said he wasn't interested in anything besides a working relationship. He said he fired another PA for coming on to him. Is that what he is going to talk to me about? Am I getting fired?

Crap. Why did my thoughts have to go there?

Declan's probably going to come in here and give me the speech that I've heard all my life. He'll tell me we can never do what we did again. He will say he doesn't find me attractive and that he doesn't think of me in that way. Or worse, he's going to tell me we need to remain just friends. There's nothing worse for a bruised ego than the "I just want to remain friends" speech.

Is it possible to have a platonic relationship with someone you fantasize about on a nightly basis? If he lets me keep my job, then I will do my best to push the thoughts of my boss out of my head.

I inhale a deep breath and reach for the door as he knocks again.

"Glad you didn't just go to bed and leave me out here to freeze." He takes a step into the warm room, causing a chill to float through the air as he walks past. Looking down at my night clothes, he leans away.

"I didn't keep you waiting long, did I?"

His question and gaze make my modest choice in pajamas feel frumpy and unattractive. I wrap my arms around my mid-section, hiding all imperfections. "I wasn't in bed. I wanted to get warm and comfortable. I must have picked up a little chill from earlier at the tree lot. I'm just trying to get warm."

I'm lying, of course.

"Let's move over here and get the heater going." He moved further into the room and flipped a switch on the wall. The light on the heater lit up like a fireplace, and within seconds, flames danced behind the glass.

"Here. Sit." He tapped the arm of a chair that he angled closer to the warmth. He took a seat on the floor facing the chair.

I sit and snuggle into the armchair throwing a small lap blanket over me. I need the cover of a security blanket to help with my insecurities.

I drag my gaze over him as he sits on the floor between me and the faux fire. His face is turned toward the glass watching as the flames flicker back and forth. My gaze trails from his facial profile down the side of his thick corded neck, taking in the strong muscles that run under his smooth skin. My gaze lingers a moment on the collar of the flannel he's wearing unbuttoned over a plain white shirt.

Leaning back, he bends one leg at the knee, stretching the other out in front of him. He oozes power and self-assurance, reminding me once again he's so out of my league.

"What did you want to talk about?" The sooner this conversation starts, the sooner I can go to bed and lick my rejection wounds alone.

He doesn't look at me as he begins. "I think we need to clear the air between us. What happened earlier this afternoon was...."

I brace my hands against the arms of the chair, waiting for the blow to hit.

"...amazing."

My gaze snaps to his, and he turns toward me and smiles. After a long, drawn-out pause, he smirks. "What did you think I was going to say?"

I shake my head. I don't want to tell him the whole truth. "I wasn't expecting that."

"Judging from the shocked expression. What did you think I was going to say?"

"I shake my head. "Nothing. It doesn't matter."

"Does to me. You looked like you were ready to take a pretty big blow."

I shrug my shoulders but smile at him. "Honestly, I didn't know what you were going to say." I tease. "But so far, so good."

He nods and continues. "I want to make a few things clear between us. There are some things about me I haven't told you."

If we are clearing the air, I need to tell Declan about my stay at the hospital and my past. "There's something I want to tell you too."

"Okay. Shoot."

"Nope. You first."

Stretching out further, he leans back on his elbows, looking relaxed and comfortable. "It's no secret I've been struggling to overcome my loss. I'm trying but, I'm struggling."

"No one expects the process to be easy for you. I think you're doing great, considering."

"Thank you. But that's only part of it."

My cheeks burn a little with heat not caused by the heater. Ducking my gaze away from his, I wait for him to continue.

"I'm aware I'm struggling, but I want to tell you that since you have come to work here, you have made dealing with life easier for me. I like having you around. I don't always show it or say it. I know I seem annoyed a lot of the time, but it isn't because I'm annoyed with you. I get...overwhelmed with everything. But the more we hang out and the more we get to know each other, the easier this all feels."

"I agree. We don't have the awkwardness anymore."

His fingers slide through his hair as he sits up toward the chair. "I feel like I can be open with you. Something I had only found in Dani. She never judged me or thought less of me, and you won't either. A few things from my past may come to the surface if I ever come out in public. It's one of the reasons I never came out as an author. But the more we get to know each other, the more I want to confide in you. One of my secrets is I dabbled in a different lifestyle years ago. A sexual lifestyle. It was when I met Dani. She knew all about that certain part of my life."

Holy shit!

That would explain the erotic romance writing.

"I found that world because I was researching a paper I was writing in college. I was invited to meet people in the BDSM lifestyle and there was something about it just clicked with me. I would have stopped after I met Dani, but she wanted to learn and try for me. She became my submissive. Most people don't understand the life, and they think it's all just a sexual kink. But to true Dominant and submissive, it's a lifestyle."

"You haven't practiced since?"

He shook his head. "I never had the urge to after Dani. But here lately, the need is awakening inside me as if the beast had been sleeping all this time."

"So, you think you might want to return to the life someday?"

He turned his head to stare at the fire, and he remained quiet for a long moment before he answered. "If I find the best person willing to open herself up to learning the life, then I like to think so."

Holy shit. I swallow hard, and it occurs to me he must see how nervous I am.

"I just want you to know, I have a past that I can't and won't deny."

"You should never deny what makes you happy."

He nods before looking back at me. "What did you want to tell me?" He asks, letting go of a sigh.

Shit.

I took a deep breath in, filling my lungs with the intake. Trying to calm my nerves. I've never talked about my past with anyone outside of my doctors and counselors. It isn't something I go around advertising. No one cares how broken I am.

"In case it comes out somewhere else, I want you to hear from me first."

He sits up until his back is straight. Raising one knee to his chest, he wraps his arms around his kneecap and gives me his full attention.

"Before I tell you, I need you to believe me that I no longer need to do any of the things I'm going to tell you about. Okay?"

Even though he nods in agreement, I can tell by his dipped brow and questionable look in his eye that he's also a little confused.

Taking a deep calming breath, I move my right arm out from under the lap blanket, revealing the whitened scars that I try so hard to keep hidden from others. I watch Declan's face, waiting to see the moment he realizes what they mean.

Pushing himself to his knees, he knelt in front of me, taking my wrist into his hands. He ran his thumb lightly over the pinched scar that runs the length of my vein on the inside of my wrist.

He's silent for a moment as he gazes over my skin. "How old are these?"

I swallow. I haven't talked about my scars to anyone in a long time. They show a part of me I don't want people to see. The insecurities I had from weight and body issues hold nothing to the shame I have about these scars— proof of my weakness.

"I've had them since high school. It was during a hard time in my life and cutting was a way I could deal with the stress and my teenage emotions."

Without looking at me, he continues. "Was that the only time?"

Why did he have to ask the one question I wish he hadn't. I pull my other arm out of the blanket, tugging my arm free, and turn my palm up to show him the matching arm.

"I had already moved to California for work the last time."

His gaze slid to mine, seeing his pained features stare back at me. "Why?"

Why? The question everyone asks and wants me to answer. The one question, I can't. No one understood. My parents. My friends. None of my family members. No one knows what it is like being an outcast or being trapped in a body you can't change. The insecurities are not something I can snap my fingers and get over. I'm never going to get over it.

"The first time in high school, I struggled with self-image issues. I have since I was a kid. I've always been a heavier girl, which doesn't go over so well in middle and high school. Kids are cruel."

I drop my gaze back to my wrists as he traced small circles over my scars with the pad of his fingers. The touch is so small and so innocent, like no other touch I've felt.

The tiny hairs along my arms stand up as he massages the sensitive skin along my scarred arm. My heart beats wildly, and my lips go dry under my panting breath against them.

"What happened in California?"

My gaze stays on his fingers as he draws circles over my skin. I sucked in a breath to calm my nerves. "I had been in California for a few years working for a family. Both parents were in films, so they always had people coming and going from the house. The house was big, and it wasn't uncommon for family and friends to crash there." I pause to take another breath. "One night, while their kids were gone for the weekend, they decided to host a huge dinner. I wasn't supposed to be there, but my plans fell through at the last minute. I don't normally hang out when they have all their Hollywood friends coming over. So I decided to go downstairs to my room. There were four rooms down there. All of them were for people like me who worked for the couple. So I was in my room when my boss's brother came barging in. He was high and drunk, but I had met him before, and he seemed like a nice guy. He stayed in my room for a while talking, and he tried to get me to drink with him. I refused, and that was when he started getting handsy." I pause the retelling and peer up at Declan, whose face had grown hard as stone, and his eyes were staring off. I continued.

"I asked him to leave me alone, but the more I did that, the more he pushed me. I fought him as hard as I could, but he overpowered me." I stop to wipe a tear from my cheek.

"After that night, I tried to tell my boss what happened, and of course, the story got twisted. He said I came on to him. I don't have the money as they do, so fighting them in court was useless. The only thing I could do was leave. They agreed to let me out of my contract and still give me a letter of endorsement, but all I had to do was drop the matter and never bring it to court again."

"Fuck. You let those assholes get off with nothing?" He yelled, squeezing his hands into fists.

"Honestly, I didn't know what to do, so I agreed and came back here. I don't say the words. The scar speaks for me. A few weeks later, I try to...."

"Was that the last time?"

I nod my head holding his gaze. "Yes. After that, my parents checked me into a hospital for ninety-days so I could get the counseling I needed to work through the trauma."

"Do you ever have the urge to hurt yourself anymore?"

"The truth? Sometimes. I would be lying if I said I never thought about it because I have. I'm strong enough to not act on it, though."

"Why are you telling me this now? Why didn't you say something before?" His thumb ceased moving, and his hand fell away from mine. I want to protest and demand he touch me again. But I remain quiet.

"I don't want my past issues to cause problems between us. I guess it's why I'm telling you now. I want to be honest with you. I also want you to believe me when I say everything is in my past. When I was going through those times in my life, I never believed I was good enough for anyone. Not even myself."

"How are you not good enough for other people. What I know of you, Quinn Abraham, you are a great person with a kind heart."

I give him a weak smile. "Thank you. I don't want you to think that you hired an unstable person."

"I never thought that about you. You're amazing and sweet...." his face sober. "About this afternoon...."

I stop him before he has the chance to continue. "Don't worry about it. We both just got caught up in the moment."

He sits back on his heels, staring at me. His brows furrow, making the lines around his eyes harden his face.

"Is that what you think happened today? That we just got caught up in the moment. Because it sure as hell hasn't felt like that for the last few weeks."

I'm confused. Is he upset with me for giving him an out?

"All I'm saying is I understand how the moment got carried away."

I scan his face, and the annoyance I find doesn't make any sense.

"Are you saying this because you didn't like the kiss or because you think I need an excuse for what we did? Because clearly, I would need a reason to want to kiss you?"

I shake my head. Saying it out loud makes it more real.

"Answer me, Quinn." His voice is low and firm.

I don't want to argue, but I just ranted about honesty.

"I want to give you an out without you feeling like you were hurting my feelings. If you need one...."

"Will you stop already?" His words slice through mine, stopping me from continuing.

"I didn't ask you for an out, did I? Don't assume you know that I want or need excuses. I'm not sure what this is between us. I'm not sure how far we might take this. All I do know, is I haven't felt feelings like this in a long time, and honestly, I don't want these feelings to fade. This is all as new to you as it is to me. Let's take it one step at a time and let nature take its course, whatever that may be." He says, moving his hands down to interlock his hand with mine.

"I understand. I'm not sure I can explain why I can share my scars with you and no one else. I've never even shared them with my parents." I said, looking down at our entwined fingers.

"I'm glad you choose me." He let my hands drop from his grip before pulling further away from me. I want to protest the loss of his warmth, but if he needs a minute to gather his thoughts, I won't stop him. We just dropped bombs on each other. To my surprise, he doesn't move far, lifting himself to the arm of the chair I occupy.

His fingers graze through the hair that has fallen to the sides of my face, and with one gentle movement, he brushes it back behind my ear. I turn my head and smile up at him. An awkward silence falls over us, and for a long-paused moment, neither one of us speaks.

Instead, we both gaze at the flames as they dance over us.

"Quinn, can I ask you for a favor? It's going to sound odd, and I won't blame you if you say no, but I need to ask." His voice trails off as if he's about to change his mind.

I don't want him to give up and pull away. That reason alone must have been what prompted me to answer. "Anything."

Do I mean anything? Yes. Whatever he needs, I'm prepared to give him.

He suddenly looks nervous as he runs a shaky hand through his hair. His cheeks blow out as he slowly re-leases a large breath. He's nervous. What does he have to fear from me?

"It's been a-awhile since I've had a good night's sleep. I haven't slept in my bed in two years."

I'm not surprised. Rachel told me he moved out of his bedroom after Dani died.

I wait for him to continue. I'm not sure how I can help him.

"Would you mind if I... if I stayed for a few hours. Here? With you?"

"With me?"

Does he want to sleep here? With me?

His hand flies up into the air. "I'm not looking for sex. I was hoping that having another person beside me will make a difference."

It is a weird request, but I quickly realize there isn't a lot I won't do for him. I want to help him any way I can.

"Of course." I offer him a smile and wave my hand toward the only bedroom. With a relieved grin, he grabs my hand and pulls me to my feet before dragging me after him into the adjoining room.

Once in the room, Declan toes his shoes off, leaving his jeans and shirt in place before climbing onto the mattress. I stand at the edge of the bed, staring down at the beautiful man. He pats the comforter, inviting me to join him. His fingers hook around the top edge of the blankets, yanking them back to expose the clean, crisp sheets awaiting me.

Nervous butterflies dance in my stomach as I turn to take a seat on the bed. I snuggle down into the bed, noticing that he remains on the top of the blanket.

Rolling to his side, Declan rests his head on his bent arm while his other hand falls to the bed between us.

"Thank you for this, Quinn. I hope it's not too weird for you."

I roll my head toward him and watch as his heavy eyelids slide closed and his breathing relaxes to a steady, even tug-of-war.

A smile curls over my lips. Happiness fills me at the idea of this man, this handsome, lonely man, needing to be close to me.

# Chapter Twelve

Bright rays of daylight poke through the thin lace curtains spreading its warmth over my face. I shield the brightness with my hand as the final traces of sleep leave my body. I lay still for another minute before stretching out the tight muscles in my back and pushing sleep away. For the first time in a long time, I woke up...rested. I finally got needed sleep.

My arms drop back down and brush against warm softness.

Quinn.

She's lying on her side, facing away from me, and I let my gaze drift down the length of her body. I take in the entire beautiful sight of her. The swell of her hip in the air. The dip of her hourglass waist and the curve of her ass as she lays in a curled position.

Last night had been about no longer being lonely. I try to convince myself anyone could have served the purpose but...who am I fooling? Quinn has worked her way under my skin these last few weeks, and I like it. Hell, I can't seem to get enough of her. She has been digging her way into my thoughts these last few weeks. Ever since Thanksgiving. Ever since that kiss.

It should bother me that I allow this closeness between us to continue, but I can't or won't do anything to stop it.

At least the guilt of being a piece-of-shit cheating husband has finally eased. I don't like the thought of Dani knowing I've been with another woman, but Dani would want me to be happy. I also believe that if they had the chance to have met, Dani would have liked and approved of Quinn.

I roll to the far side of the bed and swing my legs over the side. Glancing at the clock on the table, I wince as I read the late morning hour, no wonder the sun's already up.

I need to head back into the house and check on Rachel. She will no doubt be awake and wanting breakfast by now. Pushing myself off the bed, I run my hands through my hair, turning to gaze back at the woman sleeping undisturbed. A light smile curls up the corners of my lips as I gaze down at her. I wish I knew what spell she has over me.

I never thought Quinn could be my type of woman, yet I can't stop thinking about the next time I see her again. From the moment I leave her sight, I'm counting down the seconds until she'll walk back into mine.

My gaze drops to her wrist, peeking out from between the pillow and her head. Her hand is turned up, showing the small white scars. I could never understand the breaking point she had to push her to the desperate point where she wanted to end her life? I can't imagine that amount of self-hate and pain, and I had to watch my wife die right in front of my eyes.

Even though we are different people from two different worlds, it's beginning to make sense how we are both broken pieces of the fucked-up puzzle of life. Both of us are just trying to find our place.

I leave the warmth of the bedroom, closing the door softly behind me. I head out into the sharp cold and over to the main house. I can hear the echoed mutters of voices coming from the surround-sound speakers embedded in the walls telling me the living room Tv is on.

Rachel's awake and probably waiting for me.

I grab a water bottle from the fridge, twisting the cap off as I round the corner and head straight for my sister.

She's awake and sitting propped up on a pile of pillows. Her gaze is glued to the television screen. I recognize the classic Christmas movie we once watched every year as kids.

Stepping over to the other end of the couch, I take a seat near her feet and hand her the bottle of water I moved off the cushion.

"How long have you been awake?" I ask, gazing up at the movie. I'm not paying attention to it as much of a way to avoid eye contact. I don't want to see the disappointment in my sister. She knows where I've been all night, but what she doesn't know is why.

"Long enough to notice that my brother hasn't been in the house all night."

I don't say anything. She sucks in a breath, and I turn to face her as her eyes grow large.

"You didn't." her open mouth curling into a smile. "Did you sleep out there?"

I can't help but smirk at her childish attempt at getting information. "Yes, all right. I slept out there, but last night is not what you're thinking. Nothing happened."

"Wait a minute. You two shared a bed? All night?" Rachel's look of shock surprised me.

I guess to her; the truth would sound shocking. She couldn't possibly understand that I was looking for a solid night's sleep. To be able to keep the ghosts away long enough to sleep a good eight hours is something I didn't think would ever happen again.

"Whatever your thinking, stop it. It wasn't like that, Rachel. More like...two lonely friends who...." I pause as my sister nodding in a humous way. "Forget it. You won't understand."

Her features soften for a second as her humor fades. "Declan Palmer. Do you think I don't understand the shit you are dealing with? Because I do. I mean, I have never lost a spouse, but Dani's passing tore your heart out, and I know you're still mending but don't you dare for a minute think I don't understand."

Pausing for a minute, I think she's finished until she draws in a breath and starts in once more.

"Everyone has problems. I have them, you do, and even though I don't have all the details, I know Quinn does too. Here I am on my brother's couch, trying to keep this baby inside me to give it a fighting chance of surviving while my boyfriend is out of town on business. I'm lonely, and I'm scared, but I have other people to help me."

"The difference between us is that your man will come home. My wife will never walk through that door again."

Her chin falls to her chest, releasing a loud breath. "Declan..."

"Don't. Rachel, I'm okay. At least, I'm beginning to be. Here lately, I've felt different. I'm no longer betraying Dani by living while she can't."

"Oh honey, is that what you thought?" She asks, leaning toward me gripping my shoulders. She pulls me into her arms and holds me tighter than she ever has.

I pat her forearm and pull away from her. "I did, but not anymore. It's weird. The only way I can explain it is, I feel like I was stuck in a nightmare the last two years, and I'm finally waking up and pulling myself out of the fog of that nightmare." I hesitate because I'm unsure how Rachel will react to the rest.

"I think I'm feeling this way because of Quinn. I think having her around is good for me. She's upbeat, fun, and her cooking is more passable than yours."

We both laugh, but when I glance at my sister, instead of the disappointment I fear would be on her face. She's smiling.

"I'm happy to hear you say this because I think she is too. I didn't think I would be able to convince you of it without letting you see it for yourself."

I turn my gaze back to the holiday movie on the TV, but I can feel Rachel's gaze still on me. "What?"

"Do you like her?"

My shoulders lift with a heavy sigh. "Yeah, of course, I do."

Reaching over, she smacks my arm. "That's not what I'm talking about, and you know it."

"Nothing is going on between us. We are working on becoming friends and learning about each other, that's all. Don't be pushy, Rachel. Don't make me sorry I let you stay on my couch instead of kicking your sorry ass to the curb."

Her smile is warm and sisterly. She knows I would never kick her out and that I'm just giving her a hard time.

"Are you sure she knows this thing between you is nothing? I mean, girls have a way of over-thinking things."

That makes me nervous. What if Quinn does think last night meant something more? I don't want to hurt her feelings.

Shit!

I'm confused about what last night meant to me. Is it wrong to want the closeness of another person without wanting the relationship that typically goes with it?

Rachel's eyes soften as she looks at me. "I don't want to see her get hurt. Quinn is wonderful at her job, and she's great at not taking any shit off you. I like her, and I want her to stick around."

"You're just saying that because you want more time off when this little one comes." I put my hand on the front of her rounded stomach. It's the first time I've ever felt her growing belly. I can't remember one time that I've shown any interest at all in my sister's growing family. Put it down as another thing I've sucked at in the brother department.

"I would love to take some time off. What new parent doesn't wish to stay at home with their baby? But I also know you, brother. I know you can't make it that long without me." She's teasing, of course, but the truth is, I can't blame Rachel for wanting more time off. Hell, she deserves to have a year off. Although being a mom is what she's always wanted to be, she will never abandon me for that long. "You're going to be a great mom. You're already a great sister."

I watch moisture gather in her eyes before she drops her gaze to her lap. I don't want her to cry, but I also know a war of hormones rages inside her. I pat the top of her leg in my brotherly attempt to keep her from shedding tears.

"How about breakfast? Does the little one want anything special this morning?" I ask, pushing off the couch before turning to look down at her. Her face has suddenly transformed into a wide goofy grin.

"The baby wants an egg scramble with toast and chocolate milk." She giggles as she hides her smile in the blankets.

"Man, my sister is a garbage gut. Remind me to bill your old man for groceries."

"Put it on my tab," Rachel yells with laughter as I leave the room.

Twenty minutes later, I carry a tray of food into the living room and place it over Rachel's lap. She barely takes the time to look away from the Christmas movie to glance at her food.

"Before I forget, will you be willing to do some shopping for me today? Just a few last-minute things that I need. I had no idea the doctor was going to put me on bed rest. Christmas is next week, and I want to have Max's gifts wrapped and under the tree before he gets home. Plus, I haven't gotten anything for mom and dad yet." She huffs with an eye roll. Shopping for our dad is easy. Shopping for our mom makes me prefer a hot poker to the eye instead.

"What did you get them?" She asks.

"Nothing, yet. I haven't thought about shopping."

"Take Quinn with you. She has good taste. She can help pick something out from both of us. My list is on the table." She points to a piece of notebook paper with scribbles written across it. Picking up the paper, I glance through her list. She has to be joking.

"Rachel? There are like a dozen items on here. Who are you buying an iPad for? And where in the heck am I supposed to find a leather satchel? This list is crazy. How many people are you buying for?"

She glances away from her movie and shrugs. "The iPad is for Max's niece, and some of the other gifts are for his sisters. We buy them one each."

My eyes narrow on my con-artist sister. "You haven't even started any of your shopping, have you? Admit it."

"And when would I have had time for that. I work all the time, and when I'm not working, I'm eating or sleeping because I'm pregnant, and that's all I seem to do."

I can hear the tears welling up in her voice and telling me it's time to get out of here before she goes into a full-out crying fit.

"Okay, I'll go. I'll ask if Quinn wants to go with me, but...."

"She will. I texted her a minute ago. She said she will be ready in fifteen minutes." Why did that not surprise me?

Taking her ridiculous list in hand, I turn and head back into the kitchen. I had planned on making Quinn and myself breakfast. It looks like I no longer have time for that. My sister has put her boss to work.

*Quinn*

Shopping with Declan turned out to be a far better experience than expected. I thought going in and out of multiple stores would be miserable for a man such as Declan, but instead, he seems to be enjoying himself.

It's nearing one in the afternoon, and we're nearly done with Rachel's list, and I've picked up my last-minute gifts. I even succeeded in grabbing a gift for Declan without him noticing.

We duck into another store filled with customers hustling to get their shopping done. I feel the soft brush of a hand slide over the small of my back just above my hips. Realizing Declan has laid his hand on me has me turning my surprised eyes toward him. But he isn't looking at me. Instead, his gaze is focused on the crowd and getting us through the lines.

I can barely feel the heat of his palm through my jacket. Yet, I can't stop the heat rising inside the rest of my body. How does this man have the ability to flip all my switches? All he has to do is give me a look, a glance, or a slight touch, and I'm melting like butter. I'm not proud that this man, who has no interest in me beyond our work relationship, holds so much control over me.

We talk, shop, and laugh for the next hour as we pick up the last of Rachel's list.

"What else is left?" Declan asks, taking the shopping bags out of my hands so I can pull the paper Rachel gave me out of my pocket. I groan silently on the inside. "Only one left is your parents."

I smile as he rolls his eyes. "How about the gift of love? Think they will go for it?" He asks.

Smiling, I nod. "Send them on a very long trip somewhere." I laugh at my ridiculous idea, but when I glance his way, he's holding a seriousness on his face forcing my smile to fall.

"I'm sorry. I shouldn't have said that. I..."

"No. That's a terrific idea. Rachel and I can send them on a trip for Christmas. My dad's been wanting to go on a ski trip to Colorado. Let's get back to my house and look up ideas on the computer."

Getting back to the car, we unload our bags into the trunk before sliding into the seats. Declan started the engine and merged into traffic.

"Thank you for today. I mean, my feet hurt, and I spent way too much money but other than that, I had a great time with you today. It was nice."

Declan gives me his sexy panty-melting grin, turning his head toward me. "I enjoyed today too. And that's saying something because I hate shopping, but you made it bearable." He reached over and picked up my hand lying on my thigh. He slips his fingers between mine before resting our conjoined hands back to my leg.

A blush heats my cheeks, and I have to get it under control.

After we get back to the house and unload all our items, I head into the kitchen to start dinner. Declan busies himself on the computer looking at trips for their parents, and Rachel's on the couch squealing over all the gifts we purchased on her behalf.

I don't have the time to make a gourmet meal since we were out most of the day, but I'm able to throw together a few items in a skillet, and before I know it, I have a stir fry nearly done.

"How did shopping go?" Rachel asks, coming into the kitchen. She stops at one of the high-back stools at the island and plops herself down.

"You shouldn't be up and moving around. I'll bring dinner to you. Better go back out there and lay down before your brother sees you."

She waves a semi swollen hand at me, settling further down on the stool. "I can't stay down all hours of the day. I'm going nuts. I'm eating dinner right here in this chair." She smacks her palms against the countertop. Her words confirm her unspoken threat that she dares anyone to tell her different.

"Okay, but as soon as you eat, you are back to bed. Don't make me get your brother on my side." I laugh off my empty threat turning back to the food on the stove. She knows as well as I do that my words are empty.

"I think he's already on your side."

I look over my shoulder at her. "That's because he knows you need to be down."

"That's not what I'm talking about. Declan would be on your side no matter what the topic."

I lay the spoon I'm using down and turn to face her.

"What are you talking about?"

She grins. "My brother is finally softening those rough edges of his, and it is all thanks to you. Since I've been staying here, I've seen a huge change in him. A change for the better. You have done more for Declan in a few months than our family could accomplish in two years."

Her words warm me. It's sweet that she thinks I have anything to do with Declan's transformation. Of course, I have noticed the changes. Hell, he just went shopping for his sister's Christmas list today. Something tells me he wouldn't have done that three months ago.

"That isn't my doing. I haven't done anything to help. I wouldn't know how."

Rachel shakes her head. "But you have. You being you is enough."

I turn back to face the stove and shut the burner off. Heat rushes over my cheeks, and my heart melts. I wish

I could take credit for Declan's turn-around, but all of his progress is his doing.

"Dinner is done," I say over the lump in my throat.

"It's booked," Declan announced, carrying his laptop into the kitchen taking a seat next to his sister.

"Where are we sending them? Better yet, when are we sending them?" Rachel asks, grinning.

"I just booked a week-long ski trip in the Rockies. They fly out Christmas day and return after the new year."

"So, they won't be here when the baby comes?"

Declan's gaze turns to his sister. "Is that a problem?"

Her straight lips curl up at the corners. "No. It might be better if mom's not here to mother me in the delivery room. As it is, I told Max to have security on standby just in case I need her removed."

"You two are awful." I tease. Loading up three plates, I set one in front of each of them before taking the last empty stool next to Declan.

For the first time in an exceedingly long time, I feel whole again.

# Chapter Thirteen

♥

I stare down at the beautiful sleeping woman that I can't seem to stay away from. The last two nights, I've allowed myself to follow Quinn to her bed. There's been nothing sexual between us, not that my body hasn't taken notice of the woman lying next to me, but I remind myself I'm here for the comforts of another person.

There is something about being with Quinn, lying close to her, that has me so at ease that the nightmares are no longer plaguing me. Tonight is no different as I pull the blanket away from the pillows and slide between the cool crisp sheets. They smell like Quinn, and I groan when blood begins to run south to my cock. I've slept over the blankets the last two nights, giving Quinn the privacy and security of the sheet between us. But tonight, I move in next to her. The night air is cooler, and a chill has fallen over the room. We will need our body heat to stay warm. At least, it's the excuse I'm telling myself to justify my actions.

After slipping in behind her, I pull the blankets up to cover my bare chest. I roll to my side, rest my weight on my arm, and face Quinn. My chest is inches from her back. She doesn't make a sound even as the bed groans under my weight.

I like to believe that after the first night, my little mouse has grown used to me crawling into her bed at different hours of the night. There is an unseen force pulling me toward her, and I already know she will be a hard habit to break. What if I can't sleep without her? What if she is the reason all the nightmares are gone?

Quinn's lying on her side with her back to me. She's wearing a cotton nightshirt long enough to fall to the top of her knees when she stands. The large open neck is pulled to one side, exposing a slim bare shoulder.

No matter the late hour, sleep is still too far away, so I lay still listening to her steady breathing. The side of my cheek rests on the empty pillow next to hers. My gaze caresses her bare skin and into her soft hair fanned out under her. I'm thankful for the back porch light positioned exactly right outside so the soft glow peeks through her window. Her hair bathed in the light like a halo around her head.

My fingers tingle to feel those silky strands slide through them. The muscle in my arm twitches as I fight the urge to drag the back of my fingers over her bare skin. I wonder if she is as soft as she looks.

I shouldn't be having these thoughts about Quinn. I shouldn't be in her bed. She let me sleep here the first and second night because she's too nice to turn me away. But tonight, she doesn't know I'm here. And God, I want to be here more than anything. My body and my mind need to be here—with her.

I find being in her presence comforting and alluring. It's crazy because I never thought I would feel a pull toward another person like this again. Or that I would want to feel that pull. And yet, here I am.

With my nerves knotting up in my stomach, I slowly lower my hand to slide across the sheet. My heart pounds in my chest as I inch closer. I'm afraid my nervous breathing will echo in her ears loud enough to wake her. The tips of my fingers edge the smooth surface of her nightshirt and move up the length. The back of my fingers grazes the bare skin of her shoulder, and her head shifts against her pillow. Her closed eyes flutter as sleep still holds her.

I draw small circles over her skin, loving the soft sounds of her moans as her body shivers under my touch. I want to be closer. I need to feel her skin against mine.

Giving in to my urges, I shift my body until my chest presses against her back. Slowly I raise my head, bringing my lips down to her warm exposed skin. This is crossing the lines that no employer should ever cross. Yet, all I know is, if I don't taste this woman soon, I'm going to go crazy. My body is alive and hard. My jeans are tight and growing uncomfortable thanks to my erection pressing against the zipper, but there's no way I'm moving away now.

My lip's part against her shoulder, and my tongue pokes out to taste the ivory skin calling to me. A throaty moan escapes her lips, and her head rolls toward mine. Her eyes remain closed, and for a moment, I stare at her. Her face is soft and relaxed. She looks so beautiful that I feel a flutter in my chest. This girl doesn't know how beautiful she is.

I began working my way along her neck, stopping at the slight dip next to her collarbone. Her lashes flutter, and her lids open just enough to peek at me. My gaze catches hers, but I don't pull my mouth away. I watch her watch me as my tongue and lips caress her skin. Moving further up, she lets her head fall to the side, allowing me access to the tender skin there.

I move my hand to cup her cheek and turn her face toward mine. Lowering my mouth, I take her lips. She tastes sweet, warm, and familiar. I sink hungrily into her with a groan. She opens to me, and within seconds our tongues are feverishly dancing and stroking each other. My mouth opens wider, and I take her fully with mine pulling back for a moment to take her bottom lip between mine. Her gaze darts up to mine, and I hold her there. Her small pink tongue darts out to run over her bottom lip to moisten it. She looks like she's about to say something, but I hush her words by placing a finger lightly over her lips.

We're not going to have sex tonight. Not because I don't want to, but because we're not ready to give ourselves fully to each other. There's a connection between us that neither of us can explain. I know you feel it too. I shouldn't be here like this. It's not right, but I can't stay away." I give her a moment to think as I lean down and kiss her lips once more, waiting for her response.

If you want me to stop, I will. I'll go back to my room right now, and we never have to talk about this again. All you have to do is say the words."

Staring up into my eyes, she nods before wrapping her arms around my neck and pulling me back into her. It's the green light I've been waiting for. Grinning, I lean down and place another kiss on the tip of her nose.

As I retake her mouth, my body jolts alive. The ache to be inside her is maddening. My cock is unbearably hard to the point of pain. As long as I keep a barrier between us, I won't be sinking into her warm wet heat. I groan as my mind drifts there.

I want to touch, kiss, and explore her body. I want to know and taste every inch of her skin, but I don't want to scare her away.

I rock my hips, and a moan escapes me as my cock rubs against her thigh. Holy fuck.

"Is this, okay?" I ask, needing her approval.

Her nod is forceful as she grabs my face with her hands and pulls my mouth back to hers.

Fuck, this is hot. I want Quinn to go crazy with desire for me. I want her panting and moaning along with my own. I want to sink inside of her until she begs me never to leave.

And as foolish as I am. I want to promise that I won't.

*Quinn*

There are no words between us as Declan claims my mouth like a starving man.

Rolling onto my back, I give him better access to the front of my body. I wrap my arms around him, encasing him to me and holding him closer as our mouths move over each other with a fierce hunger. He moves until he's lying on top of me. His arms are holding his weight above me next to my head. He is pressing me further into the mattress, and it feels incredible to be dominated by him.

His hands move to the sides of my face holding me still while his kiss devours me.

My heart beats heavily in my chest. I've never been so excited and nervous at the same time because I don't want to disappoint Declan.

My fingers find their way to the sides of his ribs, and I trail softly down his skin, smiling as the muscles ripple under my touch. He has such an incredible physique. A perfect body. A body of a man who should be with someone better than me.

That thought has my arms freezing at his sides, and my hands stop moving. I can feel my shoulders stiffen with tension. Declan must have noticed, too, because he stops kissing me and brings his head up over mine to look down at me. "What's the matter? Did I do something wrong?"

I try to smile, but I have a feeling it's coming off as weak and not believable. "No, it's nothing. I'm just a little nervous, is all."

Leaning down, he kisses my lips before meeting my eyes again. "You don't need to be nervous. I got you."

I can't tell him what's scaring me. There are so many parts of me that think I'm not good enough for him. He had perfection with Dani. I'm not even a close second to her.

A familiar ringtone pierces the quiet of my tiny bedroom forcing us to look toward the cell phone on the bedside table. "What the hell?" He groans before shifting his weight away from me.

"That's Rachel. We have to answer it." Leaning over, I grab the phone.

"My sister has shit timing. I hope she knows that?" He says.

I press the call button and raise the phone to my ear without an answer. "Rachel? Are you okay?"

Declan jumps from the bed, and we are already straightening our clothes before his sister has a chance to answer.

"I'm fine, but, um...." Rachel's voice drops low as if she's trying her best to keep her voice down on purpose. "Could you have my brother come in here, please? He has a guest."

"A guest?"

"A guest?" Declan's head turns at my words. I give him a shrug telling him I have no idea either.

"Okay. We'll be right there."

Declan's already out the door before I finish with my clothes, but I manage to follow close behind. "Who in the hell would show up this time of night?"

We hear two women following him through the kitchen before I see anyone. One voice belongs to Rachel, but the other is one I haven't heard before.

Rounding the corner, I see a beautiful young blonde. She's wearing a white tailored jacket and skirt combo with tasteful gold heels with a designer name purse draped over one shoulder and a sizeable tablet-sized phone in the other.

"Declan! It's so good to see you. It's been, what, two years?" The newcomer sings with a squeal of happiness.

"Jaclyn?"

Declan looks confused. With a nod, he snaps out of the awe and throws his arms around the girls' waist, hoisting her up against his body.

Placing her back on her golden heels a moment later, Declan turns around, and it's in that moment I see a genuine smile on his lips. A smile I've only seen once or twice before.

"Quinn, I want you to meet Jaclyn. Jaclyn, this is Quinn. She's my new assistant. She will be taking things over for Rachel for a few months."

My lips drop a little as my smile fades. It shouldn't surprise me that he introduces me as such to others. After all, that is what our roles are to each other. Employer and employee. But why does it feel like he just slapped me across the face with those words?

Rachel must have noticed the shift in my presence because she offers me a reassuring smile when my gaze meets hers. The smile you hand out to the runner-up.

"Quinn, this is Dani's baby sister." Rachel offers since neither of the other two does the introductions.

"Baby isn't the word. I'm in my twenties now and not looking much like a child if I do say so myself." She giggles as she spins and bends in a half curtsy, all while never taking her eyes off Declan.

"It's so great to see you. What are you doing here?"

"I came home to be with the parents for a holiday. Mom goes a little crazy this time of year. You know how she can be. This is the first year they're putting the Christmas party back on after taking the last few years off. Since I'm here, I thought I would pop over so we could catch up. I should have called first, but I wanted to surprise you. Sorry about the time. My flight just got in an hour ago."

"You haven't seen your parents yet?"

She waves the question away with a hand. "My parents act like their eighty. They go to bed at eight o'clock. It would have been a waste for me to go there first. I remember you used to keep late hours before, so I hoped you still did. I guess I was right."

"I'm always happy to see you. You're family. You can stay in one of the guest rooms tonight. I'm not sending you off to a hotel this late."

"Um, could you grab my things? I left them by the door?"

A moment passes before I realize Jaclyn is talking to me. She wants me to carry her things. What was I, a bellhop?

"Jacks, Quinn isn't a maid. She works with Rachel. I'll grab your things." Declan tells her leaving the room to grab her belongings. Jaclyn turns her long-lash hazel eyes to me. "I'm so sorry. I didn't mean to imply anything."

I smile at her and tell her it's okay. What else am I supposed to do? It feels like an insult, but I can't be petty even though I want to snarl and be spiteful. I'm not getting good vibes from Jacklyn. Something about her makes me want to scratch her eyes out, which is weird. I don't even know the woman.

"I'll take these to the guest room you used before. You remember which one, don't you?" Declan moved across the hall and headed toward the stairs to the second floor that was never used.

"Thanks again for letting me crash here." The perky blonde aims her adorable smile toward her brother-in-law.

"I'm going to stay here a while and get all caught up with Rachel. I missed out on so much." Jaclyn removes her coat, tossing it on one side of the couch. Rachel shoots a surprised glance my way as if she's secretly begging me not to leave her alone with this woman. I have no idea how to respond. There's something about Jaclyn, something I can't quite put a finger on, that rubs me the wrong way, but she's family to Declan and Rachel. I need to remember that.

"You want to catch up with me?" Rachel asks. Her large pregnant self all but falls back onto the couch.

"Sure. I mean, we didn't get a lot of time to spend together before, but I would love to change that. I know how close you and Dani were. She used to tell me how you two would sit and talk for hours. You are the only sister I have now to do that with."

Even I felt the sting of guilt slap poor Rachel in the face.

Jacklyn takes a seat on the other end of the couch, tucking a bent leg under her body. Looking as if she is hunkering down for hours' worth of girl talk. "Tell me everything I've missed."

With an apologetic smile toward Rachel, I give her a short wave. "I'm going to leave the two of you to catch up. It was nice meeting you, Jaclyn. I hope we will have a chance to talk before you leave."

"Quinn, you don't have to go." Rachel pleads.

"Night," Jaclyn tosses over her shoulder without so much as a glance my way. I sent Rachel a soft smile before ducking out of the room. I make it as far as the kitchen when Declan comes back downstairs.

"This should be an interesting night." He says, looking from me to the living room.

I can hear the sarcasm in his voice. It makes me smile. "It's only for the night. It can't be that bad?"

He lets out an uneasy breath while shaking his head. "Jaclyn can be a handful at times. I'm sorry about tonight and that we got interrupted again."

"Don't worry about it. I'll head back out and give you guys' time to visit. I'll see you tomorrow. We have a full workload ahead of us if we want to be ahead before Christmas."

His eyes soften, and a smile slowly curls on his lips.

"Are you bossing me around now?"

I laugh. "I told you, Rachel's teaching me everything she knows."

"I'm going to talk with her. I'm not sure how I feel about having two females around here as bossy as my sister."

"If I truly were anything like your sister, this is where I would tell you to suck it up, cupcake. It's too late now."

# Chapter Fourteen

♥

Early morning fades into mid-afternoon before I have a chance to catch Declan alone. He had been gone most of the morning. Jaclyn insisted he drive her over this morning to her parent's house and drop in to say hello.

I try to keep myself busy getting my work done to launch the new book. Emails are rolling in that need Declan's attention. Questions about the final stages of scriptwriting for his up-and-coming series. Rachel tried calling his cell three times with no answer, and on her fourth attempt, he was walking through the door.

"So nice of you to join us." Rachel snapped at him, sounding bitter.

"I'm sorry. I didn't mean to be gone for so long. What was I supposed to do? Her parents kept me talking. I can't be rude to them."

Rachel dropped her gaze as if ashamed of her crankiness.

"I'm sorry. Quinn's been calling you all morning. Your script is in. You need to go over it and get it back as soon as possible. Things are finally moving along. This is great news."

"I'll be in the office for a while looking this over. I'll be out before dinner." He says without so much as a sideways glance my way. His eyes turned down as he walked from the room.

The all too familiar feeling of doubt and rejection began to crawl up my insides.

NO. I can't have those damaging feelings and thoughts return. Years of therapy have taught me that I can't control how other people will act and that it has no reflection on me. But it still stings.

Especially when it's Declan, his opinion matters to me, and I value his views above most others.

I follow him into the hall. "Are you ignoring me today?" My words stop him, and he half turns to face me. "Why would I do that? I'm anxious to start on the script, is all. This has been a long time coming for me. The studio wants to start production after the holidays."

"I've been around the last few months. I know how important this production is to you." What can I say? That I'm worried? Upset? How do I tell him I want to be important to him too? Am I crazy for wishing and hoping things between us could be so easy?

Fear liquefies my insides, and my feet are frozen to the ground. I never want him to regret anything between us.

The one thing I fear the most since our little involvement started is that he's going to realize I'm not good enough for him. And by then, my whole heart will already be fully invested.

"Hey? What's that look for? I'm sorry if it seems like I'm brushing you off. I promise I'm not trying to. I just need—to think is all."

Struggling with a heavy lump in my throat, I force a smile as I try to push back the ugly internal voice of self-doubt that always tries to take over my mind. The voice that fills my head with all the insecurities.

You're not good enough. You'll never be enough.

What makes me think a man like Declan would ever really want someone like me?

Self-doubt creeps through the cracks in the armor I have in place around my heart.

"I'll, um—let you work. We can talk later."

I return to the Living room and sit with my computer on my lap, staring blankly at the screen until I can no longer make out the words. My screen is nothing more than a blend of black and white swirls.

"Sweetie? What's the matter? Did my dipshit brother say something?" Rachel asks. She takes a seat with her laptop, scooting to the end of the sofa cushion. Teetering on edge, she looks as if she's ready to fly across the room and attack me with questions.

"No. He's working on the edits on the script, so I want to leave him alone." I give her a practiced smile.

Her eyes narrow. She's trying to get a read on me. On my emotions. "You sure?"

I nod and begin typing on the keys hoping she will drop the conversation. I don't know what I'm typing. I'm avoiding her because I don't want to tell her that Declan's acting weird ever since he returned from taking Jaclyn to her parents.

Did something happen when he was there?

Rachel relaxes back on the couch, and I feel her gaze on me. I pretend not to notice. And we work for the next couple of hours in near silence, speaking only long enough to ask or answer questions about work.

My gaze continues to drift toward the hallway. I'm numb, sad, and a little defeated.

Declan doesn't owe me anything, and he sure as hell doesn't owe me an explanation. He doesn't need to explain himself. I'm his employee. If he needs time to think, I'll give him space. There are no promises made between us.

"Look at this," Rachel announced, drawing my attention away from my pity party.

"Did you see who the studio has in mind to play the leads for the Dark Desire series?" She turns her computer around in her lap, showing me a picture of two well-known young movie stars. They are both perfect fits for the part of the characters.

"When is the casting final?"

"We are supposed to hear by tomorrow. They give them until Christmas eve to be back to the studios."

Christmas is coming up fast. My mom has called twice already, ensuring I haven't changed my mind about coming home for the holiday. I don't want to hurt her by telling her I don't want to be home. So, I promised to try my hardest to make it home in the next few days.

Maybe I should have agreed to go home. Is it possible that Declan wasn't as ready to move on as we all hoped he was. It wasn't like we had made any promises to each other. There had been no words spoken between us of a relationship. Why had I believed otherwise?

Because you're a dumb, naive girl.

Rachel and I stay busy for the next several hours updating social media, answering emails, and overall catering to the needs of a writer. Reviews need to be written, and blog posts are waiting to be drafted and edited. Beta readers are sending in their reply sheets from the latest novel, getting ready to hit the editor's desk and

Rachel stays in touch with the company handling all things production.

Besides making an occasional trip into the kitchen to throw a bag of popcorn into the microwave, we didn't move from our seats for hours.

"Crap. I need my cords. My laptop is about to die." Rachel said, setting the computer away from her lap.

"I think it was plugged in over there with mine." Pushing myself off the sofa, I go over to the wall next to the couch and hand her the cord.

"I need to go over a few things with Declan. Would you mind going to get him for me?"

Going into his office was the last thing I wanted to do.

Knocking on the door softly, I wait for his usual one-word reply, but it never comes. I would never interrupt him while he's working if Rachel hadn't needed him. Knocking again, louder this time, there was still no answer. Ignoring my better judgment, I push the door open wide enough to poke my head in.

"Declan?"

He's sitting at his desk hunch over the top of his computer, holding his head in his palms, head cast down.

"Declan?"

No reply

I step inside his office, closing the door behind me with a soft click. Moving closer to his desk, I ease to the side, placing my palm on the curve of his shoulder. My touch doesn't pull him out of the misery he has fallen into.

"Declan? Is there anything I can do? Do you want me to get Rachel?"

His head shakes softly, making the front portion of his hair fall forward into his eyes. "No. Don't bother her with my problems."

I want to reassure him that he could never be a bother, but instead, I just tell him what I was sent in to do.

"Rachel needs to talk to you. She sent me in here to for you."

No answer.

"Declan? Please tell me what's wrong? Did something happen? Did something happen earlier at Jaclyn's parents?"

His palms fell from his head, slamming into the top of his desk on either side of his computer.

"I just..." Pushing back his chair, he bounces to his feet. I take a step back to avoid getting hit by the chair.

"Shit. I'm sorry. I didn't mean to...."

"It's okay. There's something wrong. You came home acting different and... I'm starting to worry. Is it because of what happened last night?"

He turns and grips my shoulders with his hands. "No. You didn't do anything wrong."

"Then what, Declan? You're acting weird. You came home upset about something. If it's something I can help with, I want to. If you want me to butt-out and leave you alone, tell me."

"Trust me when I say I want you here, and I like knowing you're here. I like it a lot."

"What does that mean...." my gaze darts to his, and I see the uncertainty in them. He has to be struggling to understand our relationship just as I am.

His lips silence my words. His mouth takes mine as if he wants to drink me into his body. His palms lift to the sides of my face, sliding lovingly over my cheeks. He holds me in place as he takes what he wants. I want him to have everything I can give him. And I let him.

There's nothing I want more than to let this man have all of me. There's not going to be giving just a piece here or there. It's all or nothing.

I open my lips for him, and his tongue glides inside. If my eyes weren't already closed, they would have rolled into the back of my head.

The taste and smell of him have me locked under his spell.

My hands lift to the front of his shirt. My fingers caressed the plain cotton of his undershirt. The muscles on his chest flicker under my touch, but he doesn't pull away from me.

One of his hands works its way around my head, spreading his fingers through my hair before closing into a fist, gripping me with force, the pain just enough to catch my breath but not cause pain. The purr that comes from my chest doesn't sound like me. Yet the sound has rattled from deep inside of my chest.

His lips slide over mine, dancing, and penetrating. I love it.

His head moves from one side, then to the other like he's eager to find the closest fit. Like he can't get close enough.

As much as I want him to throw me down on his desk and rip away our clothes, I know that can't happen.

Forcing my mind to return to reality, I press hard against his chest drawing our bodies apart. "Declan?"

My voice is low and breathy, but it's done the trick. Like ice-cold water to the face, Declan releases my face but doesn't step away.

"This right here is what I mean. I know I shouldn't be thinking about this, but I do. You walk into the room, and you're all I can look at. You leave a room, and you're all I can think about. What kind of spell do you have over me?"

His words make me speechless. I can't move for fear I'll wake myself from this dream.

Immediately my mind begins to betray me. I'm desperate to push the negative thoughts away, but I'm not fast enough. Self-doubt creeps in. I step out, breaking our warm hold and wrapping my arms around my middle section.

I drop my gaze to the floor. I can't meet his eyes. "Declan...?"

He lets out a breath running a hand through his hair. "As I said before, I like you, Quinn. My life would be a hell of a lot easier if I didn't. It's why I was a jerk for those first few weeks. I tried to tell myself you were all wrong for me. Not my type. But the truth is, the more time I spend with you, the more I realize you are exactly what I want. But I'm afraid of liking you."

"Why do you like me? I mean, I'm not pretty like...." I don't have a chance to say her name before he interrupts me.

"Stop." His voice is firm as the determination of the word completely freezes me. He closes in the steps that separate us, and he grips my shoulders and lowers his head to rest against my forehead. His eyes drift close, and so do mine. For a long moment, we stand there unmoving, listening to our breathing as our bodies sync with each other.

"First, you have womanly curves, and I happen to think they are sexy as hell." His hand slides down my ribs and over the swell of my hip as if proving the essence of my body.

My throat closes around the air in my lungs at the dominant low tone of his voice. "And as for you not thinking you're pretty, it alarms me that you don't know how beautiful you are. You have a beauty inside that radiates off you and onto others. Your skin glows in it, your eyes sparkle with it, and I swear beauty is in your voice. Every time you turn your little crooked smile toward me, I find it harder to breathe. I could go on forever telling you all the little things that make up the whole beautiful package you are but, I don't think I need to. I need you to accept that you are indeed my perfect little mouse."

Unshed tears sting my eyes. Even through my closed lids, the moisture fills my eyes.

"Is that what's been bothering you today?"

He steps away, pushing his fingers through the length of his hair and letting out a breath. "I'm sorry about that. Today was rough. Being around Jacklyn again and going over to Dani's parents' house after all this time was weird. I mean, weird in a good way. Being there and talking with her parents and sister was refreshing for me. We can finally talk about old times without me getting crazy with anger. I know what I'm saying sounds stupid, and hell, maybe I'm not making any sense, but for the first time since I buried my wife, I've been able to look toward the future and smile about it. You did that, Quinn and I'm feeling torn about it."

"Why?"

"Because I think I should feel guilty for wanting to move on, but I don't. Not anymore. I used to stay up all night thinking about her. For these past few weeks, I've been awake thinking about you. And that scares me. I'm broken, Quinn. I can't guarantee I have it in me anymore to give you what you would need in a relationship."

"There's no shame in being broken, Declan. We all have our scars."

His gaze drops to the floor. "What I'm saying is, I don't know if loving someone again is possible for me. If that's what you need from me...I can't give you that."

Hurt seizes my insides. Yet again, loving me proves to be something another person can't do. I should be used to it by now, although it doesn't make the pain any less hard to swallow.

I plaster on the best-practiced grin I can manage, determined not to let myself get hurt again. "Who says I'm looking for love?"

His eyes slide closed as if he's trying to see through my words for the lie. They are.

"Let's not talk about this now. It's almost Christmas, and we have a lot to do so we can enjoy the weekend. We have all the time in the world after the holidays to figure things out. Plus, your present should be arriving soon. I can't wait for you to see it."

I follow his lead with a change in topic. My face heats up with warmth at the thought of Declan shopping for me. I'm giddy as a kid knowing Christmas is coming soon.

"You have something being delivered to me? You didn't have to do anything for me. What is it?"

He smiles at my childish behavior. "I can't tell you that. You will have to wait and see. Now go back out there and finish your work because you're going to want the rest of the week off."

"To enjoy my gift?" I ask, hoping to get some slight hint of details out of him.

"I'm not saying a word. Now go."

I playfully stick my tongue out at him, leave his office, and bounce back into the living room, where Rachel's fast asleep on the couch with her laptop resting on the table next to her. I'm beginning to think she's the ultimate puppet master pulling all our strings. I wouldn't put it past her to have made up the excuse to get me into her brother's office. She probably never needed anything from Declan. I smile at her cunning ways. She's too good, and when she wants something, she's not too proud to go after it no matter what others think or say.

There's a lot I could learn from her, but until then, I'll work on decoding the gift Declan has being delivered to me. I can hardly wait to find out what it could be.

# Chapter Fifteen

Max surprised Rachel by coming home on Christmas eve morning. Three days earlier than expected. To say she was surprised and happy to see him would be an understatement. By the time she got through smothering him with her welcoming kisses, her cheeks were stained with tracks of tears.

The loving couple sat embraced on the couch, holding each other, cooing into the side of each other's necks. After exchanging hellos with Max, I sneak out of the room and into the kitchen, giving them time alone together.

I pour myself a cup of coffee and duck into the fridge to grab creamer. In the middle of pouring the sweet vanilla cream into my cup, the back-door swings open, and Luc bounces in with Declan right behind, wearing a bright smile on his face. His happy expression is so contagious that I can't help but smile back.

"What has you so happy this morning? Coffee?" I ask.

He shakes his head. "I've already had my coffee and breakfast this morning."

That surprises me. "Already?" Looking at the clock on the microwave range, it's only nine-thirty. "Isn't it a little early for you?"

"I had things to do this morning." his shoulders lifted with a shrug before grabbing a water bottle from the fridge door. Twisting off the cap, he turns and presses his back against the counter.

"Oh, well, those two are smooching it up in there, so I thought I'd give them some time alone. But if you have things to do today, I'll head out to the pool house. Since I'm officially off this weekend for the holiday."

"Rachel, let you have the whole weekend off, huh? Good. I told her she should. You deserve a rest. I was talking about taking a few days off, but production starts soon, and there are too many last-minute things that need to be signed off. You and I are going to be busy starting Monday."

I take a sip of my coffee in the hopes of shielding my smile. It's crazy the way this man makes me feel, and the thought of working side by side with him for the next few weeks has me feeling giddy with happiness. It's confusing that I want to like him, and I do, but I know I shouldn't. I'm beginning to think this is more than a simple crush.

I watch him take another pull from his water bottle. As he swallows, he leaves the bottle opening against his lips and grins at me. His other hand finds the edge of the counter behind him and leans his weight against it.

"Are you going to tell me what you're grinning about? Is there something you would like to share with me?"

The front doorbell rings just as I ask the question, echoing through the house.

"Who could that be this early on Christmas eve?" Declan asks, taking a long pull from the bottle again. The doorbell rang again.

Knowing he's up to something, I remember he told me something was being delivered to the house for me. With a tiny squeak of excitement, I pivot on my toes and run to the front door. On my way, I glance towards the couple on the couch wrapped in each other's embrace and smiling like fools at me. What the hell? Do they know what my gift is too?

Getting to the door, I turn the knob expecting to see a freezing delivery man waiting to drop off his first of many packages today but what I find standing there instead takes all the air out of my lungs. My throat closes, and I suck back a sob as I cry out.

"Kit Kat?"

I throw myself against my sister's chest wrapping my arms around her neck and holding her as tight as I can. Hot tears sting my cheeks, but all I can do is stand here and breathe in the familiar scent that is my sister. Kate has always been the do-good beauty queen that never had a hair out of place. She lives for her work. She's a make-up artist by choice. My sister has never met a lipstick she didn't like.

"What are you doing here? You said you were working through the holiday." I sob against her shoulder.

"I was going to. But my manager got a call a few days ago asking if there was any way my company could spare me for a week over the holiday for another large production piece. It wasn't until Declan called me himself that I found out it was him who hired me."

"Oh my god. I can't believe you're here for Christmas. We haven't been together in so long."

"I know. Can we go inside? I'm freezing my butt off out here. It took you long enough to answer the door."

"Oh my god, yes." I hurry us through the door and close it quickly against the early morning chill.

Luc barks from down the hall, and Declan appears in the kitchen doorway holding a coffee cup with steam rising.

Turning my sister toward the living room, I give out the introductions.

"Max, Rachel, this is my sister, Kate. Rachel is Declan's sister. Max just got home this morning from a business trip. It looks like we both got a surprise." I say to Rachel. But I can't forget the one person I owe for the best gift I've ever gotten.

"And this is Declan. My boss."

"We've met. I mean, we've talked over the phone a few times in the last week. And we had a nice long talk in the car from the airport this morning."

I turn quickly to stare at Declan. "So that's where you were off too so early this morning."

I turn back to Kate. "Where are you staying? Are you going to mom and dad's?"

"Declan suggested I stay here with you. We only have a week together, so I want to make it count."

I smile. "Yes! Oh, it's going to be so fun. We haven't been together for Christmas in forever. But, crap, I mailed your gift to you. I don't have anything for you here, and I doubt anything is open today."

"Are you kidding me? Being here for Christmas with you is my gift. Besides, I'll do what we used to do and wait until the sales after Christmas, then I'll make you buy me something."

"Deal. Come on. I'll show you the pool house."

Taking her hand, I drag my sister through the house and out the backdoor.

"Wow. I can't believe you're living here. Look at this place." Kate said as we entered the pool house.

"And Declan...whoa. Is he hot or what? You told me he was good-looking, but you didn't say he's sex on a stick." We both laugh.

"That's probably because he's my boss, Kate." I don't dare tell her that not just once, but twice, I've made out with my boss. I'm not sure why I don't tell her, she's my sister, and she would never judge me. Maybe it's because I'm not sure what this thing between us is.

She shrugs off her coat and throws it and her purse on a nearby chair. "So. When has that ever stopped anyone?"

"You mean, when has that ever stopped you? I still can't believe you're here. It's crazy we haven't seen each other in what feels like forever." I head over to the tiny kitchen and flip on my small single-cup coffee maker. I need a new cup since I left mine sitting on the counter in the kitchen.

"I know. It's weird how life just drives you to do your own thing. I'm so busy going from location to location I haven't seen mom and dad in a year."

"At least you call them. I can't bring myself to dial the number unless I have to. You know how mom is. And dad...he's slowly coming around."

We both know how our father has treated me ever since I tried to end my life. I had been close to my dad at one time, but after that night, my relationship with my father has never been the same.

"I think we should go over there and surprise them. It is Christmas, and I'm sure your boss won't mind you leaving for a few hours. He has his family here after all."

I turn back toward my sister and fill her in with the lies I've told. "I kind of told mom I was working over the holiday, and I didn't have time to come home."

"Quinn..."

I shrug in defense. "You don't know what it's like being here in the same town as her. She calls and checks in with me all the time like I'm a child, and she's afraid I might...well, you know. All that is behind me now, but they still want to watch me as if I might take my shoelaces out any minute and find the nearest ceiling fan. I can't deal with that over the holiday Kate. I'm finally feeling good about myself, and I like the place I'm at in life for once, and I can't let them drag me down."

She closes the distance between us and wraps her arms around my shoulders, pulling me closer to her in a hug.

"I love you. I had no idea you were still struggling with this. But if mom and dad make you too crazy, then I'll go alone. I'll keep up your story and tell them you are neck-deep in... whatever it is you do." She pulls away enough to catch my gaze. "But I'm telling them you will be at the Abraham's New Year extravaganza. The theme this year is the sixties. I'm not the only one that will be there in flower power bell-bottoms."

I groan as I think of my mom's New Year's party. She's been putting it on for as long as Kate and I have been alive. Mom and dad invite their colleagues and friends and party it up as they ring in the new year. When Kate and I were little, mom would let us stay up until ten. Two hours past our usual bedtime. She and dad would shoo us up the stairs, where we would sneak out of our rooms and sit at the top of the stairs for hours listening to the music and the party carrying on without us. Once we turned fourteen, we could stay for the entire evening. After Kate and I left for college, we hadn't made it back home too often to attend many of their parties.

The two of us sat together for the next three hours, talking, and catching up on life, jobs, and each other. After lunch, Kate borrowed my car to visit our parents but promised to be back by dinner.

Heading into the main house, I found it eerily quiet. Rachel and Max were no longer in the living room, and no sounds were coming from the back bedroom. I head toward the back of the house to Declan's office to see if he's left, but when I poke my head into his office, I find him feverishly typing away on his keyboard. Luc's asleep on the floor next to the desk, oblivious of his master.

I'm about to turn to leave when his head pops up, and he offers me a smile that could quickly melt my heart.

"Mouse! I thought I would get ideas and an outline down for a new book idea while everyone was out. How's it going with your sister?"

"Good. She's on her way to our parent's house right now to visit." I walk completely into the room, closing the door to the office behind me.

"You didn't want to go with her? They might want to see you too."

I shake my head. "I can't handle my parents on the holidays. It's better if she goes without me. Where's Rachel and Max?"

"They wanted some alone time and headed for her bedroom an hour ago. Knowing my sister, she most likely took this chance to nap since she can't do anything too strenuous."

"Guess that leaves just the two of us, huh?"

His head turned until he was facing away from the computer screen. "Looks like."

There's that smile again. The smile that makes my stomach fall and my heart pound.

Swallowing my nerves, I move closer to him, edging my way toward the desk. I trail my fingertips along the smooth wooden perimeter as I walk.

"I want to thank you for my gift. It's the best present I've ever gotten. I've missed her so much."

"I know you have. You always look so miserable when you talk about missing your sister. Honestly, she's the one that made this happen. I just told her boss I wanted to hire her for a job. She's the one that made all the arrangements and kept the secret."

"And if you knew my sister, you would know that's a sacrifice. Regardless. Thank you."

I'm standing so close in front of him that his knees brush against my thigh. He leans up in his chair, bringing our bodies closer.

"You're welcome." He says. He doesn't move toward me, leaving the decision to close the gap between us up to me. With my newly found comfort, I take full advantage of it.

Leaning close, his intoxicating scent enters my nostrils, and my heart quickens. My hair falls forward, framing my face as my lips lightly brush the side of his cheek. Slowly testing the waters, I linger a second longer than I would if this were merely a friendly peck. Declan's hand rose to the back of my hair, allowing his thick fingers to sink into my strands. He turned my mouth to his lips, meeting mine halfway. His soft pillow lips against mine. The heat from his body crawls along and covers my skin. My eyes slide close, and his palm moves to the side of my cheek, keeping me in front of him, taking and giving everything we both need.

His lips part against mine, and as if we are responding in slow motion, I manage to open to his invading tongue. Ever so lightly, he kisses and caresses me, worshipping me with his mouth. A soft groan escapes the back of my throat, and I begin to fall forward, bracing a hand on the arm of the chair to catch myself. I'm plucked off my feet and settled softly against his chest, cradled in his lap before I have a chance to right myself.

One arm wraps behind me, and I'm braced against it as the other falls from my cheek to the side of my neck. His mouth doesn't leave mine.

"I feel like I've waited weeks for this. We are finally alone." His hand slips up my leg to settle over my knee, his nose skims the side of my neck, and he buries his face in my hair. The heat of his warm breath purrs against my exposed skin, and my eyes close. I want to be skin on skin everywhere. I like the heat from his naked body under my hands, but I know this is a lot for him.

"Remember the night you came to my room? You told me sex wasn't what you're looking for and that there are other things we can do. Tell me what you were thinking."

The hand on my cheek falls as he drops our hands to his chest, pressing my palm against the stiff muscles there. The pounding of his heart vibrates against my skin.

"We can start by touching each other. It's been a long time since I've had anyone touch me."

My stomach tightened at his words. I want nothing more than to give him what he needs, but I'm nervous. Spreading my fingers wide, I began inching my hand toward the collar of his shirt, tracing the folded ends with my fingertips. I start to pop the buttons free of their holes and work my way to another. Declan's mouth swiftly claims mine again. This time there's a forceful hunger behind it—a hunger I've been needing and waiting for.

My fingers work the last of his buttons, free ripping his shirt apart, exposing the tight muscled chest underneath. My nails skim lightly over the tight ridges leaving faint red marks in their wake.

His hiss sings as his hand reaches for the back of my neck, pulling my mouth down to his. My palms flatten against his chest, and I sink into the taste of him. His mouth opens over mine. Controlling and demanding, I give everything to him. I do. My fingers trail to the front of his pants, feeling the increased pressure of the bulge behind his zipper. Knowing that I arouse him to this state makes my insides tingle more. My body's waking up as if it's been asleep for years.

The tips of my fingers brush the length of him, and his body responds with an impulsive thrust into my hand.

"Awe, baby, it's been so long since I've had anyone touch me there." The affectionate name causes me to pause slightly.

"Then we need to remedy that. I've been dying to touch you for a long time, but I've been too afraid...."

He stops suddenly, gripping my face between his palms. He brings my gaze to face his. His eyes sparkle with tiny hues of copper in his chocolate eyes as he speaks. "I never want you to feel afraid or ashamed to talk to me about anything. Whether it's about you, us, or anything that's going on in that pretty little head of yours. I need you to be open and honest with me about everything."

His spoken words are exactly what I need to hear from him, and as if their magic, they begin their work over me. I can feel myself easing out of all stages of embarrassment.

He leans in, bringing his lips to my forehead before moving the soft wet kisses down to each cheek. His mouth glides across the tip of my nose before capturing my mouth once again. Heat fires in my belly, and my heart races, throbbing so loud in my ears, it would be hard to hear anything else. My hand works over the front of his zipper, and with each passing motion, I can feel him growing thicker and thicker. I want to feel his skin against mine. I need to have the heat of him against the soft, delicate pads of my palm. My fingertips reach for the metal pull at the top of the zipper teeth and give it a tug hearing the hiss of the metal.

His hand shoots to mine, his fingers wrapping around my wrist, stopping me from continuing. My gaze snaps to his. I'm pleading with him silently to let me finish. To help him feel good under my touch.

"If we do this, it changes everything, Quinn. It changes our work relationship; it changes our—friendship."

My body stills. I can't and won't let him think I'm not a hundred percent into this. That there's nothing, I want more than him.

"I know."

Our gazes hold each other for a lingering moment as we both wait for the other to move first.

"If we're going to do this, we're going to do this right. Tonight, I want you in my bed. Come to my room and don't make plans after because I don't intend to let you leave my room until morning."

# Chapter Sixteen

As it turns out, I'm enjoying my Christmas eve.

My parents are out of my hair and starting their vacation. My future brother-in-law is back from his business trip, making my needy pregnant sister no longer my top concern, and to top it off, a beautiful woman is waiting to share my bed tonight. Yes, I would say a great Christmas indeed.

Quinn's sister, Kate, returned from their parent's house an hour ago and the two of them had been in the kitchen ever since getting dinner finished up. I made myself stay in the living room with Rachel and Max, knowing full-well if I venture into the other room, all I would be doing is getting in the way and staring at the clock until the time came to head to our rooms for the night. Nervous excitement fills my stomach like I'm waiting for my first time to happen all over again.

It has been a long time for me. Just thinking about Quinn naked and spread out on the bed waiting for me has me pressing hard against my zipper again. This afternoon had been hell trying to separate myself from her. She left my office to busy herself with Lord knows what, while I had the pleasure of suffering all afternoon with her taste still on my tongue and the tingle of her touch lingering on my body. It was hard to let her go knowing she would only be a few steps away from me all day. I've thought of little else than laying her out across my desk and feasting on her body.

I busy myself with work sending back emails to producers on the upcoming mini-series. They want me to fly out to Denver to begin filming two days after Christmas. I haven't had a chance to talk it over with Quinn, but of course, I'll need her to go with me. Rachel's too close to the due date for the baby to travel. Not to mention the bedrest she's on. Looking at her now makes my mouth water with the need to kiss every glorious curve and twist of her beautiful body.

"Dinners ready. We set the table in the dining room." Quinn announced, walking into the living room with a wine glass in her hand. She smiles my way, and I can't help but hope that she's thinking the same thing I am. That she's been watching the clock all day and counting the minutes until we can finish what we started earlier. I shouldn't be trying to intrude on Quinn's visit with her sister, who has only arrived this morning. I should give her this time and wait another night or two, but I can't. I've waited long enough.

"It smells great in here. This little one is taking everything I eat, leaving me with nothing. I'm also going to eat at the table tonight too. I'm not sitting around on this couch eating off a dinner tray." Rachel announces, waddling her way into the dining room.

"The doctor said...." Max started in, but she didn't let him continue. "The doctor said bed rest until the baby comes. We are in the clear now. The baby can safely come any day now."

I follow my sister and Max over to the table and take up the chair at the end. Dinner is placed over the surface, and I'll admit, Quinn has outdone herself again. The formal table is beautifully decorated with Christmas décor. Three tall white pillar candles stand in a row down the center of the table, casting glows off the green and red foliage weaving in and out of the holders. It couldn't look any better if a stage designer set the room themselves.

A large golden glazed ham demanded our attention from the middle of the table but, I couldn't focus on the food when my gaze found the beautiful creator of tonight's dinner sitting at the far end of the table. I harness every ounce of willpower I own to not drag her out of her seat like a caveman and lock her away inside my bedroom.

At dinner, platters were passed around, and everyone's plates were as complete as possible. Max takes a moment to stand from his chair, clearing his voice to draw our attention.

"I know tomorrow is Christmas, but I can't wait any longer to give Rachel her present."

My gaze moves to my sister's, and the surprise on her face matches the rest of ours. She has no idea what he's about to say.

"I can wait until tomorrow, Max," Rachel says, grinning with anticipation. The look in her eye tips her off that she's just as excited to receive an early gift as Max seems to be in giving her one.

Max turns away, disappearing out of the room for a moment returning with a shiny red box with a green velvet bow attached to the top. Handing it to Rachel, he stands off to the side, waiting for her to open it.

Next, she pulls out a smaller velvet black box. Pulling on the ribbon, it falls from the box, releasing the top from its home. "This had better not be what I think it is," she says, her voice cracking with unchecked emotion.

"How about you open it before you yell at me."

She flicks the top open and gasps as a bright sparkle glares up at her from the light of the chandelier.

"Are you kidding me?" She moves a shaky hand to cover her mouth.

"Rachel May Palmer, I love you. I've loved you since the moment I ran into you and spilled my coffee down the front of your suit. And even though you were pissed at me, I know that was the moment you fell for me too."

Grabbing her hand in his, Max knelt to one knee next to her chair and raised the hand to rest over the top of her swollen belly.

"We are about to become parents together, and you already have all of my heart and love. I can't wait to be a parent with you, and I can't wait until we have another one on the way. I want a large family, and I want to have grandbabies with you. I know we always talk about getting married someday, but I want to make it official. Rachel May, I want you to be my wife."

We all watch as a lone tear slips down her cheek. "I thought you never actually wanted to get married. What happened to marriage is just a piece of paper?" she asks, her voice shaky with emotions.

"I still feel social or social standards shouldn't define marriage; I think if two people love each other, who cares if they agree to love and obey each other. And I know how much it means to you, and there's nothing

I wouldn't do for you. I love you. If a wedding and the exchange of rings is what you want, I want that too. What do you say? Marry Me."

"Oh my God. Yes!" Rachel jumped out of her chair despite being pregnant.

We watch the couple embrace and kiss while the other two women at the table clap and swoon at the large rock Rachel pulled free from its sheltered velvet box.

"Congratulations, you two!"

As if I had just poured a giant bucket of ice water over my sister's head, her gaze swings back to mine before dropping to the newly placed ring on her finger, then up to Max then me once more.

"Declan. I didn't think..." she trailed off, gazing at her hand again with the palm turned down.

"What?"

"Oh, shit. Man, I'm sorry. When I thought of proposing tonight, I just wanted Rachel to be surprised. I didn't think about...."

It took me a minute to understand. Didn't they think I would be okay with someone talking about marriage and happiness around me? I could laugh at the looks on their faces. I fought the urge to laugh and wondered how long I should keep them on the hook.

"I think it's wonderful. I mean, you guys have been together forever, it seems, and you're having a child together. It makes sense. Besides, why shouldn't the two of you be happy? This isn't about me." I'll admit, it's a little embarrassing. Is this how it's been since Dani? Has everyone been tiptoeing around me?

"You're not upset about this?" Rachel asks, motioning between her and Max in the air. After taking a moment to take note of all emotions in my body, I realize that yes. I am happy for my sister.

"I'm happy for you two. Now, come over here and let me see that rock that's blinding me since you pulled it out of the box."

Rachel's smile lit up the room as she hurried over to my side. I don't think I've ever seen my sister this happy, and she deserves to be. This is her moment, and I don't want to ruin it by everyone being concerned for me. She's been right by my side during the loss of Dani. No matter how I tried to push my sister away, she never went too far. And for that, I owe her everything.

After making their rounds of hugs and showing off her ring, we all finally settled back into dinner by heaping our plates and taking our seats.

Everyone who interacts with me daily is all sitting around my table. As I stare at the large amounts of food that is in no way going to all fit in my stomach, a familiar soft buzzing and vibration flicker across my thigh from the side pocket of my jeans. Taking the cell out, I light the damn thing up to see who's sending me a text. Hoping it isn't production saying they are pushing things further back; I slide the tips of my fingers inside the pocket and pull out the cell. Sure enough, there is a missed call and two texts waiting for me, but they're not from production as I feared. They're from Jaclyn.

Reading through her texts, anger begins to swirl inside my chest.

Fuck.

I rush back a text letting her know that her texts and calls are not appreciated and that she needs to spend this time with her parents, not spent texting me.

Another one pings my phone, and she's asking to see me this time.

Shit.

She's beginning to piss me off.

The texts started soon after I left her parents' house yesterday morning. She tried her best to touch or feel me anyway she could. Doing her utmost to get close and get her hand on my thigh that she all but pretended a shocking accident after I called her out on the move. I should have known she was up to something since the entire car ride over to the other side of the city to her parent's house.

What did she think she was doing? I should be like a brother to her. What am I saying? I am a brother to her. For the five years, Dani and I were married, I had been her brother-in-law. In my eyes, thinking of Jaclyn as anything more than what she already is to me is wrong and weird.

I glance around the room to see if anyone is watching me or notices I'm not engaged in the conversations. Looking toward my sister, she's too busy glancing at that rock Max slipped on her finger to realize anything. Lifting my eyes, I locate the one person who would take notice, and sure enough, her gaze is cast down toward the cell in my hands. Looking back down to the lit screen, I fire back a response typing a couple short words telling her I'm done with the conversation before I shut the screen down and slide the device back into my pocket and pick up my water glass for a drink to cover my frown. Another vibration and soft buzz hum from the cell in my pocket, and I curse under my breath. When is she going to get the goddamn hint that she's like a sister to me? I shouldn't give it another thought. Ignoring her might be the best answer, but I can't seem to leave it alone.

I pull the damn thing out one more time, and this time her response isn't as nice as the others had been. This one is full of colorful words, and she's all but demanding that I come to pick her up since I'm the one who left her there with her parents and that she can no longer stay at the house with them.

I don't respond. I shut the phone off and pushed it back into my jeans. My gaze shifted up to the other side of the table to Quinn. I offer her a smile as her eyes find mine over the top of delicious-looking food she spent all day preparing. After a minute, a smile that reaches her eyes spreads over her face, and at that moment, she looks happy. And after learning new things this morning from Kate, she more than deserves to be.

The ride with Kate this morning proved to be helpful and informative. Quinn might not like to open up about certain things from her past, but Kate's a little more forthcoming in her telling. She wouldn't go into details about anything, saying that those were Quinn's stories to tell, but she talked about how her sister tried to take her own life and how she had been a cutter before in her teen years.

I was unsure what the term meant until I googled it as soon as I got home. Learning it's a form of self-harm that is most likely rooted in her eating disorder. She had mentioned once before she struggled with weight issues all her life, before the rape in California.

Kate also touched lightly on Quinn's stay at Western State psychiatric hospital after her suicide attempt. I don't know all the details, and someday I hope Quinn will be comfortable enough to tell me but knowing that she's just as scarred on the inside as I am, makes me feel closer to her. As if she, above everyone else at this table, knows my inner pain. Our stories may be different, but our scars are the same.

*Quinn*

I wipe the granite countertop down with the wet soapy rag making sure all dinner traces are no longer visible. Turning around, I face the kitchen looking again to make sure that the room is back to how it should be. Or maybe I'm just stalling.

My sister has long since gone off to the pool house to sleep off the jet lag that had her eyelids drooping all through dessert. Rachel excused her and her new fiancé to her bedroom where they could spend alone time.

I glanced around the room once more before heading towards the small table in the far corner and to the small overnight duffle bag I tucked on the chair beside it. The bag that contains my overnight clothes and personal stuff is awaiting me to pick it up and join Declan.

My stomach launches to my throat, and the tangled mess of nerves doesn't help my stomach come back down.

I'm acting crazy.

The man said he wanted me and was ready to take things between us to the next level. What am I so nervous about? Taking in a shallow shaky breath, I flip the switch turning the lights out, forcing darkness to fill the kitchen. Grabbing my bag, I turn and head down the hallway toward the quietness of the bedrooms. The tight bundle of nerves stays in my throat as I come to stand at the bedroom door where the soft, shallow light is spilling over the carpet and into the hallway. The room he uses now isn't the room he shared with Dani. He had moved out of that room not long after she passed since there were too many memories lingering between those walls for him. Placing my palm on the smooth surface of the wooden door, I pause to wonder if I should knock before barging into the room.

As if he can sense me in the hall, the door is pulled open, and there he stands in front of me. I let my gaze sweep over him from his bare chest down his cotton pajama bottoms to his bare feet.

"I was beginning to think you weren't going to come." He said, stepping to the side of the doorway, opening a welcome path to enter. I peer up at him as I walk past, meeting his eyes. My gaze locked on his, letting him know I'm not only here but that I'm confident in having this night together. He closes the door behind me, and I hear the click of the lock engaged.

Looking around the room, I notice nothing fancy about it, with a king-size bed and matching end tables on either side. It holds little, if any, personal items. There's an on-suite bath opposite the bed with a walk-in closet right beside it. What little décor in the room speaks about him, from the simple black and white photo of a beach and ocean that hung over the bed to the pair of matching silver lamps on either end table. Even the simple white down comforter looks sleek. No-fuss. No thrills. Just like him.

"I like what you've done to the room," I say, not knowing what else to talk about.

He let out a sound resembling a snort and chuckle. "Thanks, but it's been like this ever since we moved into this house. Are we going to discuss room décor?"

My gaze falls from his and lands on the floor. "No, sorry. I'm not sure what else to say. I'm nervous."

"Me too. It's been a long time for me. We will lean on each other. We don't have to do anything we're not ready for." He closes the distance between us until we are standing toe to toe. His hands raise to my shoulders, brushing the backs of his knuckles over the bare skin exposed at my collarbone. His touch is softer than excepted but not as rough as I fear I need. It's been so long since I've been touched and loved that my mind and body are having difficulty debating between what I need and what I crave.

Leaning onto my tiptoes, I bring my lips to him, brushing a soft kiss across his mouth. His hands lift to the sides of my face, trapping and keeping me encaged against him. I love the feel of his warm fingers against my skin. Opening against me, his hot mouth draws my lower lip between his, suckling before letting it slip back out. Parting my lips more, I allow him inside, sweeping my tongue in a rhythmic dance against his. Flames and heat begin to course through my body, starting at the core of my stomach.

I become aware of the heat and wetness between my legs growing as his hands slide down my shoulders to find the bottom of my shirt. He lifts the shirt over my head, exposing my bra. His fingertips trace the thin lines of fabric covering my breasts and smooth a light caress over my cleavage, sending shivers along my skin.

"You are so beautiful, Quinn. And you hide away under all those layers of clothes." His hands slip down the length of my arms to interlock our fingers together. He extends my arm out at our side, and his eyes sweep across the bare skin of my stomach.

Still holding my wrist, he brings my palms to his lips once more. His pink lips stand out against the small white scars decorating my skin as he brushes the softest kisses against the raised skin that have shamed me the most. I try to pull my wrist from his grip, but he tightens his hold. "How did it start?"

I don't ask him what he means. I know he's asking why I started cutting.

"I haven't talked about this in a long time with anyone who wasn't my doctor."

"That's okay. You don't have to tell me. Knowing you're all better now, is what matters."

I draw in a deep breath, feeling relieved that he's not making me talk about it, but I realize I want to talk with him. A part of me wants him to know about my scars and my past. As Kate's been convincing me for years, that there's nothing to be ashamed of. These scars are just as much a part of me as anything else in my life. Shaping who I am and who I have become. I let his touch and closeness give me the support I need to speak.

"It started my freshmen year in high school. Some of my friends were accepted on the following year's cheer team. They had all made it. They were all thin, beautiful, and had rhythm. Me at that age, I was a little more of a mess. I had a few pimples on my face and one too many cinnamon rolls for breakfast. My friends spent the summer convincing me to try out for the team when school started, so we could all be together. After spending the entire summer talking and planning with my friends, I agreed.

"We spent weeks working on a routine they all learned while at cheer camp that summer. I managed to lose a few extra pounds and practiced like crazy for weeks. When school started, tryouts were on the first day, and when I got there, I froze up and forgot all the moves. I also fell on my face when I tried to kick my foot in the air. Needless to say, I didn't make the team."

I pause long enough to take a breath. My nervousness was returning, and I began to think twice about telling him for a moment. But the light rubbing of his fingers along my wrist is strangely encouraging for me to continue.

"At the time, I didn't know that I was not only trying out in front of the cheer team but the entire football team as well. Kids at that age are assholes, and I didn't know how to handle the bullying. I already had image problems, and their cruel comments were like gas on a fire. I started cutting as a way to deal with the pain from the teasing and bullying that followed me for years."

Leaning down, his palms hold my face as he lowers his mouth to press a kiss to my forehead, the tip of my nose, and finally, my mouth.

"All that's behind you now." He raises my wrist to his mouth, kissing the scars once more.

"All there is ahead of us is the future now. Let's focus on that instead. And I want to thank you for trusting me with your past."

His lips crush over mine again, forcefully taking what he wants, and I'm happy to give. Pressing myself against him, I push my bra-covered breast against his bare chest, feeling the heat from his body through the fabric. His arms wrap around and behind me, fanning out across my back, pressing me tighter against him. Flames from the new urgent fire crash over me, and the need to feel his skin on my skin, heat to heat, is overpowering.

Pressing my hands against his bare chest, I let my fingers slip lower to the waistband of his pajama pants. Pulling at the elastic waist, I open the band far enough to allow my hand and wrist to slip inside freely. I immediately feel heat meeting my skin before the back of my hand brushes along the tip of his hard erection. My gaze flies to his, holding the dark brown orbs as I wrap his rock-hard erection in my hand.

A graveled moan escaped the back of his throat as his hips surged forward, grinding his cock further into my hand. I tighten the hold, squeezing my fingers enough to let him know there's no turning back. I'm not letting go, not this time. His eyes slowly roll back before his heavy lids fall closed and his head falls back, and his hip pulse harder into my fist. Slowly at first, I begin working with him. I work my hand to slide from base to tip using the pad of my thumb to sweep over the ridges and the small slit at the top.

"Jesus Christ, Quinn. I'm not going to last if you keep that up." His eyelids open, and the heavy desire staring at me at the moment nearly melts the rest of my clothing from my body. Gripping my wrist with his fingers, he pulls my hand free of his pants.

"If you care at all for your clothes, you have five seconds to get those pants off before I rip them off you."

Standing in front of me is a turned-on man that hasn't had a woman in over two years. I smile as heat rolls over my body but quickly fades when I see that all teasing and playing has left him. Oh, Lord, what have I done?

# Chapter Seventeen

Her female scent is driving me wild. Being this close to Quinn, kissing and touching her, it all seems too good to be true. For weeks I've thought of little else and crave every day after tonight.

The small tight smile began to fall from her lips as I held onto my promise. "One…"

"Are you serious?" she asks, taking a step back toward the bed.

"Two. Completely serious. Three…"

Her fingers drop to the button of her jeans, flicking the metal button out of its home before I hear the hiss of the metal teeth descending. Before the zipper had a chance of making it to the bottom, she froze. Looking into her gaze, I could see the fear buried deep. Shying away from me is no longer an option for her.

"Hey, look at me. It's only the two of us in here. Your safe."

"I…" her hands and fingers shake, and her gaze falls away from mine. I take a step toward her bringing my hands to her upper arms to help steady her.

"What's the matter, Quinn. Tell me so I can help you." Her whole body is now trembling under my touch.

"I've nervous about being naked in front of you."

Christ. Why didn't I think of that? I know she had problems in the past with her self-body image. How could I forget and demand that she expose herself to me like that?

"And still, you were willing to try for me."

Raising her eyes, she meets my gaze again. "I want this. I want to be with you. I just don't know if I can stand naked in front of you yet. Is that crazy? I'm sorry I...."

I don't let her finish. I take her downturned face between my hands and kiss her quietly. Moving my mouth softly over hers, I can feel her anxiety melting, allowing her to relax against me, and her trembling eases as she melts into my mouth.

"Listen to me. I'll never ask you to do anything that you're not comfortable doing. I promise you that. If you still want to continue tonight, we can get into bed and under the covers. You are beautiful and have nothing to be embarrassed or ashamed of, and I also know that those are your battles to fight. Just know that I will be here waiting for my chance to see every beautiful inch that is you when you're ready."

Trailing a kiss from her lips to her cheek, I take a step back, taking her hand. I lead her to the bed where the comforter has been turned down and waiting. Pulling it the rest of the way down, I direct her to slide between the sheets, settling her in the middle. Her gaze glued on mine, and I held her there as she lay back against the pillows. My hands drop to my bottoms' waistband, and her eyes flicker to them. I smile to myself, knowing I'm going to give her an eye full, but I've never had a problem with modesty or the image of what my body looks like.

Her gaze stays locked on my parts, and I push my bottoms down over my hips, feeling the cold air touch my cock as it's released from behind the warmth of my clothing. Stepping out of the cotton mess, I kick them toward the side and close the distance to the bed. Her eyes are on my erection, and the knowledge of her enjoying what she sees gets me harder. Stoking the fires that burn inside me into an inferno.

I reach for the edge of the sheet, but her one word stops me.

"Wait."

Her hands disappear under the sheets, and judging by her movements, she's slipping out of her jeans and panties. Realizing she's completely bare, not more than a foot from me, makes my cock throb with hunger.

She pulls the pants free from the closed space of the blankets and tosses them to the floor next to mine.

"Are you sure?" I ask, giving her one last chance to stop. Not that I wouldn't be damn pissed off if she did, but I would respect her wishes and not push her further. Lifting the sheet, I barely get a glimpse of her flesh before sliding in next to her. Leaning on my forearm and elbow, my chest presses along her side, and she gazes up at me.

Without a word, she leans forward moving her hands to the clasp at her back, pulling her arms free of the small strips of fabric holding her bra on falls away, exposing gorgeous breasts. Strands of hair fall to the sides, shielding her plump flesh and rosy nipples from my view, and I'm not having any of it. I push the lock of loose hair back, tucking it behind her shoulder as I turn her face toward mine. I lean into her, kissing her lips until she opens for me, allowing me entrance into her warm mouth.

Quinn falls back against the pillows, and for the first time, I finally get a good look at the beautiful breasts and blush pink nipples that have been plaguing my thoughts.

"You are stunning," I say, kissing and caressing her neck and shoulders, working my way further down. I take one rosy tip into my mouth as my hands find the hot skin of the other breast smashing it against my palm. I squeeze and rub at the heaviness in my fist before rolling the tight nipple in my fingertips. She moans as her eyes drift shut and her head sinks further into the pillow. Swirling the tight tip around with my tongue, I close my mouth around her breast and hollow out my cheeks as I give it a hard suck.

Her fingers find their way into my hair, curling around the short ends at my neck. I shift my weight until she's fully tucked in beneath me.

I release her flesh with a pop and begin to work my way down to leave a trail of wet kisses along her skin as my mouth seeks out her other breast. My hands hungrily roam her body. I crave to see her naked creamy flesh lying against the white sheets from breasts to stomach.

"You feel and smell so incredible."

Sliding my hands down the length of her sides, I brush the smooth skin of her thighs, silently urging them apart to allow the width of me to nestle between them. She complies.

As I move into place, I can feel the heat of her core pressing against my stomach. Her warmth seeped through me, causing me to pulse with need. My fingers move to the inside skin of her thigh, inching closer to the moist center heat of her. She moans as I brush against the outside of her and my nostrils flare as the womanly scent of her fills the air. My mouth waters to taste her and my fingers itch to sink inside her. I need to pace myself. After all, we have time to learn every inch of each other.

I urge them forward, finding the wet heat between her legs, and slip a finger inside. I nearly come at the tightness of her inner muscles around my finger. Moaning, I pull my hand back but return with a second digit to stretch her opening. It's been a long time since she last had sex, and I don't want her to have any discomfort. I know the more Quinn is prepared, the better it will be for both of us. The wetter she becomes, the easier it is to adjust around my size.

She gasps as her hips lunge off the mattress and her fingernails find the skin at my shoulders.

Christ, she's so tight. I'm going to lose my shit once I slide inside her. I work my fingers in and out, letting her body relax and adjust to the size of my digits. I need to get my body under control before I'm too far gone. I don't want to be too rough and not be able to hold back.

Quinn moves under me, her hips bounce off the bed, and her legs fall to the sides, leaving her wide open and exposed. She's more than ready.

"Look at me, sweetheart." I urge, keeping my gaze on her face as I pull my fingers from her. I can't wait another minute to have even the slightest taste of her sweetness. I allow myself that small pleasure by lifting my soaked fingers to my lips. I suck them clean with a groan at the taste and smell she leaves on me.

Holy fuck. It's been a long time since I've been this hard. My cock's throbbing with the need to be inside her.

Sucking in a gasp, she watches me enjoy her flavors, her gaze locking on mine, and at that moment, there's nothing else in the world besides the two of us—a knot forms in my stomach and flip-flops around. I haven't felt feelings like these in a long time, and to be honest, I miss it.

Her hands move to the front of my chest before her fingers slide down to my groin. Wrapping her fist around my cock. I can feel the heat of her palm against the pulsing head, and the sensation gives me the need to thrust into her hand. It's too much and so good that I jerk away and out of her hold. I don't want to come before I even get inside her.

"What's the matter?" She asks, her eyes gazing up at me with a slight look of concern.

"Nothing, you make me feel...so good." Lowering my mouth, I graze her lips with mine. My body is knotting up with anticipation. My mind is no longer mine to control, and my chest feels like there's a wrecking ball threatening to bust through my ribs. My heart is pounding, and it's like I'm back in high school all over again and waiting for my first time. I just hope this doesn't turn out as that did. That sad excuse of an act of sex lasted a total of five minutes thanks to the half-hour of four play beforehand.

"Declan, I need you. I can't take this. I'm burning up."

"I know, little mouse, I am too. But I can't get inside you until I'm sure you're ready." My hand falls back to the hot wet center of her, and as I slip my fingers back inside her heat, I groan as her hips and back bow off the mattress, trying to get just as close to me as I need to be.

She's ready.

Moving to my knees while staying between her thighs, I reach for the nightstand drawer grabbing the small box sitting just inside. I pull out a foil packet and use my teeth to rip it open, and within seconds I'm rolling it over me.

"Last chance to say no, baby. If you want me to stop, you need to say something now."

"I don't want you to stop. I never want you to stop." Her feminine purrs pull me back down against her chest. I was sinking into the comfortable niche of her body that feels molded to fit my size. My hand slid between our bodies and down her stomach to her moist core, where our bodies are not yet joined. I take my cock in hand and guide it to her opening, pressing inside slightly. I hesitate a moment, but Quinn doesn't have it. She's done waiting.

Raising her knees to a bent position, she places her feet flat on the mattress to gain strength to thrust her hips toward me; she impales herself on my cock.

"Oh. My. God." She wails, closing her heavy-lidded eyes as her head rolls back on the pillow. I couldn't have thought up better words myself at the moment. Sinking into the tight deep depths of her is like a jolt, lightning zapping life back into my body. A lightning bolt of energy I've been missing. That I've been needing.

My eyes immediately grow heavy and close for a moment as I savor every intoxicating inch of her tightness. I can't move. Not yet. I stay buried deep, needing a moment to gain my barring first, or I know the second I move, I'm going to lose my shit like some teenage adolescent child.

⦚Declan?" Quinn's voice is rushed and shallow as she twists and turns, thrusting her hips toward me, trying to get closer and lodge me even further inside. A moan escapes my lips before I can bite it back in a weak attempt at keeping my voice down. The need to move is overwhelming, and I immediately withdraw until only the tip remains. The cool air touches the wetness wrapped around me and makes me eager to get back inside her warmth. Sliding back home inch by slow inch forces a whimper from her throat. I want to take my time with her. I want this to last, and the last thing I want is to make her feel rushed and hurried, but I don't think I can hold off any longer.

My hand sneaks down to the crease at the back of her thigh, lifting her leg high and wider allowing me more freedom to thrust harder and deeper.

⦚If this is too much for you. You need to tell me."

Her head bobs against the pillow, and her free leg finds its way around my hip, pressing the heel forcefully into my ass.

"I can't stay still. I need you too much." I say, sliding in and out. I pick up my tempo by slamming back into her, yet she's taking everything I'm giving to her. Her heels dig in, and her arms wrap around my neck as if she's getting ready to hang on for the ride of her life.

"I'm going to come, Declan. Oh god." She whispers into my ear as I thrust into her faster. Her inner muscles tighten around me, and they're milking me. I'm close to the edge, but she goes over first. She's taking me down with her.

"Come, baby. Let go and come for me."

Burying her face in my shoulder, she lets loose a muffled scream as her muscles tighten once more around me and squeeze against me. I lost all the strength I've been holding on to.

"Shit! Now, baby. Give it all to me now." With a cry that sounds more like a passion-filled war cry, her body jerks, and thrusts against me a couple times before finally going still for a long-drawn-out moment. I can't keep myself from the beautiful bliss any longer. I'm falling off the same cliff and into my ocean of ecstasy, soaring over the edge. I release inside the warm lining of the condom, and I damn the barrier between us at that moment. I know why it's there and understand its necessity, but it doesn't make me hate it any less.

My breathing slowly returns, and I roll to the side and get out of bed. Walking naked to the bathroom, I disregard the used condom and wash up before heading back in.

We both need a shower, but that can wait until morning. I don't think I have the strength to hold my eyes open long enough. Judging by the satisfied look on Quinn's face, she couldn't care less either about waiting.

Quinn is on her back. Her hair spread out over the pillow behind her, looking like a halo around her head. Crawling in beside her, I wrap an arm over her stomach, pulling her tight and settling into her scent. Leaning forward, I brush a light kiss along her neck and the back of her hand before resting my head on the pillow next to her.

Sleep had come quickly to claim Quinn, and within minutes, it came for me too.

*Quinn*

Christmas morning was everything I've ever imagined it could be. The tree stood brightly lit with white lights that shimmered off the glass balls and brightly colored ornaments. Flames roared in the fireplace in the living room, giving off a comfy warmth. Rachel and Max joined Declan, Kate, and me for morning coffee before we hurried over to the presents under the tree like a group of children awaiting our surprises. The morning was spent with oohs and ahs as we opened our gifts. To me, Rachel and Max's gift is a beautiful gold chain with a teardrop pendant and a gorgeous champagne pearl in the center.

Kate gave me a beautiful Kate Spade purse, making me feel worse that I don't have a gift here for her. I know she'll love the pro-beauty brushes and carry case I sent to her. Her gift will be there waiting for her when she gets back on location.

"How's your Christmas morning so far?" Declan asks, handing me a cup of fresh hot coffee. I smile up at him as a ping of heat touches my cheeks. The memory of the events from last night brings warmth to my face.

"Good. I mean it. It's been a great morning."

He takes a step toward me and closes the space between us, bringing his hand to my cheek. "A great morning to go with a great night?" he says, causing my cheeks to burn hot with the remembrance of the night before.

"Yes, today has been wonderful, and last night was...amazing. I just wish we had more time before you have to leave. I should have got you on a later flight."

"Why don't you come with me? You can do work from the set." He said, leaning closer to brush a soft kiss over my lips.

"I would love to, but Rachel is too close to delivering, and someone needs to run things here. Plus, we're expecting another shipment of ARCs to come in, and they need to be mailed out to the beta readers. Besides, you're only going to be there for two weeks. You'll be back before you know it." Raising my hand to his chest, I can feel the heat against my palm.

"Let's spend the day lounging around and watching old movies together." He says, leaning down kissing the side of my neck. His arm wraps around my back, and his hands find their way to my ass.

"Ugh, I wish I could. Kate and I are going to our parent's house this morning. We will probably be there for most of the afternoon. Mom wants us to stay for brunch. I'm sorry, but I'm all yours afterward."

"Don't be sorry. They're your family. Go. Have fun with your parents. We have time to hang out together after I get back. It's only two weeks. Tonight, I want to give you, my gift."

"I thought Kate was my gift. You didn't have to do anything else. She is more than enough."

"She was one of them," he says, grinning.

"I have to wait until tonight for my other. Why can't I have it now?" I ask, knowing it will kill me to wait all day to know what Declan got me.

He smiles and gives me a peck on the lips. "Nope. You have to wait because I know the suspense will eat you alive."

An hour later, Kate and I are sitting in our parent's living room, opening presents our mother dumped into our laps. Dads in his recliner, half paying attention to us and the tv at the same time.

Our mom piles the gifts as Kate, and I unwrap. "Geez, mom. How many gifts did you buy us? We don't need all this."

"I'm going to have to buy another suitcase to get all this back with me," Kate said, ripping open another beautifully wrapped package.

"Oh, you girls, just stop. I'm your mother, and it's my job to spoil you on Christmas."

"Mom, we didn't get you this much stuff."

"Don't worry about that. You both being here is the best gift I could ask for. And I love the purse and clothes you girls got me. It's about time I updated my wardrobe, and both of my girls have such great taste in style." A loud beeping interrupted from the kitchen. Mom jumped to her feet. "Shoot, the ham. Kit Kat, will you help me, honey."

"Sure, mom. I'm coming."

Both Kate and mom left the room, leaving me alone with dad, who was trying his hardest to act as if I wasn't even in the room. What's new there? It's been years since my dad, and I have had a one-on-one conversation.

"What are you watching?"

"A Christmas Story. Damn, the movie is on all day."

"You watch it every year."

"Yep." Is all he said, followed by silence

"Did you have a good Christmas so far?"

"I guess so." More silence

I'm not sure why the silent treatment is bothering me more today than any other day. Maybe it's because of all days. Christmas is the one time I feel he should give me a break. Enough is enough.

"Is this the way we are going to spend the rest of our lives, Dad? Me trying, and you ignoring me?"

My dad turned away from the tv for the first time to stare at me.

"What the hell are you talking about? I don't ignore you."

I know denial when I see it. If he wants to pretend everything's fine, that's on him. "Okay, Dad. Fine." I get up, planning on leaving the room, but he calls out, stopping me.

"No, wait, come here. What are you talking about? You think I ignore you?"

I roll my eyes as I turn to face him.

"Are you kidding me? That's all you do, Dad. You and I haven't talked in a long time. Not since that God-awful year. When are you going to forgive me? Mom has."

He sat up further in his chair, folding the footrest closed. "What are you talking about? Forgive you? Forgive you for what?"

I can feel tears starting to build in the back of my eyes, and I will them to go away. Why is he acting like this? He knows exactly what I'm talking about, but if he wants to pretend like it never happened, then okay.

"Nothing, never mind. We can go on pretending we have a healthy, happy relationship."

"Stop with the bullshit, Quinn. I have no idea what you're talking about? But obviously, I've done something. I don't ignore you. Is that what you think?"

All the feelings bottled up for years all came rushing back to me at once. It was like a damn breaking on a river. The overflow was too powerful to contain and began pouring out.

"How can I not. If I'm in the room, you don't talk to me. If I try to talk to you, all you do is pretend you're watching tv or reading the paper. Admit it. You have never been able to forgive me since that night. Mom has, Kate has. Why are you still punishing me? I'm finally healthy and happy, and you want to keep living in the past. You have treated Kate and me differently for years."

Mom came back into the room, looking between dad and I. Kate, following behind her. "What is all the yelling in here about?"

"I'm waiting for dad to admit that he hasn't forgiven me yet, and that's why he treats Kate and I so different."

"Forgiven you for what, Quinn?"

"That's what I'd like to know." My dad said, scooting to the edge of his chair, looking like he was about to leap up at any minute.

"How many times do I have to apologize for that night? I was hurt and confused. I didn't know how to deal with that kind of shit." We never talked about the night I tried to commit suicide as a family. It was a night none of us would ever forget. It's a night we all would love to forget.

"Awe, honey, there's no need for apologies. That's in the past, and you are healthy now. Your father loves you and just wants you to be healthy and happy. That goes for both you girls." Mom said, closing in the distance and wrapping her arms around me.

"Fine, mom. We will all just pretend everything is okay. You, of all people, should know what bottling this kind of emotions up can do to a person. But let's keep pretending that the elephant in the room isn't there."

"There's no need to get smart about all this. Your better now, and that's what matters."

"Then how come dad can't talk to me? Huh? Why can he talk to Kate about her boyfriends and her jobs? How come he can talk to the damn neighbor's kids about their lives, but he doesn't know that first thing about what I'm doing and never asks me about my life? Can you tell me that, Mom? Because he can't." I said, pointing a finger at my dad. I'm yelling now at mom, but there's no way I can keep the anger at bay.

It's my dad who reaches out to me first. "Quinn, you listen to me. I've followed you through every big and small step in your life. I know about your jobs and your schooling. If I seem distant, it's not because I don't love you any less than your sister. It's just I'm not good like your mom at talking out my problems. When you girls do come home, you talk to your mom. I always figured it was easier for you to talk with her than you to talk to me. I had brothers growing up, so raising girls was the hardest thing I ever had to do. There are times I have no idea what to say to you two. And as far as that night goes..." he pauses for a moment before he continues. "I know what that bastard put you through, and the thought of him doing that to you just makes me...." He swallows hard and keeps going. "And then you didn't know how to handle your emotions, and we had to watch you sink deeper and deeper into your depression. Just to think that one of my beautiful babies was hurt and lost in life was the scariest reality of my entire life, and I never want to relive it again."

We all are wiping tears from our eyes. "And as for the woman you are today, standing right here, right now, I couldn't be prouder of you for the growth and accomplishments you have overcome since that horrible night. I love you, don't you ever for a second forget that.

You and Kate have always been my biggest and best accomplishments."

My tears run down my face as I throw my arms around my dad, burying my face into his shoulder. He wraps me in his arms, pressing his cheek to my hair. His scent is warm and familiar. A smell I haven't had the pleasure of being this close to in a long time.

"Maybe I didn't love you, quite as often as I could have." Dad sang the words into my hair.

"You were always on my mind. You were always on my mind."

A sob ripped from my chest at the words of the famous song hit my heart. We just stand there in each other's arms and cry. Mom and Kate are watching us wrapped tight into each other as their tears roll down like mine. Besides all the crying and yelling, it's turning out to be a Christmas none of us are going to forget for a long time.

# Chapter Eighteen

♥

Declan called while Kate and I were still at our parents to let me know they had taken Rachel to the hospital. As it turns out, she had been having sharp pains since last night and now acknowledges it could be contractions. I offer to drop Kate off first, but she insists on going to the hospital with me, so we head straight there from our parents.

"I'm going to put this one down as the weirdest Christmas yet. You cried, dad cried, mom cried. But to be fair, mom always cries. All in all, I think it turned out better than I thought it would once you started in on dad. I thought things were going to get ugly for a minute."

"Yeah, it was definitely different from all our other Christmas's, that's for sure."

"What made you decide to confront dad today finally? I mean, it's been a year since all that crap happened. Why today of all days, couldn't you just ignore it?"

Glancing over at my sister, I caught her eye before turning back to the road.

"I don't know. We were just sitting there, and something came over me. I can't explain it. It pissed me off that we were in the same room and, yet, we never said a word to each other."

Kate smiled and nodded. "Good for you. Probably not the day I would've chosen to confront our parents, but it all worked out in the end. Now you and dad can work on strengthening your relationship, and you can stop avoiding going over there."

"I have been busy the last few months, if you haven't noticed."

"Oh, I've noticed. It's not hard to see what's keeping you busy, either. You and Declan have some serious chemistry together. Not to mention you never returned to the pool house last night."

I give her a shy smile, but I don't confirm or deny what she already knows.

Kate and I got to the hospital just in time to find Declan pacing nervously up and down the hallway.

"How is she?" I ask, stopping beside him. Declan stops and lets me comfort him with my hand on his back.

"I guess she's okay. They kicked me out of the room to get her in a gown and hook the monitors to her. Max is in there with her, so there's not much for me to do. I'd just be in the way.

"Let's find some seats in the waiting room. I'm sure Max will let us know what's going on. As soon as he can."

The three of us moved down the hall into the smaller waiting room for the families of the delivery ward. There's a nurse's station and a set of double doors you have to be buzzed through to get to the rooms.

"So, how excited are you to be an uncle?" Kate asked Declan. We took seats in a small row of chairs and with me in the middle of my sister and Declan. His look passed me and over to Kate.

"I'll be excited when she's no longer pregnant and biting my head off all the time."

"She wasn't that bad," I said, smiling at how his eyes grew wide and round as if he couldn't believe I was saying those words.

"What are you saying? It was horrible. I barely escaped with my life." To that, Kate and I laugh.

A few minutes later, the double doors opened, and Max came walking out looking around the room until he spotted us across the hall in the waiting room.

"How is she doing?"

"Good. The doctor was just in to look at her. He said she's dilated to an eight, and if she keeps this momentum up. He said she could be ready to push within the next few hours, and I'm going to be a dad!"

I stand from my chair and wrap my arms around Max in a friendly hug.

"Congratulations. I can't wait to meet your little girl." He takes a deep breath and gives me a tight squeeze before stepping back.

"Thank you."

"We will be right here waiting for the updates. Get back in their dad. We want to know as soon as we can go in and see momma and baby."

Max leaves the three of us to return to Rachel. Kate excused herself, saying she's going to find the cafeteria for coffee, and promises to bring us both back a cup if she finds it. That leaves Declan and I alone for the first time since last night.

"I never got a chance to give you my Christmas gift." He says, slipping his hand into mine.

"That's okay. It's been a crazy day. A Christmas, I'm not going to forget."

⫽How did things go at your parents?"

⫽Considering I confronted my dad about our relationship, and we were all crying, I think it was pretty okay. I accused him of loving Kate more than me, and I also accused him of never forgiving me for the night of my incident."

⫽Wow, and here I thought Christmas with my mom and dad were tense. How did he take it?"

⫽After, I yelled, and Dad yelled, Mom tried to intervene. We all cried, and my dad told me he was proud of me and that he doesn't hate me, and he wasn't trying to make me feel shut out."

Sliding his fingers from my hand, he touched the inside of my wrist, feeling the slight scar that lay underneath. "You never told me about that night. You don't have to if it's too much."

⫽No, I want to. I've learned over the years of therapy that it's better to talk about it. And if we are to be together, whether it's for work or whatever it's better that you hear it from me." I pause long enough to take a deep breath to calm my sudden nerves.

⫽I told you how and why I got depressed and what happened in California, but as for that night, I had been pushed to my breaking point for days leading up to it. I had withdrawn from all my friends and family. I even pushed my sister away from me. She had no idea I was suffering as much as I was. I told everyone around me when they asked, that I was fine. Kate says if she had known, she would have done something to stop me. But the truth is, there was nothing she could have done.

⫽I didn't want to talk to anyone. I just wanted to be left alone. I was in a dark place and being among the living was making me miserable. The happier people were around me, the more I hated them for feeling the way I didn't.

The night I did it. I took the blade out of one of my dad's carpet knives he kept in the garage. The edge was new and sharp. I remember cutting my finger, trying to get it out of the holder. I went back into the house, and my parents were cooking dinner, and I remember they were laughing at something as they cooked dinner together. I told them I would take a bath before dinner and went upstairs, closing myself into the bathroom. I filled the tub, stepped in, and...." I let my words trail off as I brought my wrist up, so we could both look down at the white two-inch scar running the length of it.

Kate found me by accident. She came barging into the bathroom trying to get ready for a date and saw me lying there. I drifted in and out of consciousness after that. I was alert when the EMTs got there and I knew they were wheeling me into the emergency room, but everything else faded out. The one thing I can't stop thinking about was the look on my parent's faces when I woke up in that hospital room. After that, I spent a month in a hospital working with counselors to get better and work out my problems. My parents didn't lock me in there. It was my choice to go. I wanted the help."

When I was done telling the story, Declan leaned over and brushed a kiss on the side of my forehead. "Thank you for telling me. It means a lot to me that you feel comfortable enough to tell me your story."

I nod. "I've never told my side to anyone before. Not even the doctors. They all knew why I was there, but not why. You are the only one I've ever told."

I'm happy you told me. That you trust me enough to tell me."

We sat there together holding hands until Kate returned carrying three coffees and a brown bag of pastries. The three of us waited the next two hours before the double doors opened again, and this time when Max walked out, his face looked paler than last time, and I could see sweat visible along his hairline and across his forehead. We all jumped from our chairs as he got closer.

"So? Is there a baby yet?"

"Six pounds seven ounces. We named her Reagan Danielle. The doctor just finished cleaning up the room. You can come in and see them."

Rachel's sitting up in the bed with a small pink blanket bundle cradled in her arms when we walk into the room. She looks tired, sweaty, and wrung out but happy and still beautiful.

"How are you feeling?" I ask, moving to the far side of the bed to let the others have room to see the new baby.

"Good. Sore, but of course, that's going to be normal for a few days. Did Max tell you the name we settled on?" Rachel asked, looking to her brother.

He gave her a soft smile. "Reagan Danial. Dani would have loved it. Thank you."

"We didn't do it for you. She was my sister-in-law, and the reason Max and I are together, to begin with. I wanted to honor her in our lives, so I felt this way she will always be with us."

Declan didn't speak. He just cleared his throat and bent over to peek inside the wraps of blankets. "So, are we going to get to see this Christmas baby, or are you keeping her all to yourself?"

"Sorry, I'm a new mom here. I'm going to be stingy for a while." She hands baby Reagan to her uncle, and I watch as Declan awkwardly takes the tiny bundle trying to place her in his arms. I step over and help adjust the baby, but he still stands stiff and unsure, holding his arm bent and tight, so her tiny head can rest in the crook of his arm.

Standing on my tiptoes, I peer into the middle of the blankets. Starring back at me are the rounded pinkest cheeks of the cutest sleeping baby.

"Oh my gosh, Rachel, she's beautiful!"

"Isn't she?"

"Looks just like her mom," Max said with a proud new dad expression.

We all coo and take turns holding little Reagan for the next hour. When the nurse came in to tell Rachel it was time to try breastfeeding again, it was our cue to leave.

Getting back to the house, Kate heads off to the pool house, calling out the good night before closing the back door behind her, and Declan and I were left alone.

Not waiting for him to make the first move, I head to the sizable on-suite bathroom of the room we shared last night and start filling the tub with a hot bubble bath. I can hear Declan in the room behind me. I take my time undressing. My nerves twist into a heap in the pit of my stomach at the thought of him watching me get undressed and seeing me naked. It's a milestone I want to reach, that I need to reach, to move forward in my healing.

After stepping into the hot bubbles, I pin my hair on top of my head and settle back against the tub.

"I'm going to finish packing first. Then, do you mind if I join you?" Declan asks, leaning against the door frame of the bathroom watching me.

"Not at all. I was hoping you would." I say with a shy smile as I lift a leg out of the water and stretch it into the air. I watch as the soft foam bubbles run down my thigh and disappear back into the water.

"Screw packing. I can do it in the morning." He was already tugging his shirt over his head and tossing it aside before attacking the buttons on his pants. He was naked in seconds and stepped into the over-sized tub built to hold two people. Spreading my legs, I allowed space for his body between them as he sunk his lower body into the bubbles, his gaze finding mine. His hand found my foot in the water and began to rub his thumb along the sensitive bottom muscles before working his strong fingers up my ankle and along the silky skin of my calf.

"Are you sure you want to leave your packing for the morning? Your flight is early." I asked, lifting my leg to place my foot on his chest. His gaze drops to his fingers, watching as he runs them up and down the length.

"Are you trying to get me out of your bath?" He asks, grabbing my foot between both of his hands.

"No. I just don't want you to be in a rush in the morning. As it is, you're likely not going to get a lot of sleep."

One eyebrow raised in question. "I'm not, huh? And why is that?"

My gaze drops to his hands as he pulls my foot out of the water to bring to his lips. He places a tender kiss on the top of my foot, and a scorching heat lights up my core making my muscles tighten and clench.

"Hum? Is there a reason I won't be getting much sleep tonight? Do you have plans for me that I'm unaware of?" He asks again, running his thumb up the bottom of my foot from heel to toe.

"I was hoping we could spend our last night— together."

"We are together. Are there other things you want to do together that we're not already doing?" The corner of his lip's curls into a smile, telling me he's enjoying the teasing.

I bite my lip to keep from shouting out for him to take me to his bed and do all the dirty kinky things he can think of to me. Instead, I push myself up to a sitting position and wrap my arms around his neck as I move my body to straddle his lap. His hard erection presses against my core, and I thrust my hips back and forth to gain friction against him. Water and bubbles splash over the sides of the tub. His hands slide behind my back, pressing me closer until my breasts are flat against his chest. My nipples bead into hard nubs at the soft tickle of his chest.

His mouth drops to mine, opening his lips enough to suck my lower lip into his mouth. His teeth bite lightly on the soft tissue sending another prickly shock wave to my core. My tongue pokes out to slip into the warmth of his mouth, and my hands hold his face controlling the kiss as I sink deeper. His cock pressed against me, and in one small twist, his tip nudges against my clit, sending an excitement revving my heart.

"Mouse, you're driving me crazy. I need to get inside you." His mouth is hungry and demanding against mine.

"Take me to bed," I whisper against his lips.

Wrapping his arms around me, he lifts us from the tub, splashing water from the side and onto the floor. He holds me against him, urging me to wrap my legs around his waist as he carries me from the bathroom and over to the bed. We land in the middle with legs and arms intertwined, mouths fused, and fingers seeking out each other bodies.

Reaching between our bodies, I wrap my fingers around his cock, stroking the length of him.

"If you keep that up, I'm going to come before I get inside you."

I move my hand to trail back up his stomach. "We don't want that."

Leaning away from me, he reaches for the bedside table and retrieves a foil packet ripping it with his teeth. Within seconds he's covered and entering me, thrusting in as far as he can go before, he stops and peers down into my face.

"I want to go slow and savor the feeling with you. I'll need the memories to hold me over for the next two weeks."

"Two weeks will be over and done before we know it," I say, wrapping my arms around his shoulders drawing him down to my mouth. He begins a slow and tortured game with our bodies as we kiss. Going slow and gentle, the motions are agony on my nerves and clit. My body is on edge, and I need the friction to pull me into that state of bliss I'm chasing. I need the fierceness I know he can give me.

"Faster," I purr against his shoulder. He takes a moment to pull back and look at me. "Are you sure?"

My head bobs. "Yes. God, yes. I want to feel everything you have to give me. I want it all."

"I don't want to hurt you."

A sexy smile curls over my lips, and I wrap my legs around his hips, digging my heels into his ass. "Trust me. You won't."

He doesn't need any more coaxing after that. Bracing his weight on his forearms, he increases his thrust and continues the delicious torment until we are both panting and calling each other's names.

Our night didn't stop there. Declan and I made love one more time in the early hours of the morning before he had to climb out of bed and head for the shower. His plane left in three hours, and he still needed to pack. I fell back asleep, and the sound of water lulled me back to slumber only to snap awake in what felt like mere seconds to sweet soft kisses along my cheek and lips.

"I'm leaving. I didn't want to wake you, but I had to kiss you goodbye."

Through my sleep-heavy eyes, I peel my lids open and smile at him, lifting my head from the pillow to access his mouth fully.

"Have a good trip."

He laughs, swatting my ass before leaving the room. I'd see him again in two weeks. It wasn't a long time. I could handle fourteen days.

I didn't have a choice.

# Chapter Nineteen

♥

A week into our two weeks apart, I made myself stay primarily busy by getting the long list of chores done. There were books to mail out, websites to update, and a million other things that never seemed to be finished. Rachel was only a phone call away if I needed her. But she was at home with baby Reagan and not due to come back for another few months. I'm left running all things behind the scenes.

Kate left to return to work a few days after Declan left, and it was bittersweet taking her to the airport. It's funny how I never noticed how much I missed having my sister around until she left me, knowing it could be months before we get to see each other again.

A knock on the front door grabbed my attention from the list I was looking over. Opening the front door, I find a woman standing on the front step dressed in business attire and a leather case over her shoulder.

"Hello, are you, Mrs...." the woman pauses as she opens her case and pulls out a piece of paper. "Sorry. Mrs. Palmer? I'm Laura Glenbrook with Evergreen Bay reality. I have an appointment to see the house." She says, holding out a business card for me to take.

"To see the house. No, I didn't know you were coming today. Who did you say called to set up an appointment?"

She looks back on her paper. "A Rachel Palmer. Is that not you?"

"No, I work for Rachel. Please, come in. I'm sorry, I had no idea you were coming today. Rachel must have forgotten to tell me she had an appointment with you today. But she did just have a baby, so she most likely forgot. Let me make a quick phone call to see what's going on. Please, come in." Grabbing up my phone, I dial Rachel.

"Hey, what's up?" She answers

"I have a Ms. Glenbrook here from Evergreen Bay Reality."

"Oh, I forgot to tell you she was coming by. Do you mind showing her around?"

"Does Declan know about this? It doesn't seem right to show his house if he doesn't know she's here."

"Relax. I'll handle my brother if he finds out. I'm not selling his house. I just want to know what he could get out of it in this market. I've never hid that I want him to move into the city. And he did admit he had thought about selling once. That place is too large for just him. But now that he has you...." her words trail off.

"She's here and waiting for me, so I'll call you back once she leaves." I smile at Ms. Glenbrook from over the edge of my phone.

"Thanks, Quinn. If I don't answer right away, it's because I'm trying to get this baby asleep. Once I do, I'm taking advantage of the peace, and I hope to take a nap myself."

After we hung up, I turned back to the broker. If Rachel is taking responsibility, I'll do as she asks.

⟊Do you know much about the house? I already know the room count and all the important stuff from looking up the listening from the last time it was up for sale. But it's nice to see if any updates have been made over the years, and it looks like this place has been kept in good hands." She adds, looking around the room.

⟊Yes, Declan takes great care of this place." Thinking of Declan selling this house gives me mixed emotions. Maybe he could finally move on from his past. Was I naive to hope for something serious between us?

A lump formed in my throat, and I pushed it back with a smile. I don't want to come off as a crazy person by grinning uncontrollably.

⟊I'd be happy to show you around. Do you need to take pictures as we go?"

⟊We don't do any marketing like that until we have signed paperwork. The house isn't on the market yet. I wanted to come out and look around to offer up a listing price and talk over terms."

⟊We can start down here and work our way up and out to the pool house."

I showed Ms. Glenbrook the entire house and out-buildings. She asked me questions, and some I knew the answers to, but others I didn't. I gave her Declan's number, telling her she could call him if she had more questions or when she came up with a listing price.

Later that evening, I stayed busy stuffing envelopes with advance reader copies of Declan's newest book when my cell phone rang in my pocket. I quickly pulled it out, hoping it was Rachel with the to-do list for to-morrow, but after glancing at the name on the screen, my heart skipped a beat, and I squeal a little to myself as I rushed to accept the call.

⦸Hi. I didn't think I'd hear from you again so soon after spending so long on the phone last night. I thought you would be too busy to call. How are things going on the set?"

The other end of the phone remained silent for a lingering moment until Declan's voice broke through. "I just got off the phone with an agent who had a question for me about my house? Did you show a real estate agent around my house today?"

His voice held irritation and anger. Dread seized inside me, and for a second, my thoughts froze. I didn't know how to answer him. Hadn't Rachel talked to him about the broker?

⦸I...uh..." Was all I could get out before I heard what sounded like the words un-fucking-believable from under his breath. I immediately jumped to my defense.

⦸Declan, I did show the broker around the house this morning, but I didn't...."

His words cut me off before I could explain any further. "I can't believe this. I thought you were different, Quinn. You know how hard all of this has been for me. You, of all people, should know what it feels like for people to push you into things you are not ready for. You know you can't just move on simply because others want you to. And yet, here you are, throwing it back in my face. I thought I could trust you."

He didn't know about the house. There has been some mistake. Tears threatened to fall as they grew heavy and began to sting my eyes.

"Declan, listen. I did let her in the house, but...."

"Just stop. I'm so tired of everyone in my life telling me how I should feel and how I should be over Dani and moving on. I told you why I didn't want to sell, and that didn't matter to you. You think just because you're a woman I fucked a few times, which gives you the right to sell my fucking house and make those decisions for me? The house I had with my wife. The one person who meant the most to me in this fucking world. I can't begin to explain how angry I am."

There was a brief pause on the other end of the phone. I could have taken that moment to explain myself and plead to him that I had nothing to do with it, but I was stunned silent with the harshness of his cruel words he so easily threw at me.

With tears running down my face, I realized at that moment that he wasn't interested in my side of the story. He wanted someone to blame, and in his mind, I was the likely candidate. I had meant so little to him that he was ready to point his finger at me without first asking a few simple questions.

Was that all I am to him? Some girl he fucked? My heart broke at that moment. The stabbing pain shooting through me felt like physical agony. I'm stunned, silent. I hear him rambling on over the line, but now I only hear the sound of his voice. I'm no longer listening to the words.

My eyes burn with glossed over tears blinding me as familiar pain and rejection come rushing back over me. My limbs grow numb, and even though I remain standing, my legs are heavy. I make it over to the couch and sit down before the muscles in my legs decide to give up.

I hold the phone to my ear, hearing, seeing, and finally feeling-nothing. Unable to defend myself and not caring if I ever do again.

⧄I think it would be best if you move out before I return home. I'll have Rachel give you a reference, but after that, it might be best if we don't contact each other again."

I hear the phone click off on his side, and the phone falls into silence. The only sound I can hear is the pounding of my heart and the shattering echoes of my broken, battered heart.

*Declan*

"You want me to give Quinn a what?"

Rachel all but screamed the questions at me over the phone.

"A reference. I'll need it emailed to Quinn by the end of today."

"Why does she need a reference? Where the hell is she going? I just had a baby, Declan. I can't go back to work right now. What happened? Did something happen between you two? She was fine a few hours ago when I talked to her. She was getting things done."

"I don't want to get into it with you right now, Rachel. I'll figure something out, so you can still have time off. I'll consider hiring someone else."

"Hiring someone else? What the hell is going on, Declan? Where is Quinn going? She didn't say anything about a new job. Did you try to sweet-talk her into staying? I can't believe this."

"No, I didn't talk her into staying. I'm the one who asked her to leave. And before you start screaming at me again, I'll...."

"What the hell did you do that for?"

"Things were moving too fast with her. We wanted different things from each other."

"What the hell are you talking about? Last I checked, you were both all lovey-dovey. What the hell did I miss while I was napping?"

"She had a fucking real estate broker come look at the house this morning, Rachel. Who does that kind of shit? I sleep with the girl a few times, and she puts my house on the market? Without talking to me. I wouldn't let you talk me into selling. Why in the hell would I let her do it? She admitted to showing them around the house."

The other end of the phone remained eerily silent, and I started to wonder if my sister had hung up on me.

"You there?"

"Oh, Declan." Her voice broke with the crack of a sob. I didn't think she would be this upset over me firing Quinn. I know they have become good friends, but that didn't mean they couldn't remain so. If she's worried about the work, I'll hire ten people if that's what it takes to keep her at home.

I take a deep breath in as I try to calm my anger. "Look, Rachel, we will find someone to replace her, okay. Don't worry. You will get the time you need to be with your baby. Let me worry about all that."

"Declan, I'm not worried about that. This is not how all of this was supposed to happen. I swear, if I had known you were going to freak the hell out like this, I wouldn't have called her."

"Called who? What the hell are you talking about?"

"Declan, I'm the one who asked the broker to look at the house. Not Quinn. She called me to see what was happening when the lady showed up. Quinn just showed her around because I asked her to. She's the one who didn't want me to do it and was against it from the beginning. She said it wasn't right without you knowing. I told her I would take the blame. God, I wish you had called me first. Didn't she tell you she wasn't the one who called the real estate company?"

Fear and dread consumed me. It took a full minute to understand what she had just said.

"No. Fuck. I didn't give her a chance. I think she tried, but I wouldn't let her finish."

If she had been the one that hired the broker, then I accused Quinn of...

"God damn it."

"Declan don't be mad at me, please. I wasn't trying to sell your house. I just wanted to know what you could get in the city that is a little smaller. Plus, with things developing between you and Quinn, I thought that maybe being in a new place would be a great way of making a new start for you. You seemed so happy at Christmas that I had...hoped. Dani wouldn't want this for you. She would want you to move on and fall in love again. And she would have liked Quinn. Don't you think? Keeping that huge expensive house is just another way of keeping ahold of Dani. You only bought that place because she loved it. You won't be hurting memories of her if you sell it. She wasn't that kind of person."

Silence fills the phone. I can't respond, thanks to the lump in my throat. After a minute, Rachel speaks again. "Look, keep the house, sell the house, whichever you want to do. Just don't blame Quinn because I finally became that sister to meddle in your life. I'm sorry that I did."

Shit.

My heart is pounding heavily in my chest as I think back to the words, I'd said to her. Oh Christ, what have I done? She finally opens herself up to someone and drops her defenses, and I crush them like a wrecking ball in a single moment. She's already fragile and, yet I spit harsh words at her.

"Shit, Rachel, the things I said to her— I don't think...."

"What did you say to her?"

My words come crashing back to me. "I asked if she thought because she was a woman, I fucked a few times meant she could sell my house."

Hearing the words spoken aloud has me closing my eyes at their harshness. The sudden pain and regret start seeping through my pores to consume me. To think of the hole, I must have ripped into her trust. She has to be crushed. I need to talk to her. I need to explain to her that this was a huge misunderstanding and make her understand what an asshole I am.

"Rachel, I'll call you back. I need to talk to Quinn. I'll deal with you later."

"You better gravel, brother."

After hanging up with Rachel, I hit the call button under Quinn's name. It rings six times and goes to voice mail.

Shit

I call right back. Six rings and voice mail. Where the hell is she?

Calling right back this time, my call is sent straight to voice mail. That only happens when the person you call declines your call. I can't blame her for being mad. I would be too.

Hell, I was pissed. Unfortunately, I took it out on the wrong person. The person who had tried to set me straight while I accused her of stabbing me in the back. I never gave her a chance to confirm or deny what I accused her of. I never asked her if she was guilty. I just assumed she was.

This will set her back on the trust I had asked her for. What have I done?

My phone suddenly rings in my hand, and I quickly answer it, hoping it's Quinn returning my call.

"Hello?" I say, mentally getting my apology ready.

"Declan?" A soft shuddering sound follows my name, and I quickly recognize the voice belonging to Jaclyn. I curse under my breath, trying to quickly come up with anything that will get me off the phone with her.

"Declan, I need your help. I don't know who else to call."

"Jaclyn, look. I told you already. Nothing is going to happen between us...."

"It's not about that. It's my dad. He wants to kill me."

"What the hell are you talking about?"

"My dad and I got into a fight over Dani, and he said it should have been me that died. Not her." She sobbed into the phone. Closing my eyes, I let out a breath releasing some of my frustration. No matter how she's been acting lately, no one deserves to hear that from their parents. And she's still Dani's sister, and Dani would have my balls for not coming to her little sister's aid.

"Where are you now?"

"At the airport in Denver. I came to see you. When I left my parents, I didn't know where else to go."

"You're here? Why didn't you go home? Back to school?"

"I just couldn't be alone right now. Please get me or give me the address, and I'll get an uber. Either way, I have to see you before I leave."

I might be making a huge mistake, but I need to find out what happened and get Jacklyn back on her way so that I can get my life back in order.

"You can stay, but only for a day. Then your back on a plane and heading back to school."

"Absolutely. You have my word. I'll see you soon."

# Chapter Twenty

"Quinn? Please pick up the phone."

Silence

"I know I jumped to conclusions and blamed you without talking to you first, and I'm sorry."

Silence

"Quinn, I..."

"Message deleted. End of messages."

The automatic female voice came over the line as I hit the number two button to erase his voice. I don't care what he has to say. He made it crystal clear how he felt about me. After all, I'm just some woman he fucked a few times. Pain from his words shook me again as I threw the last of my clothes into my suitcase. I glanced over to the pile of bags and suitcases by the door, making sure nothing was forgotten. I grabbed my coat and swung it around my shoulders, stuffing my arms into the sleeves. I pull it tight around me and sling my overnight bag over my shoulder and leave the pool house.

"There you are. I'm glad you didn't leave yet." Rachel said from her seat on the high back stool at the kitchen island.

"What are you doing here? Shouldn't you be at home with the baby? Where is Reagan?"

She smiles and turns her body more, pointing to the other side of the room. "She's over there in the car seat. We decided to stop here first before heading home. Max wanted to get the rest of my things, but he had to take a conference call when we got here. He's in the bedroom now. How about you? It looks like you're leaving anyway, huh?" She nods toward the bag slung over my shoulders.

"Yeah. I told your brother I would be gone before he got back."

"He doesn't want you to go, you know. He messed up. What can he do to make you stay? Besides, I still need you."

"I'm sorry, but it's not that easy," I say, shaking my head. With a shrug of my shoulders, I add. "He didn't even ask, Rachel. He didn't ask me if it was true. He had it set in his mind that it was and that I would betray him. He thought the worst of me and didn't even think twice about it. Not to mention he made it clear that our relationship up to this point wasn't as important to him as it was to me, more like just passing the time for him. I don't know what I was thinking about getting personally involved with a job. I know better." I say, mentally kicking myself for the hundredth time.

"Quinn. He doesn't feel like that. He jumped to con-clusions."

"No, Rachel. You didn't hear him on the phone."

"He was upset."

My temper was rising the more she defended Declan. I understand he's her brother, and she's standing up for him but damn it, he hurt me.

"He referred to me as just someone he fuckcd. It sounds to me like he doesn't believe too strongly in a common relationship."

Her face falls.

"He said that to you. What a creep. I'm going to kill him." Her words softened my anger, and a soft smile touched my lips.

"It's sweet of you to offer murder, but there's no sense dragging you off to jail over this. Besides, I'm heading to my parents for the night. Then I'm joining Kate on set for a few days. But before I leave, I want to see that adorable baby of yours again."

She doesn't question the change of subject but instead turns to new mom mode for the baby. Rachel smiles and hops from the stool.

"Here she is." She says, lifting the car seat to the top of the table. Looking inside under a pile of pink and white blankets is the tiniest, cutest, chubby cheek sleeping baby.

"Oh my gosh, Rachel. She's beautiful." I say, gently pulling the blankets away from the baby, revealing more of her face.

"Do you want to hold her?"

"Of course, I do."

I spend the next twenty minutes cuddling the adorable baby, and in those moments, my heart softens from the anger I was holding earlier. Peering down into the face of a sleeping Reagan, I couldn't help but to want to help her mommy.

"If you need me to, I'll keep working with Declan to cover for you, but I'll only stay until you find a replacement for me."

Rachel squeals, wrapping her arms around me.? "Oh my gosh, Quinn, that's great. Thank you."

"Wait a minute. I do have a few conditions."

"You name them."

"I'm staying in the city, so I'll be working from my parent's house. I don't want to have meetings here at Declan's. If we need to have a meeting, it must be somewhere else. I can't come back here."

If she had doubts, Rachel didn't voice them. "Sounds good. I'm so glad you're not leaving me. If I had to do all this on my own and take care of a baby, I would lose my mind."

"We can't have that, now, can we?"

*Declan*

I shove two fingers into the front pocket of my jeans and pull out the ringing phone. Scanning the name, I press accept.

"Hey, sis. What's up?" I ask, catching the eye of the second co-producer, who gave me a dirty look before pointing up to the red light over the sound set, indicating that filming is in progress. Holding up a hand to apologize, I slip from my chair next to the scene writer and slip out the door.

"Hey, what's going on? We're in the middle of filming."

"I should be asking you the same damn thing. What the hell is going on out there, Declan? Is Jaclyn out there with you?"

Shit. I knew this was going to happen if Rachel found out.

"She is. She fought with her parents, and she didn't want to be by herself. She called me crying. She was already here before she called me. What was I supposed to do? Leave her at the airport? She's still Dani's sister, Rachel. I can't just act like she's not family."

"Family? Declan, have you seen any of the social media Jaclyn's been posting?"

"You know I'm hardly on those damn things. Why?"

She was silent for a minute before she asked. "Can you put me on speaker and log into your social media. There's something you need to see."

I glanced over my shoulder to ensure no one was around me or that my phone call wasn't interrupting the filming. I turned the volume on my phone down, placed her on speaker, and logged in.

"What am I looking for?"

"Log into your sister-in-law's page and see for yourself."

After typing in Jaclyn's name, I wait as post after posts come to life in front of me. There are pictures of behind-the-scenes of my production—some of her sitting next to me in the stage chairs on set. I had let her come to sit with me yesterday because she promised not to get into trouble, not to mention she all but cried when I refused to join her in her hotel room last night. We agreed that she could come to the set with me but only for one day.

Then I saw it. The post that would have anyone raising a questionable brow at. It was a picture of me, Jaclyn, and a few of the actors in the mini-series, and the caption on the photo said. 'Spending the day on the set with my man.'

My stomach dropped. I had the sudden need to hurl.

"What the hell?" I asked out loud.

"Do you see it?"

"Yeah, I'm looking at one right now. Rachel, I don't know what she's playing at here, and I have no idea what's going on. I've never touched her other than a brotherly hug."

"Don't you think I know that? I also know that she's had a thing for you for years. Dani used to think it was cute...."

"Wait a minute. Dani knew about her sister having a crush on me?"

"Declan, it was nothing more than a little sister crushing on her older sister's boyfriend kind of thing. No harm. But all that was years ago when she was younger. She's an adult now, and she knows better. She's up to something, and I don't like it."

"Christ, I don't need this. What the hell am I going to do?" I ask, closing the app on my phone. I couldn't look at it another minute.

"You need to get her out of there. Put her ass on a plane and send her home. Her demons aren't yours, Declan. She will make rumors happen for you that we don't need. Remember, they said reporters could start digging if they thought they might find a story. The mini-series is already getting serious attention. We don't need bad attention getting out on the media."

This was so fucked up. I ran a hand through my hair, pulling on the ends, embracing the pain for a moment.

"Okay, I'll do it today. Can you get a plane ticket online up for her, please?"

"I'll call Quinn and ask her to...."

I cut her off. "Quinn? I thought she was gone. I never heard back from her." It's been two days since I last spoke to Quinn. I spent every minute I could yesterday calling and leaving messages, but they all went unanswered.

"She's going to continue to work for us, but she's only going to stay until I find a replacement for her. I just didn't tell her how long that was going to take."

"How is she doing?" I miss her. I miss talking to her, even going over the simple day-to-day stuff.

"Good. She's on a little vacation with her sister. Last I heard, there was something about a beach party, lots of beer, hot guys, and body shots." She laughs on the phone, but I don't see the humor in her torment.

"I'm kidding. Quinn's on set with Kate for a few days, but she said I could call if I needed anything. I'll have her book the plane ticket."

"Don't do that, then she'll know Jaclyn's here, and she'll think...."

"She knows." Her reply was so matter of fact that it seemed on purpose.

"Shit."

"She thinks that's why you haven't tried to call her again. You know because you already moved on."

"I did try to call. I left a shit ton of messages. I stopped trying because she wasn't answering. Did you tell her that?"

"No." She sounded so matter of fact. "Look, I love you. You're my brother, but until you're ready to move on from the past, I don't think you should be around Quinn. She's too good of a person to be treated carelessly. She likes you, and even though she hasn't said it, I think she would love to have a future with you. So until you're ready to let the past go, you will only hurt her more. If you need more time, that's okay. You'll be ready when it's the right time for you. And I promise you; I will no longer push you into anything you're not ready for. It's your life, and anything you do in it is solely up to you. I love you, dork."

It was hard to hear those words. But she was right. There were things I needed to figure out in my life myself before I ever should have brought someone else into it. It wasn't fair to Quinn, and if the roles were reversed and she was the one pining after a lost husband, I would want her to get things straight before moving on to me. I owed it to her to get my shit together.

"Thanks, Rachel. Your right. I need to get my shit straight."

She giggled. "Of course, I am. Was there ever any doubt?"

# Chapter

# Twenty-One

"There you are. Have you eaten anything yet? I was hoping we could go grab a bite downstairs." Jaclyn announced as soon as I walked into my hotel room. I dropped her bags at the door before entering the small apartment-sized room adjacent to mine.

"Jac's, please come in here. We need to talk."

The smile she had been giving me slowly falls as she joins me in the small living room.

"What is it?" she asks, taking a seat on the couch.

"What was your goal in coming here?"

"What do you mean?"

"Don't do that. Please don't pretend you have no idea what I'm talking about. We both know what you have been doing ever since you got here. The whole damn world has seen it on social media by now. So, I'm going to ask you again, what is your goal here?"

"Declan, please don't be mad at me. All I've done is post a few pictures. No harm."

"Calling me your man is no harm? You are like a sister to me. What will our parents think? If they haven't already seen it?"

"Well, I'm not your damn sister anymore."

Her confession pisses me off. How dare she be so casual about this. She acted as if her sister hadn't died but had moved to a different country.

"Listen to me. Even though Dani is gone doesn't change anything between us. You will always be my sister. NOTHING more."

Her face scrunches together, and her brow dips. "No one understands. No one knows the pain I'm in all the time with missing her."

Her words are suddenly cut off with a sob she tries to mask by turning her head away.

"You understand. You're the only one who does because she left you too. Maybe in some weird way I thought since she was close to the both of us, somehow if we were close to each other, it would be like being close to her again. Neither of us can forget her. We could help each other with our pain." She swiped at a tear that ran down her cheek. "We don't have to have a sexual relationship. We can just be here for each other. Like she was always there when we needed her."

I'm stunned and speechless by her confession.

"Jaclyn, I'll always be here for you because we're family. Losing Dani doesn't mean you and I, or you and Rachel, can't still have a connection. I think Dani would love the idea of the three of us staying close. She loved you so much. But I will never have anything more than brotherly affections toward you."

"I know. I mean, yes, I used to have a crush on you, and I still think you're pretty hot, but it does feel wrong when I think about it. I'll take the posts down."

I grin at her to lighten the mood. "That's because it is wrong, weirdo," I say, bumping my shoulder into hers until she smiles back at me.

"I think it's past time we both start to move on from the past. We can't keep going on like this, it's not fun or healthy for either of us. Rachel keeps reminding me that Dani would never want this misery for us. She would be upset with how hard we are both fighting this. What do you think she would say?"

Jacklyn glanced up, meeting my eyes. "Dani would say to go live life for her. She would kick our asses if she could see us now."

"Yep. I think she would. She would want you to find someone you love and get married."

"She would want the same for you," Jacklyn said, peeking up at me.

"Yes, she would. I can honestly say I have begun to think about the possibility of moving on. Besides, I've started seeing someone."

A cruel smile lifts the corner of her mouth as if she's been waiting to put her two cents in. Showing her hurt and sting to her ego, "Don't tell me you're referring to Quinn because that's a joke."

Her words are all it takes for my anger to flare to life. "What the hell does that mean? You know nothing about her."

"I know she's not your type. You married my sister, who was beautiful and perfect. And I'm sure Quinn is a nice person but come on Declan. She's plain and chubby. You need someone more...."

"What, more like you?"

"No, I told you that's all wrong. But somebody that isn't her."

This girl is unbelievable.

"There's nothing wrong with the way Quinn looks. I happen to think she's a beautiful woman. And not that I need to defend her to you, but she has a perfect body that I like very much."

Leaning back against the sofa, her aggressive smile stays in place.

"Really? Then where is she? How come she's not here with you? Because you can't bring yourself to move fully on, can you? I understand what that feels like, Declan. She never will. Everyone wants us to be over Dani and for us to just forget about her. I can't do it, and I know you can't either. Misery loves company."

Yes, losing Dani was the hardest thing I've ever experienced in my life. She was the best thing that ever happened to me so far in life. But Quinn has made me realize Dani won't be the last. And Jaclyn helping me see once and for all what everyone sees when they look at me. A broken crazy man who chased a ghost.

"You're right. I haven't fully been able to move on from Dani yet. I will never fully get her completely out of my system. Your sister was the love of my life, and I miss her every day." I pause as I push myself to stand. "But I need my life to move past this. I never thought the day would come that I would ever say those words, but here it is. And I have Quinn to thank for opening my eyes. I like her, Jaclyn, and I hope someday in the future, you will like her too because no matter what you may think, even with Dani gone, you are still my family. And I want nothing more than for you to be happy as well. Now, pack your bags. Your plane leaves in two hours."

*Quinn*

Glancing around the cemetery, I shiver as the cold slips beneath my coat, causing me to snuggle deeper into the warm lining. January weather in Washington state is cold. Rain, wind, and freezing cold, make it hard to concentrate on what I've come out here to do.

Two weeks have passed into the new year and even though I haven't talked to Declan in all this time, being here is still something I need to do.

Rachel has helped keep me busy and my mind off her brother. She calls daily needing things done, or we get together a few times a week to go over items that require one or both of our attention. But mostly, we spend time together and talk about the baby. I love going to her place to see little Reagan, and surprisingly things haven't been weird between Rachel and me, but my heart still hurts for Declan and the friend I lost in all this.

I miss him.

How did I allow my heart to get so far gone? I knew better than to become involved with my boss and make my work life personal. I'm not new to this lifestyle. I know the rules. I've lived and breathed them my entire adult life. I've been able to keep my heart locked away with every other job, but this one blindsided me and took my breath away.

Yesterday, Rachel sent a text telling me Declan would be home in a few days and I should talk to him. I don't think that's a good idea. Besides, he hasn't made any attempts to set things right. He called me the first few days, and I childishly refused to answer, but I was still angry. Now that the anger is gone, it has left just hurt feelings. Rachel tried to bring him up in conversation the other day, but I threatened to walk out of the room if she did it again. My stubborn pride and bruised feelings make it impossible for me to see him.

This morning, Kate tried over the phone to convince me I was being stupid. She also asked how I expected the man to talk to me let alone apologize if I avoided him at all turns? Of course, I didn't have an answer for her because she was right.

I'm embarrassed.

He hurt me. In those few short hurtful words, he made me relive the sharp pain and humiliation of my youth, the attack, and all the self-doubt all over again. Last week Kate admitted she was afraid I would start cutting again. I told her not to worry because the truth was, I was past that. But that's not to say I haven't thought about it.

The world doesn't know about or refuses to acknowledge certain disorders, even ones like cutting, are no different from a junkie trying to remain clean. The urge is there and will always be. It may be buried, but it stays with you. I have good days, and I have bad. Never enough to bring me close enough to the darkness I was in when the pain of cutting was all I wanted.

I haven't been back to those depths in a long time, and I have no plans on ever returning there. Not after Declan threw me away without a backward glance, I want to find my happiness again and to do that, I can't carry anger around with me like weighted chains anymore. Forgiving Declan is the best thing to do. I've rehearsed the lines of my speech to him over in my head a hundred times. I practiced what I wanted to say to him.

I want to tell him he hurt me. That he made me feel small and unimportant to him, and that after the days, weeks, and months we spent getting to know each other, I have never liked, loved, and hated another person as I do him. I want to tell him that I understand he misses his wife and that it kills me that I find myself jealous of her.

Those thoughts make me mad because I should never take it for granted that I'm still here among the living, and she has lost her battle. And it kills me to know that given a chance, he would choose her in a heartbeat to be back in his life over me. I can't blame or fault him for that.

I also want him to know that I can forgive the words spoken and the pain they caused, but the one thing I'm struggling with is the fact I'm letting my old scars still hold a death grip over me just as much as he's allowing his late wife to keep his heart.

I move across the frozen ground, searching for the name I've come to know so well. Rachel told me where I could find it when I told her my plans of coming here today. She agreed it was a great idea. A good way of giving me the closure I so desperately need to move on.

It's weird to say I need closure with someone I've never met, but I do. I need to forgive Declan, but I also need to be forgiven. This was the only fitting way for me to do that.

Walking further onto the grounds, I head for the row of headstones laying in straight lines. The second one from the end, and there it was. A large monument with the name Daniel Elizabeth Palmer. Beloved daughter and wife with two hearts overlapping each other engraved across shiny black marble with tiny pink flakes embedded.

Standing in front of the cold stone felt strange. As if I was meeting her in person. My skin tingled with the sense of a presence, but after looking around, I knew no one lingered nearby as far as I could see. The morning was turning out to be cold and wet. But despite the weather, I needed to be here.

With a shaky breath, I began.

"I guess I'll start by introducing myself. I'm sure you know who I am by now." The chill in the air stung my eyes, and I brushed the sting away with the tips of my fingers.

"My name's Quinn, and I work for your husband."

Tell the truth, Quinn.

"That's not fair. I said I was going to do this right, so I will. I work for him, but I also..." deep breaths. "I'm also in love with him."

The damn wind stung my eyes again, forcing me to blink a few times to clear the blurriness.

"This is weird, but I have a few things to ask you. It's about Declan." Pausing, I clear my throat. This is crazy that I'm nervous talking to a headstone.

"He's struggling, Dani. He's keeping you locked away inside his heart, but in doing so, he's pushing others out and not opening to the chance of love again. I know you wouldn't want a lonely life for him. Rachel always tells me how down-to-earth and supporting you were and how special you thought every person was. Rachel's always talking about you. Sometimes when she's telling a story about you, she pauses as if she wants to seek you out in the room only to frown when she remembers your no longer here. She was lucky to have you as such a great friend and sister. She says you and I would have hit it off if we had met. I like to think we would have been good friends."

An emotional breath chokes me up, and I cough it away.

"I guess I'll get to the point since it's so cold out here, and I'm freezing." I shiver and hold my coat tighter around my body.

"I'm asking you, woman to woman— friend to friend. Please help him let you go. Even if that means he doesn't come to me. Please help him find peace in his heart to be happy again. I'm more than ready to love him as hard as you did, but he won't let me in. Not while you still hold his heart."

I bring my hand out of the warmth of my pocket to brush a tickle of wetness from my cheek.

"You have always held his heart, Dani, and the truth is you still do. And no matter how I try, I can't pull it from your grips. I'm not sure I can. You probably could have if the situation were reversed, you would probably know just how to capture his heart to love you."

I giggle a little. "That's okay. I'll let you have that one. I've never been any good at the whole man thing and dating. My sister Kate told me for years it's because I'm not girly enough, whatever the hell that means." I pause long enough to draw in a breath.

"In all seriousness, I'm jealous of you. It may seem petty since I'm here and you're...not. I'm sorry, but I am jealous. He holds you on a pedestal with his love to heights I'll never reach in my life. And I never want you to fall from there, I just want to be up next to you."

Then, I brush another tear from my stinging eyes and touch the moisture against the freezing stone I'm talking to.

"I wish I could have known you. But if I had. I would never have met Declan. At least, not like I do. So, in a way, I guess it's best we have never met, but I promise you this, if I get to stay in his life, I will never ask him to forget you. Not that he ever could." I tuck my hand back into my pocket as another chilling wind passes by.

"Anyways, it's freezing out here, and I'm going to head back to my car. Think about what I asked. I'm more than willing to take it from here. If you'll let me."

I close my eyes and send a silent prayer of thanks to Dani for listening. Not knowing what else to say, I turn from the cold headstone needing the warmth of my car.

"Quinn?"

I freeze at the sound of my name.

Oh my god.

It takes me a moment to regain my thoughts, and I turn toward the familiar voice and gaze over to the man standing ten feet behind me.

Oh, God. Please tell me he didn't hear any of my confession. Guilt and embarrassment consume me.

"What are you doing here? I thought you were still in Denver for another few days."

He shrugs his shoulders. "There are some things here I need to take care of first. I'm going back in a week for another week."

"How is the project coming along?"

"Good. It's weird being around all those people. I'm used to being in my office, alone. It's kind of weird to see the world that has only been in my head on the screen."

I nod and listen. A part of me wants to throw myself at him and repeat all the words I just confessed to Dani. But I don't. He hurt me. And even though I can forgive him. He hasn't tried to call me in over a week. Maybe he has decided I'm not worth the hassle and decided to give up on me.

If he would only show me a sign that he wants me back in his life. Wants me back in his bed. I would confess it all this very moment. But I can't put myself out there.

Not again.

I'm too afraid of him rejecting me again. A cold breeze flows by, reminding me of the temperature we are standing in.

"What are you doing here?" He asks to point toward the cemetery.

"I wanted to talk and clear a few things up." I let it go at that, and thankfully so does he.

"Well, I'm heading to my car. I'm freezing and soaked to the bone."

"Yeah. I'm uh...staying here a little longer."

I wave my hand to tell him he has no reason to explain anything to me.

"I'll...see you later."

I turn to leave, wishing to just disappear into thin air. I never wanted him to know that I had come out here. I sent a meek glance over my shoulder, confirming that he was watching me walk away. Great. It was like the walk of shame all over again.

# Chapter

## Twenty-Two

♥

*Two months later*

"I can't believe she's going to be two months old already. Where did the time go?" Rachel says, handing a smiling Reagan over to my awaiting arms.

"And she's already holding her head up."

"That's wonderful, Rachel. She's so adorable. She looks just like you." I say, smiling at the beaming mom.

Rachel laughs. "That's funny because I think she's a little mini-Max. She has his eyes and mouth. She already pouts like he does, too, when things don't go her way."

"Imagine that. Are you planning on coming back to work full-time or are you planning on staying part-time for a while longer?"

"I want to continue as I have been. It's been a big help to be home with her all day, and I work when she takes naps. But when she gets older, and she's not asleep all day, I'm thinking of cutting down my hours more." She glances at me from under her long, gorgeous lashes as a shy smile curl over her lips.

"Rachel, that's great. I mean, it will be hard to adjust without you, but things have been going pretty good."

"Yeah? I've been worried about how it's been working from your parent's house. I've thought if I do decide to cut my hours more, we will have to hire you an assistant to do all the hands-on stuff."

I know what she means by that. We would need to hire someone willing to go to Declan's house since I refuse to return. I haven't been back since I packed and moved out two months ago. After all, we had been through, and there was no way I could go back. It hurt too much. It was hard enough going to our weekly meetings and seeing him. Fortunately, our meetings have moved to Rachel's condo. We were given a middle ground.

"How long has it been since you and Declan have talked?"

"We talk every week at the meetings." I know she wasn't referring to work.

"I mean really talked. Not about work, but about you two?"

I shake my head, starring down at Reagan in my arms. I move my gaze to anything that isn't Rachel.

"There is no us, so there's nothing to talk about."

"Quinn. He's still trying to work things out in his head, but he's trying." Her voice is soft with empathy.

"That's why I didn't push him when things ended. He has ghosts still haunting him, and I thought I could help him cope with them, but I can't. He has to work through those alone. Besides, he doesn't want me in his personal life."

"Why do you say that? I know you think differently, but you two are perfect together—you're good for him. You brought my lifeless brother back to the living. I don't think anyone else besides, you could have done that. His family certainly couldn't, even though we all tried. Please don't give up on him that quick."

I lay a now sleeping Reagan down in the pink frilly bassinet next to the couch. "I'm not the one who's giving up," I say, keeping my voice down to not wake the baby. "I want to be there for him." I still do. "If he wanted me, he would have come after me, but he didn't."

"He's scarred."

"So am I. It's not every day that I open myself up for others to hurt or reject me. I spent my high school life doing that and part of my adulthood. I couldn't survive it again."

Rachel brushed a hand over my shoulder, giving me a genuine smile. "I know, Hon. I just hope the two of you can move past these trials of your pasts. You both deserve to be happy."

A stronghold tugs at my heart. With every week that passes, Rachel's beginning to feel more like a sister to me. "Thank you. It means a lot that you say I helped your brother. The truth is, he helped me too, when I was with him. I haven't felt that way with another person ever." Heat bloomed across my cheeks, admitting the truth. I turned away and reached for the purse I had left on the end table.

"I'm going to go. I still have a few posts to edit before going live on the blogs and emails for the book club members. Thank you for this afternoon. I need to come by more often. It's great to have lunch where we have such a beautiful view. I've never seen the city like this before."

"Come by anytime. I love the company. I don't get out much now that Reagan's here. I'm not comfortable taking her out to too many public places yet. Too many germs are floating around."

"Isn't that the truth? I will. Maybe we can make this a weekly thing." I say, heading for the door.

She follows behind me, reaching for the door handle before I can.

"Sounds like a plan. I'll see you next week. Same day?"

Opening the door, I step out into the hallway. "I'll be here." I wave goodbye and head for the elevator. The door closes as I wait for the elevator to arrive. My cell phone beeped from my purse, and I fished it out, seeing two new emails waiting for me. I busy myself with the first email when a familiar ding sounds, and the door slides open.

"Quinn?"

My head snaps up to stare at the man who hasn't left my thoughts in over a month.

"Declan? What are you doing here?" I ask before immediately feeling stupid. His sister lives here, so obviously, he's here for her. "Sorry. Of course, you're here to see Rachel."

"Actually, I was coming to find you."

"How did you know I was here?"

His lips curl into a sexy smile as he steps out of the elevator, letting the door close and leave without me. He pulls his phone from his pocket, holding it in the air.

"Rachel's been texting me. She told me you were here. I've been waiting to talk to you."

My heart races with thoughts of what he wants to talk to me about. I could only hope it has nothing to do with work. "What did you need?"

"Come with me for a minute, will you?" He asks, reaching his hand out to grab mine. My gaze drops to the hand now holding mine, and my skin around his touch sizzles. "Okay"

Grinning, he turns on his heels and heads down the hall away from his sister's door. Two doors down, Declan stops, fishes a key from his pocket, and unlocks the door pushing it open as his gaze darts back to mine.

"Who lives here?"

"Let's get inside first."

He must have read the hesitation on my face because he drops the grin. "Trust me. You're safe. I know the owner."

Taking his word for it, I step inside the condo that is a copy of Rachel and Max's. The inside is empty of furnishings or anything personal. A bottle of wine sits on the counter with a hand-written note that congratulates the purchase. It was reading the letter that made my heart begin to beat faster.

"Declan, did you buy this place?" He doesn't answer as he moves over to the counter and the wine bottle. Picking up the note, he glances over it before grabbing the bottle. He turns to face me, and my heart squeezes in my chest at the sight of him. This man is walking sex appeal. My gaze travels over his body, eating him up, knowing the muscles and lines behind those clothes. I roll my lower lip between the edges of my teeth with the memory of his naked body above me. My gaze snaps back to his, and I notice he's watching me eat him up with my gaze.

"Are you thinking of me right now?" His question brings my mind back, and a blush breaks out over my cheeks.

"Why do you think that?"

He shrugs his shoulders, and his fingers work on opening the wine. "Because you're looking at me like you want to rip my clothes off." It was blunt but accurate.

My cheeks flush warm again. The time for hiding is over. If I can't be truthful with him, we have no hope for a future together.

"I'm thinking about how sexy you look and remembering how it felt to have you above me in bed."

His face drops with shock from my words. He hadn't expected me to be so truthful. His hands stilled from working the wine bottle open. Sitting it back on the counter, it was soon forgotten as he took a step toward me. Standing my ground, I refused to back up as he came at me. He stopped once we were toe to toe and inches away from each other.

"You think I'm sexy?"

I grin up at him. "You know you are. But to answer your question, yes, I do."

His face leans closer to mine until his voice can brush softly against my ear. "You also think about me...in bed? Naked? Above you?" The last two words come out like a whisper causing my stomach to roll with excitement. My heart shuttered with his closeness. Raising my hand, I placed my palm against his chest. Not to push him away, but with the need to touch him. His hand came up to cover mine, and our fingers intertwined, keeping both our hands tight against his body.

Swallowing a lump of nerves, I steel my spine and look up into his eyes. "There hasn't been a night since our last night together, that I haven't thought about you."

I pause to take a deep breath, trying to calm my nerves.

"I understand you're scared because of what happened to Dani. Putting yourself out there after a loss like that, I can only imagine what you're feeling. But I need you to know that I'm feeling it too. I told you what happened to me in my past and how I struggle to view myself. That day on the phone when you wouldn't listen to my side of the story was like the biggest and hardest rejection I've ever had to face because it came from you. You made me like you, Declan Palmer, and against my better judgment, I fell for you. I tried not to. I knew better than having feelings for my employer, but I couldn't stop myself. You made me feel things I never have for another person. You made it okay to open up and allow someone into my heart. I was special and adored, and I thank you for that."

Declan stood silent, listening to me pour my heart out. His face held tenderness and warmth. He leaned in to brush his mouth softly over mine when I finished. A shiver slipped down my spine taking me a few lingering seconds before parting my lips and allowing him to slip inside my mouth. His tongue swept against mine, and his mouth took my bottom lip between his, sucking it inside the warmth of his mouth. He turned his head slightly to the side, angling his head to gain clear access to my mouth. His hands moved to the sides of my face holding both my cheeks in his palms, holding me still as he worked over my mouth slowly.

Pulling away, he parted just enough to peer down at me. His eyes hooded heavily with lust, and at that moment, I couldn't think of anything or anyone else besides the two of us.

"I love the way you taste. Every time I kiss you, I crave you more and more. I don't think I will ever get enough."

My stomach rolls with hope at his words. God, I wish they were true. I wished he could like me as much as I like him. But actions speak louder than words, and the problem is, there could never be anything real between us if he keeps a firm grip on the past.

With that new realization fresh in my mind, I place my hands against his chest, pushing him away just enough for his hands to drop their hold from me.

"Please don't say those things to me. It hurts bad enough that things can't happen for us. And when you say sweet words like that to me, it makes me want you even more."

A wicked smile curls one corner of his mouth. "Who said we can't make things work between us?"

"Declan, I can't have a relationship with you and Dani. She's still a part of your life, and I except that, but...."

"What would you say if I told you I sold my house?"

Those words stopped my thoughts, and I fell silent. Taking a second, my gaze glanced over to the hand-written note by the wine again, then back to him. No...

"Did you...did you buy this place?"

Closing in the tight space between us, his hands returned to the sides of my face. The pad of his thumb caressed along my cheekbone.

"I did buy this place. I also know that it wasn't you who had the realtor come to the house. It's why I didn't fight too hard when you and Rachel came up with the idea of you working from your parents. I didn't want you to know I sold my place, and I bought this one. This condo is my way of showing you that I not only want but need to start my life over again. You helped me realize I was wasting away. Yes, I loved my wife, but she's gone, and

I'm tired of living in the past. I want to live in the future. I want to live in the future with you."

I gasped as his words hit me right in the chest. "Declan..."

"Let me finish. I bought this place for two reasons. It's close to my sister, which makes her happy, and we all know if she's happy, then we're all happy. And it has three bedrooms. It's important to have that many because I was hoping you could come back and live with me. I'll understand if you want your own space for now and have your own room but believe me when I say I want you back in my room. I want you in my bed. I want you there when I fall asleep and every morning when I wake up. I know you don't think I can step out of the past, but I can. I want to prove to you. I want to move on with my life. I want to move on with you."

Tears stung my eyes, threatening to spill over my lashes. His words are the sweetest anyone has ever said to me. He wipes my tear away with his thumb.

"Why are you crying?" His voice holds an edge of concern.

Closing my eyes, I turn my face into the soft cushion of his hand. "I'm not crying. My eyes are watering." I say, trying to make light of our conversation.

"Really? What's the matter? Are you upset?"

"No. I'm not upset. I'm the opposite, actually. I couldn't be happier that you want me in your life and your bed. But I can't go on like it was. I'm falling in love with you, Declan, and if you are nowhere near where I am, then I don't think it's a good idea for us to be together. It will hurt too much to be this close to you and not have you."

Leaning over, he kisses me on the lips so soft it barely feels like we are touching at all.

"I'm not asking you to live with me as my assistant. I want you to come live with me as my girlfriend. We can take things slow. We both have issues that will take time to work out, but I want to work them out together. And Quinn...?"

He pauses long enough to brush his lips against mine again before whispering. "I think I'm falling in love with you too."

My heart seizes in my chest, and I have to force myself to stop before I hyperventilate with happiness. My arms fly up to wrap around his neck. "Now, those are the sweetest words I have ever heard." I smile, stretching on my tiptoes to reach his mouth with mine. He hadn't said he does love me but that he is falling in love with me. I can live with that for now. I'm just happy he sees me in his future.

"So, what do you say to living here with me?"

I kiss him once more on the lips before dropping my hands to my side and taking a step back. "I think I would like that. But under a few conditions."

"Anything. Name it."

"I'll move in and live here with you, but I want to continue working for you. I'll be your PA by day but at night...." I pause and take a deep breath to still my nerves. "I want to be in your bed. I don't want my own room. I want to know I matter to you and that you can't shut me out anymore. If you need your space, that's fine, but I won't have you locking me out of your life for days at a time again. It nearly killed me. I also need you to talk to me, even if it's about Dani. I never want you to feel like you have to hide her from me."

"Hum. Your conditions are valid and ones I can live with. I want to see you happy. I want to be the one who makes you happy."

"You already do."

He kisses me again, and this time it comes with a force and hunger I have been missing for over a month. The taste of him is intoxicating, and no matter how close to him or deep our kiss goes, it's never going to be enough until this man is completely mine.

Mind and body.

"What do you say we break in the Master bedroom?" He asks as he places a kiss at the corner of my mouth before moving toward my neck.

"There's no furniture. We don't have a bed here."

"I don't own a bed anymore. When I sold the house, I sold it fully furnished. I told you, I plan to start over with you. I want you to come with me to pick out everything new for our new place."

Man, I love the sound of that. Grabbing his hand in mine, I turn us toward the narrow hallway leading to what I assume are the bedrooms. "Who needs a bed anyway."

His lips curl at the corners, and his eyes darken with lust, making him look even sexier, which I didn't think was possible. I'm going to enjoy spending my days in this man's arms and him in mine. Teaching each other, loving each other, and starting our lives over. I know this is just the beginning of our story, but it's sure going to be fun filling in the middle.

The End
(For Now)